The

Rye Rooftop Club

Mark Feakins

This is a work of fiction. All the characters, organisations and events in this novel are either the product of the author's imagination or are used fictitiously.

This second edition 2021.

"Family not only need to consist of merely those whom we share blood, but also for those whom we'd give blood."
Charles Dickens

For my logical family,
Martin and Henderson,
together forever.

CHAPTER 1

*The blue door, larking about with the
French and birthday rituals.*

The ancient town of Rye was used to invaders. Seven hundred years ago it was the French setting fire to things and stealing the church bells for a lark. Then came the beery smugglers rolling around its narrow streets with illegal hordes of wool and gold. More recently it is tea-time tourists pursuing antiques and parking spaces, Victoria sponges and ghosts that haunt the dark corners of the borough. However, on this freezing November night, Ralph stood alone with the old Sussex town looking damp and surly in front of him. Not unlike the early French raiders, he wished he'd brought a thicker coat.

Across the forecourt of the train station, the glowing supermarket squeezed the last minutes of trade out of its long day. A small woman, with her yellow coat covering a pink dressing gown, scurried out of the door with a bottle of brandy in one hand and a can of squirty cream in the other.

"Just some essentials," she called when she saw Ralph watching her. "Brian, the night taxi, will be here in a minute. This late it's usually just him to meet the last train. He might have gone for chips. Going far?"

Ralph hesitated, "Erm...The High Street."

"Oh, that's just up the hill," she said, tossing her head and throwing some excitable curls of copper hair from her face. "Follow me if you want, unless you are a sex pest, then don't, just wait for Brian – you'll have your work cut out pestering him."

Before she finished her sentence she had set off up the hill towards the town. The last thing Ralph wanted was company, but moving seemed preferable to standing in the cold. So he picked up his heavy bag and followed her.

She shouted over her shoulder, "Keep up, you have to get a bit of pace going or you grind to a halt halfway up the hill, at the steep bit. People regularly slide all the way back down to the bottom. Generally, it's a spectator sport for us locals, but I'm feeling generous tonight so I'm warning you."

Ralph doubled his pace and jogged lightly beside her, marvelling at how she could keep up both her speed and a non-stop, one-sided conversation.

"I'm giving you the benefit of the doubt," she continued. "On the sex pest front, that is. You're not one, are you? No, you've got ever such nice shoes and eyes. Brown, sort of chocolatey – your eyes, I mean, not your shoes. Are you on holiday?"

They had reached the peak of the hill and she turned a sharp left into a cobbled street lined with shops.

"The High Street," she declared, waving the brandy recklessly in the air. "It's a funny old time for a holiday, isn't it? I mean, Rye has loads of tourists, being so old and ancient and medieval and everything. Wait," she stopped without warning, causing Ralph to cannon into her back. "Do you hear that?"

They listened. Ralph had no idea what he was supposed to be hearing, so just looked at the woman as she held a heroic pose of brandy bottle above her head and the can of cream clutched to her chest. After a moment or two she whispered, "There...listen."

Gradually, he began to make out a distant clanking noise, followed by what sounded like something being dragged along the ground.

"What is it?" he hissed.

"Gone," she declared and set off again along the cobbles. "It's weird, a few people have heard it. We think it's one of the duellers."

"A jeweller?"

"No, why would a jeweller make that sound? A *dueller*, you know, people who duel, sword fighting to the death, all that. Apparently, people have seen a couple of ghosts having a duel, then the victor is heard dragging the body through the town to throw it off the top of Rye Tower. I've heard it a few times lately, gives you the collywobbles, doesn't it? Don't get me wrong, it's a bloody lovely town actually. Do you mind if I swear? You'll like it. Rye, I mean, not swearing. Right, this is me," she halted outside a plain white door next to the unlit windows of a café. "I know I did Brian out of a fare from the station, but it would have been a waste of your money to get a taxi up here, wouldn't it? Plus, his chips would have gone cold, so everyone's a winner really," she took a breath at long last. "Are you OK? You're ever so pale."

"Just tired," Ralph murmured.

"Fair enough-ski," she said, giving him the brandy bottle in order to free a hand to rummage through her dressing gown pockets under her coat. "Do you mind keeping going? I've got to go inside now and would rather not have you hanging around, if you know what I mean. If you just potter up the road, I'll nip inside safely. I'm sure you're perfectly normal, what with your nice shoes and everything, but better to be safe than sorry."

"Of course, sorry," Ralph handed her the bottle and walked away. He passed a few shops, but soon stopped and glanced over his shoulder. She had gone and the road was empty, so he turned around and backtracked to the white door where she had left him.

Under the misty light of an iron streetlamp he took a deep breath. The last thing he'd wanted was a longer conversation with the chatty woman and her crazy red hair, so he hadn't said anything when he saw what he was looking for right beside her door. He took a few steps to his left and stood in front of the blank face of the abandoned shop, shivers rippling through him. What had he done?

As he stared the sound of something like metal pans being knocked together floated towards him again, then it changed to what could easily have been something heavy being dragged along the pavement. He could see no one on the street, then jumped as a sudden beam of light pierced the drizzle and he looked up at a window above the café next door, where the curtains were being held back a crack - not enough to reveal the observer, but just enough to see the can of squirty cream held in her hand. Fumbling the new set of keys from his jeans, he quickly moved to the far side of the shop where there was another door, blue this time. He opened it, made his way inside and up the creaking stairs to his new home.

* * *

In the small flat above the café, Anna dropped the curtain as the strangely silent man disappeared from view. She sighed, shook the can vigorously and hefted a large swirl of cream on to her mug of hot chocolate.

Birthdays weren't really a big thing once you were into your thirties, she told herself, which was perhaps why no-one had really bothered too much this year. Although it wasn't her birthday just yet, so she would just have to wait and see what the day might bring forth.

"Bring forth," she said out loud, enjoying the feel of the words in her mouth. It was a nice little phrase and she made a mental note to use it more often. As she did so, a little brass clock gave full vent to an enthusiastic *ting*, its neighbours on the crowded mantlepiece - three china piggy banks in the shape of communist leaders and a stuffed water vole – said nothing.

Midnight had struck and Anna was now thirty-three, "Happy birthday me!" she said to no one but piggy Karl Marx, Stalin and Chairman Mao. "I made it."

Anna knew that it was foolish, but she had always held a fear that she wouldn't live to see this birthday. Her father had died when he was just thirty-two and she was convinced that this would also be her fate. She had only been ten, but the memories of that night were still crystal clear. The faint smell of alcohol on her mother's breath as she sat carefully on the edge of her bed. The half-light of early morning on her blank face as she told her that Daddy was gone. The hollow sound of her voice, "He was just thirty-two. I ask you, Anna, who dies at thirty-two?"

Anna lay down across the cushions of her green velvet sofa and wondered how you marked the breaking of a curse? Giving thanks to the gods that had spared you, through a ritual involving some sort of sacrifice? She was pretty sure that all she had in the fridge was the breast of an already departed chicken and half a beetroot, so that may not work. Oh well, a splash more brandy and another whirl of squirty cream in her hot chocolate would do.

As she shook the can again, the lonely man outside floated across her mind. Why hadn't he said he was her new neighbour? Or was he? Perhaps he was planning to rob the place? Vandalise it? She tensed, ready to dial 999 at the first sound of suspect activity through the wall, but there was nothing. He probably wasn't a burglar, not in those shoes. Besides, the bag he was carrying was full when he arrived – wouldn't a burglar need it empty for his swag?

She rested her cheek on her hand and sighed. He was alone and looked sad, she thought, which made him all the more glamorous. It seemed that now she had lived to see it, there was the potential that thirty-three might well be a very good year.

CHAPTER 2

The Japanese kimonos, Jaffa
Cakes and running away.

As consciousness rippled slowly to the surface, Ralph lay for a while enjoying the feeling of comfortable heaviness. He shifted slightly and something poked him in the ribs, stabbing him further awake. It was his over-stuffed holdall, hugged tight to his chest. Everything he now owned was in that bag - except this place. He groaned as images of his new home above the shop played on the inside of his eyelids; shiny orange cupboards in the kitchen, furious pink tiles in the bathroom and grim, grey furniture in the living room.

Ralph gathered enough energy to open one eye, which thudded closed again as his watch told him it was not yet six in the morning. He dragged himself from the flattened cushions of the old sofa, stripped off yesterday's stale clothes and pulled his running gear out of the bag and over his shivering skin. Outside, the biting coastal air hit him with unnecessary enthusiasm and he hesitated, having no idea where to go. It was too cold to wait for long, so, for the second day in a row, he took a deep breath and simply started to run.

✻ ✻ ✻

Anna was already up and tucked into the back of the café when Ralph jogged by, so she didn't see last night's mysterious stranger with the good shoes. The strong coffee smoothed out her low-level brandy headache as she happily busied herself in the small kitchen. It was professional, practical and meticulously organised; a stark contrast to her flat and her fashion choices. Anna's style was entirely vintage and seemingly unholy alliances were formed between surprising playmates; today's Japanese kimono, in lime green and gold, was paired with land-girl corduroy jodhpurs and a striped shirt that a continental fisherman would be proud to wear as he hauled in his catch. Yet, Anna's warm, round, freckled face, with her frizz of bright copper hair, set all these styles off in such a way that everyone who met her travelled from startled to enchanted within seconds.

After another reviving sip of coffee, she tied her Magic Roundabout apron around her waist and began rummaging through a pile of baking tins. The kitchen was an odd shape, a sort of unequal triangle created when the back of the shop had been divided to add a couple of toilets and a discrete internal door that led to the flat above. Every inch of the small space was both spotless and purposeful, allowing her to create the volume of pies and cakes that her growing clientele demanded.

The kitchen was separated from the café area by a long wooden counter with a deep, rich finish that spoke of its previous life in a traditional haberdashery shop at the other end of the High Street. It had drawers and small cupboards on both sides in all shapes and sizes, previously filled with buttons, lace and thread. On the kitchen side it now held spices, wooden spoons and piping bags. The public side was the domain of Irene, Anna's fiery head waitress, who had a strict system for the storage and management of menus, cutlery, note pads, pencils and much more. Should a stray napkin appear in the doily drawer, or a confused fork find itself lounging amongst the teaspoons, Irene would launch an investigation to find the culprit that would put the Spanish Inquisition to shame. Anna had learnt to stay strictly to her side of things.

The mahogany counter-top no longer displayed elegant gloves and ribbons for ladies' hats, but the latest chrome and blood-red coffee machine, which sported buttons, grinders, steam arms and thermostats. Irene had mastered the basics of it, but still tried to steer customers to a straightforward cup of tea, in order to avoid what she described as, 'far too much faff for a milky coffee'.

The café itself was a bright, square space fronted by two large windows and a central door, topped with a stained-glass panel of lilies representing its origins as a flower shop back in the 1920's. The tables and chairs did not match, but all had their own stories to tell from defunct churches, pubs or stately homes. The rose-pink and white checked tablecloths helped to unify the disparate furniture, with a floral cushion adding comfort to each chair, ready to receive a bottom of any proportion.

Apparently random bric-a-brac clung bravely to the light, cream walls and assorted shelves. Stuffed owls settled in next to piles of pinecones and a pith helmet. Speared butterflies flew past framed vinyl LP covers from the 1980's, while china ducks, frozen on a toilet wall in their search for a warmer climate, seemed comfortable to share the space with a display of Victorian knickers. She knew exactly where and when each item had come into her possession and she enjoyed the company of their eccentricities and light dusting of memories.

Anna loved everything she had created at The Cookery - a name she had inherited, but chose to keep out of respect for the previous owner; a nice woman called Gladys, who's marriage had taken a turn for the worse when a lady circus performer swung into town and changed her husband's perspective on life forever. Anna's love for baking came from her mother, who used to make celebration cakes for the great and good of Rye, when the discrete stash of pinot noir had not got the better of her. Anna had carried on the tradition of making stunning cakes for visitors to the café as well as individual clients, but her particular speciality had become her pies. People came from far and wide for them. Just as in other areas of her life the contents were eclectic, but somehow they worked. Today's pie-of-the-day, chorizo, carrot and mango, had become a surprise winter favourite. As she rolled the pastry she hoped that she was making enough or Irene would not be happy.

* * *

Ralph was running at a good pace to get the blood flowing and keep the cold at bay. He passed a tearoom, numerous charity shops and art galleries, another tearoom, pottery shops, estate agents, more tea rooms and no less than six funeral directors. You could die of many things in Rye, he thought, but thirst would not be one of them.

He was slowly stretching out his tired, tense limbs and getting a sense of his new home. He saw tall, elegant Georgian buildings, then crooked houses clinging to their neighbours for support, walls made of fist-sized chunks of flint and plenty of sturdy oak-beamed pubs. Ralph began to enjoy the unusual, ramshackle nature of this tiny town he had never even heard of until a month ago.

As he ran under an ancient castle gate proudly framing the sea behind it, he thought of the endless nights and solitary lunch breaks spent secretly surfing the internet to find his own gateway to freedom. Not really knowing what it might look like, he had scrolled through new houses, new places, new jobs, sometimes even new countries. He looked at so much that he nearly passed over the small notice on a social media site. He knew at once that this was *it*. The illusive, game changing, *it*. Since then he had read the advert so many times that he could conjure it up word for word:

***Could The Bookery be the new start
you've been looking for?***

For sale - The Bookery: A well-established, independent book shop with residential accommodation.

A long-standing high street business could be yours in the beautiful, medieval coastal town of Rye, one of Sussex's best kept secrets. Rye's labyrinth of winding streets and passageways, dotted with quirky shops, ancient inns and cafés, are explored by thousands of locals and tourists each year. The Bookery was established in the 1930's in this literary town, with former inhabitants including renowned novelist Henry James, E.F Benson (the author of the Mapp and Lucia books), and John Ryan (the cartoonist creator of Captain Pugwash).

An excellent investment opportunity, with potential for development and growth, the business holds a strong presence within the busy high street, plus, it comes with the added bonus of a two-bedroomed flat above the retail premises. This is an opportunity not to be missed.

Three-years' audited accounts are available for genuine enquirers and the business and accommodation are priced at a competitive value, as the current owner requires a quick sale. (All fixtures and furnishings included).

Ralph knew at once that his new journey had started - if he was brave enough to begin it.

✳ ✳ ✳

Anna took her third batch of scones from the oven, these were whisky, ginger and gin, and transferred them to cooling trays. Although it was only the first of November and there were few tourists about, Anna knew she could rely on her regulars to give her a busy

Saturday. She had stiff competition from a myriad of other tearooms, but this didn't stop her dreaming of building on what she had started and expanding the business. Anna wasn't quite sure how yet and anxiety always crept in when she thought about it seriously. She would wait until she found someone to share it with, she thought, someone who knew what they were doing. Until then she was happy surrounded by the warmth of her ovens and humming along to music she imagined would have suited a pre-war Parisian brothel, but never failed to make her smile.

As she worked Anna thought about the surprise arrival of her new neighbour. Why had she talked so much? Did he think she was mad with her tales of dead bodies being dragged along the street? Thank goodness she hadn't told him about the ghostly woman in grey she had been seeing lately hovering in the shadows wherever she went. He had seemed so lost last night, standing outside the empty shop next door and she felt a familiar flutter in her stomach as she thought of this tall, handsome man who was obviously in need of her help. From long experience of concentrating romantic- ally on lame-ducks, she knew that it was hard to find a decent man amongst the lost souls (or 'no hopers', as Irene preferred to call them) she was attracted to. How- ever, all lessons learned from her past faded away, as the excitement of meeting this mysterious man with choc- olate eyes and soft dark hair consumed her thoughts, and she dreamed of their almost certain future life to- gether.

* * *

When Ralph had read the advert for The Bookery he knew it wasn't a logical choice, as he had no experience of running a shop, but something about it spoke to him. As an only-child isolated on his family's farm high in the Peak District, books had been a means of escape from the hills and mud of his immediate environment. He knew that wasn't really enough to qualify him, but at that moment it didn't seem to matter, it was everything he needed. The bookshop offered a place to live where no one knew him and a way to earn a living all rolled into one. Also, it was his for a price he could just about afford.

He knew he had broken his parents' hearts by not wanting to take over the farm, but they accepted his decision and generously gave him an early inheritance from its sale when they retired. Since then he had quietly been tucking money away to build on that foundation. Every time he got a bonus at work or a pay-rise he would put it straight into this, his secret 'Freedom Fund', without a word to Helen. They had both earned good salaries which went into the joint account each month. Their house in Barnsley had been paid for by her parents as a wedding present, so he felt he could justify the subterfuge.

Helen. The cold morning air gripped him tight as he thought about her, so he picked up speed trying to shake off its icy embrace. What was she thinking now, waking up with him gone? As the sister of his best friend from university, Helen had fallen easily into their group. She was funny, smart and a talented artist, constantly producing scribbled portraits of people as they sat in the pub. He too had spent much of his childhood doodling and sketching, adding his own illustrations to the piles of books he asked for at birthdays and Christmas. They had bonded over their love of drawing and had quickly been assumed by everyone to be a couple; him, the handsome football team captain, her, the dark beauty always at his side. It wasn't something they had discussed or even decided for themselves, they both just fell in with the expectations of those around them. Having never seriously dated anyone and been quite comfortable with his own company, he found that being with Helen meant fitting in and, for a while, he liked it.

Ralph pushed himself harder as he ran along the quayside, heavy drizzle now setting in and making the pavements shine. After the first few months of their marriage he had developed a pattern of long runs that seemed to help quell a rising panic growing inside him. Running allowed him enough time to imagine packing all of his fears behind a solid brick wall, hiding all of the feelings he didn't want to face. When he returned from a run he felt able to carry on for a bit longer, everything that frightened him tucked neatly away. However, in recent months, even the long hours pounding Yorkshire's hills could not stop his brain roaring inside his head - and then he had found the advert for The Bookery. This was his moment and he didn't dare hesitate.

He contacted the owner of the bookshop and within two weeks it was signed and sealed, The Bookery was his and the Freedom Fund was all but empty. He had an unpleasant conversation with his boss at the web design agency, telling him he needed to leave in a hurry and wouldn't be working a notice period. He paid a flying visit to his parents in their new bungalow in Bakewell, to tell them in vague terms that he had too good an opportunity to miss 'down South' and he would be in touch when he was settled – and that he was going without Helen. This information didn't seem to surprise or interest either of them greatly, as they showed him the photos from their latest cruise along the rivers of Latvia.

Ralph pounded up a steep hill and past the ancient smugglers' haunt of The Mermaid Inn. He nodded to another hardy winter runner, his face mostly hidden under the peak of a grey baseball cap. It was hard to believe that it was only yesterday that the padded envelope arrived containing the keys to The Bookery. Suddenly it was happening, no time to waste or his nerve might fail him.

In his haste he hadn't been able to find any paper at home, so, on the inside of a Jaffa Cake packet he had written Helen a heartfelt, but ultimately uninformative note, announcing his departure. He truly believed that his going would be the best thing for both of them, but he had no words to explain why he had to go, just deeply buried feelings and a need to get away. The house was already Helen's, so the car and the contents of the joint account could be hers too - leaving everything for her lessened his guilt a little. He only wanted to take what was entirely necessary and he was surprised to find that it all fitted into one bag.

It had been a last-minute decision to leave his phone, but it was full of so much of his old life and he wanted to start as close to new as he could. After a factory reset, deleting everything, he had placed it next to the chocolate-stained note, leaning against the pepper pot on the kitchen table. He remembered the final moments clearly; shutting the front door firmly behind him, posting his keys through the letter box and then beginning to run.

CHAPTER 3

The crushed coffee cups, doilies and early visitors.

When Ralph returned from his first morning run around Rye, he managed to bring the boiler to life and stood in the shower letting the hot water revive him. He had forgotten to pack towels, so dried himself with yesterday's t-shirt and headed to the bedroom but paused at the living room doorway. Although the morning sun was struggling to make itself known over the tops of the buildings opposite, the miserable room seemed more inviting in the early light. The grey, prison-like walls of last night were actually a soft chalky blue and, on closer inspection, the sagging items of furniture were actually good quality antiques. His heart took a small leap as he sensed that this place could feel like a home one day, but anxiety soon crept back over him as he thought of the bookshop downstairs. Right, time to meet The Bookery, he said to himself, and see if we get on.

His sparse wardrobe stuffed in his holdall, of jeans, t-shirts, sweatshirts and trainers, made it quick and easy to dress and Ralph thought that he might enjoy this new life of simple, limited options. There was nothing to eat or drink in the flat, so, after a large glass of water from the kitchen tap he headed down to find his way into the bookshop.

In the narrow hallway at the bottom of the stairs were two doors, the blue one in front of him opened on to the street and to his left was a plain wooden door held with a deadlock and a bolt. He slid back the bolt and flipped through the bunch of keys he had been sent, selecting two options. Luckily, the first one turned easily in the lock and Ralph pulled the door open towards him. As he stepped through he was greeted by the aroma of warm wood and old paper and he paused for a momen, taking in his future laid out before him.

He was standing at the back of the shop in a shadowy corner that looked out over a huge square room. The estate agent's photos had not given the impression of anything like the real size of it and he felt overwhelmed. The farthest wall was lined with tall, wide windows that let the weak sunshine trickle in from the street. There was a central door and running under the windows were empty display areas currently showing a collection of dried flies and an arrangement of abandoned cobwebs. Every wall was lined with sets of severe wooden shelves stretching up to a high ceiling. The middle of the floor was crammed with half-height shelf units standing back-to-back, with bedraggled pot plants crawling over them as if making a bid for freedom.

Ralph stood on a raised platform that ran the entire width of the room and filled the back quarter of the shop. There was a long wooden step leading up to it and each wall behind and beside him was covered with more tall, dark shelves. Most of them contained books, but not in orderly rows, some were piled on their sides, others lay in sad, crooked lines, while across the floor were strewn cardboard boxes over-flowing with dejected hardbacks and paperbacks. The whole place was enormous and depressing, not the dream he had created for himself at all.

He leant back against the door as the enormity of what he had done hit him. He had been completely naïve to abandon everything he knew for some hazy photographs and an optimistic sales pitch. Ralph closed his eyes and pinched the bridge of his nose, trying to focus on why he was here. He repeated the words he had said to himself on yesterday's long train journey across the country, "You have run from a life you could no longer live, from lies you could no longer tell to a place where you can reinvent yourself as the person you know you are meant to be." He opened his eyes as the sun finally rose high enough to send a shaft of bright light into the shop, illuminating the floating dust that danced in front of him.

"Come on, idiot," he said, out loud, to break the heavy silence. "You can't be beaten by this. This is all you've got now."

He peered down a set of stairs that rose from the floor behind a coffee-stained shop counter in the middle of the platform area. Through the gloom he could just make out a basement with more miserable books under layers of dust. He took a couple of tentative steps down, but froze as a familiar sound of something heavy being dragged along the ground caught his attention and he quickly retreated back into the shop. He shook his head and laughed at his reaction, the last thing he needed was for this place to be haunted.

From the corner of his eye he caught a bright green flash across the filthy windows at the front of the shop. He turned and stepped down from the raised area to see a small, wild-haired woman in a lime green kimono waving a paper cup. The copper-haired creature was red in the face, but seemed strangely familiar and pointed at the cup excitedly and then at Ralph, repeating this pattern with increasing enthusiasm until he was able to lip read an exaggerated, "Coffee. For you!".

Ralph picked up the keys from the counter and went to the door, working through them to see which would fit. On the third attempt the key turned in the lock. The bizarre coffee fairy he now recognised as his neighbour, saw his success and proceeded to push the door, but it didn't budge and her forward momentum meant that she crashed into it with an audible, "Oof", sending a spray of coffee up in the air and down the glass.

"Wait," Ralph shouted. "There are bolts too. Sorry, hang on," he reached to the top of the door and slid a bolt back, did the same at the bottom and was then able to pull the door open. "Are you OK? Did you burn yourself?"

"No, no. Nothing serious. It hasn't gone through to the bone - only kidding. It's on your door though, I'll just try and..." Anna took the plastic lid that was hanging off the crushed coffee cup and used it to catch the frothy coffee as it slid down the glass. "It's cappuccino, so you might want to wash it off quite soon or it'll stink. Can I come in?"

Before Ralph could gather his thoughts the chattering woman from last night was shimmying past him and into the shop, "Yes, sure," he muttered.

"Did you sleep well? You remember me, I'm next door? That way," she pointed vaguely out of the shop and to the left, as she trotted around the piles of books and boxes. "Blimey, there are a lot of books here. Well, I suppose there would be - it being a book shop. Ha, ha. You'd be buggered without them...sorry, language. Still, I'm thirty-three now, so I'm trying out a bit more language. Oh, how old are you?"

She stopped and looked at him, 'Calm down,' she told herself. 'You're going balmy again. Gently, gently.'

"Twenty-seven," Ralph rubbed the back of his neck as he felt a headache starting.

"Pardon?"

"You asked how old I was. I'm twenty-seven."

"Oooh, yes, good age. I liked being twenty-seven and twenty-eight, but twenty-nine was probably my best year."

"Was it?"

"Yes, it was a good one. I got The Cookery when I was twenty-nine. I'd only been doing cakes in my kitchen until then, plus pies for vile old Dew-drop Dobson. Have you met him? No, probably not, you only came last night. I hate him, so I think you should too, as we are going to be friends and everything."

She took a rare breath and smiled, so Ralph leapt in, "Can we just...thanks for the coffee...but who are you again?"

"Oh," Anna cocked her head to one side, letting her copper curls bounce. "I thought I said? I'm Anna, I'm the café next door. It's called The Cookery. It's always been kind of a pair with The Bookery, you see. So, I'm your neighbour and now we're a sort of a couple. Lucky you weren't really a sex pest, isn't it?"

He shut the shop door, "Yes, it probably is. Right, well, I'm Ralph."

Anna grinned at him, "Hello, Ralph. Am I going too fast for you?"

"Yes, a bit," he said.

"Sorry, I do that, when I get excited," she puffed out her cheeks. "I go about a million miles an hour. I've been told about it before...from the police mostly...I've got loads of points on my driving license. It's a habit."

"OK, so...Why the matching names? I mean, The Cookery and The Bookery are separate shops, right?" Ralph's head swam as he realised that maybe he should have done the full legal checks after all.

Realising that she was clearly frightening the life out of him, Anna wrapped the kimono around herself and settled down on the step in the middle of the shop, "Oh, yes, don't worry, you haven't bought me too. Although I am on offer to a good home, but..." she told herself to focus. "...That's another story. Look, both shops were owned by a married couple, oodles ago. Patrick ran the bookshop and Gladys ran the café. So, they made the shop names up as a pair, I suppose. It's kind of cute when you think about it. All went well, for years, then the circus came to town."

"The circus?" Ralph said, taking a sip of the rich strong coffee.

"Yep, literally. I don't know the full story, but it had to do with a lady circus performer. Well, Patrick fell for her and went off to join the circus, with a trump, trump,

trump."

"Really?"

"Actually, I made that last bit up," Anna said, reining herself in again. "To cut a long story - that I could easily make longer – short, they had an affair. But she left town with the circus and he was never the same again. This place fell into disrepair - he just lost interest, I suppose. Anyway, in the end Gladys had had enough and sold The Cookery to me and moved to Malaga. A few years later the circus lady fell off her trapeze and came back for Patrick, so he sold this place to buy them a lodge-home near Coventry. So, here we are, Anna and Ralph. The Cookery and The Bookery. Linked together like star-crossed lovers."

Ralph choked on his hot coffee, "Well, can't blame a girl for trying," she shrugged. "Why didn't you say anything to me last night about moving in here?"

"Oh, well, I didn't know we were actually outside The Bookery at the time," Ralph lied. "I've never been to Rye before."

"Really? And you bought this place anyway?"

"Yep," he headed to a wobbly pile of boxes hoping to prompt his guest to leave and avoid more questions he wasn't ready to answer.

Not one to be put off, Anna continued, "So, you're on your own to take over the bookshop?"

"Yep," Ralph's head now buried deep inside a box.

"That's a shame," Anna said, not feeling that it was a shame at all. "Still, you'll soon make friends – look at us, you'd barely stepped off the train and we became friends. I grew up here so I know most people and most places if you need any help, plus I've got cracking pies..."

"Not a euphemism," chuckled a deep trans-Atlantic

voice from the front of the shop.

Ralph rose from his hiding place amongst the boxes as his heart sank at the sound of another visitor.

"Oh," Anna turned, her lips tightening, not pleased to lose her exclusive access to her would be romance. "Morning."

"Morning, crazy lady," the owner of the voice stepped into the shop, revealing a strong bearded jaw, broad shoulders squeezed into a crisp shirt and waistcoat, a trim waist and well-fitting jeans that both hugged and sagged in all the right places. "Here you go, birthday girl."

Anna took a card and a long, thin parcel wrapped in pink tissue paper from him, "Oh, thanks, you didn't have to."

"Well, you have made it quite clear that I have had to for the last few years, so I'd be in big trouble this year if I hadn't bothered, right?"

"Too right," she said with a giggle. "Oh, Joe, this is Ralph. Ralph, this is Joe."

"Good to see you, Ralph. How do you make holy water?" Joe asked as he tossed a piece of chewing gum into his mouth.

"I'm sorry?" Ralph said.

"Joe, he's only just arrived, give him a break," Anna slapped Joe on one of his remarkable biceps. "Joe is known for his jokes...well, he calls them jokes."

"Either of you, how do you make holy water? No? Anyone? OK, you boil the hell out of it!" Grinning, Joe extended his hand to Ralph, "Tough crowd. I'm Joe Wells, from next door."

Ralph took his hand and looked into two deep, ocean blue eyes that made him suddenly anxious, "Are you from The Cookery too? Oh, are you two...?"

"No."

"Noooo," Anna laughed.

"Not anymore. We dabbled once..." Joe held his eye contact with Ralph. "I'm the other way, Let's Screw."

Ralph stepped back, as if stung, "What?"

Joe laughed, holding both hands up. "Let's Screw - it's the name of my hardware store. It's next door - on the other side of you."

"Another of Joe's little jokes. How the town council let him get away with it, I will never know. He's so...well, look at him...he can pretty much get anything he wants, looking like that...and does," Anna added as a bitter after-thought, blushing as she remembered her short-lived, but thrilling access to Joe's body not long after she had bought The Cookery.

"It's a purely factual statement. I sell hammers, nails, paint, screws, screwdrivers, everything for your DIY needs. So, the name fits, right?" he smiled at Ralph.

Just then a hawk-like head, encased tightly in a red scarf, appeared around the half-open door and looked at Anna, "Oh, this is where you're hiding, is it? The lazy lummox hasn't arrived yet, keep your eye out, will you?"

"Do you mean Rosie, the Saturday girl?" Anna asked, primly.

"That's the one," the head said, unabashed and turned to Ralph. "I'm Irene, by the way. I'm her waitress. Not the only one, but the only one who seems to do any work, even with my kidneys. Pleased to meet you."

"You too, I'm Ralph."

"Are you? I've never met a Ralph. It's a posh name."

"Not really, I was just named after my grandad."

"Bully for you," she looked back at Anna. "Any sight-

30

ings?"

"Oh, well, not yet today, but I'm sure she was there last night while I was locking up," Anna said.

"Hm, I still think we need to tell the cops."

"What about?" Joe asked.

Anna shrugged, "It's probably nothing, but I'm sure I keep seeing this shadowy woman in grey watching me. I just catch sight of her sometimes, but then she's gone. It's so strange, when she's there I have this feeling that I know her or she knows me. It's creepy, but also kind of comforting. Anyway, what with that and ghosts dragging dead people up and down the street..."

"You need to take more water with it," Joe laughed. "Ghost stories are only for the tourists."

"Rubbish," Anna said. "You heard it last night, didn't you, Ralph?"

Ralph blushed, "Well..."

"See, now you've even got the new bloke going," Irene snapped. "I'm off to the shop. We're low on loo roll and if we run out I don't want any shenanigans with my doilies like last time, so I'm stocking up," and her head vanished briefly, before quickly reappearing and locking her steely gaze on Joe, who took a small step backwards.

"Oh, pretty boy, I know you come from that there Canadia, or wherever, but I've told you before - stop chewing that bubble gum. For one, it'll have your stoppers out and B, if I see one spot of it on my pavement, I'll rip your gizzards out." Irene disappeared and there was a stunned silence as all three waited to see if the performance was complete, which it clearly was as her head, reattached to her thin, birdlike body, stalked past the window and off down the street.

"That was Irene," Anna said as if by way of explanation. "She's immune to Joe's appeal."

"I see. She's...erm"

Joe leant across and Ralph felt the deep tones of his voice caress his ear, "She claims to be sixty-three, but she's actually seventy-two. She has seven children, twenty-three grandchildren and six great-grandchildren. She may be tough as old leather, but she's fertile, I'll give her that."

"I see," Ralph said, tripping over a box as he tried to put some distance between himself and Joe.

"Is the rest of your stuff coming soon?" Anna said to Ralph as he scrambled to keep his balance.

"Erm..." he hesitated, seeing both Anna and Joe waiting for a reply. "Yes, soon. How did you know I...that I didn't..."

"I was with you when you arrived, remember? With just one bag, which seems a bit odd as you were moving in."

"Good lord, woman," Joe said. "Leave him alone. Let him settle for a while before you start dragging all the skeletons out of his closet."

"I wasn't dragging anything out of anywhere. Shut up," she started to move towards Ralph, who was trapped amongst boxes and shelves and unable to bck away. "Please don't think I was prying. I wasn't...what are you doing?" Joe had taken hold of her arm and gently, but firmly, was guiding her towards the door.

"I'm leaving now and I'm taking you with me," he said. "You have to watch out for the lummox, whatever one of those is? So, while you are doing that you can make me a coffee and open your gift. You'll love it, I even included extra batteries."

"Oh, not again. The charity shop refused to take the last one you gave me," Anna said as she was drawn away out on to the street.

"Just shout, my friend, if you need anything. Anyway, we'll see you at the Club, won't we?" Joe sais as he shut the door behind them and Ralph was alone.

He moved to the front door in a daze, turned the key in the lock, then shot both bolts back into place. Ralph lent against the glass, he hadn't understood most of what had been said, but Irene had scared him, Joe had unnerved him and Anna exhausted him. If they were his neighbours, then perhaps he really had made the worst mistake of his life.

CHAPTER 4

The rooftop, Charles Dickens and
a tiny velvet slipper.

R alph stretched and looked out of the shop window to see that the light was already beginning to fade. After a shaky start it had turned out to be a good day and he allowed himself a smile.

After his alarming neighbours had left and the coffee worked its magic, he had looked at The Bookery with fresh eyes. Among the apparent chaos he had discovered that the books left for him by circus-fan, Patrick, were actually an interesting selection. He thought he would probably reduce the range a bit and definitely get some more up to date titles, but it was a good start. He had spent several hours just sorting and categorising, being soothed by the gentle feel of the books and the process of bringing some order to the shop.

He found a pad of paper and a pencil and the long-forgotten artist in him resurfaced and he began to sketch an entirely new layout for the shop. His instinct told him that independent shops could only survive against the big chains by providing a different and unique experience for shoppers. He decided that he wanted the shop to become a space for creative exploration, where people would enjoy spending time and feel inspired to spend money on the books that they found along the way. He would remove some of the shelves as there was barely room to breathe at the moment, then he would paint the remainder starting with a rich, deep blue at the front of the shop, gradually using a lighter shade with each set of shelves, until the books at the back sat amongst a light, sky blue. He wanted to intruduce colour and light, lifting the gloom that hung over the place.

Ralph thought about a travel section and painting the back of some shelves like windows looking out to views of the sea or countryside, and only by picking up books would people be able to catch a glimpse through to the vistas beyond. He imagined an area for young people that was full of colour, adventure and discovery, so he designed shelves that were part of a jungle, with painted parrots and monkeys sitting amongst the books. Another area would be a fairy-tale castle with flowers growing up and princesses climbing down.

Ralph's hand flew across the pages as he sketched and planned, feeling a freedom and joy that he thought he had lost. Although he knew nothing about running a shop, his vision and creativity seemed to fit naturally with The Bookery and he began to think it might work. It had to - he had no plan B.

❋ ❋ ❋

Ralph massaged his aching hand as he put the pad aside and headed out to get some supplies. He went down the hill to the supermarket, buying some store cupboard basics and a ready-made pasta meal for dinner. On the way back he bought duvets and pillows, sheets and towels from two enormous ladies in their bedding shop, who wriggled to get as much of their bulk into the doorway as they could to wave the young man off as he left.

Ralph cooked his pasta in one of the two dented saucepans he found in the kitchen and ate it at a small table in the living room. His brain was still buzzing from his day in The Bookery and he scribbled notes as he ate, creating lists of jobs to do and the things he would need, such as paint, brushes, step ladders and old items for display to give the atmosphere he was trying to create. Then he focused on practical things he had not even thought about until now, like credit card machines, accounts with book suppliers, a business bank account, insurance and so on. With a sense of rising panic he began to plan a timetable for achieving everything he wanted to do, setting himself a goal of opening in two weeks. It was going to be tight, but his Freedom Fund was now very limited and he needed to start earning some income as soon as possible. He was also aware that there was the potential of a lucrative Christmas season coming up which he could not afford to miss.

After a couple of hours, he sat back and yawned. It had been a long day, but an even longer journey to get to where he was now. He thought about Helen and what she might be doing. His stomach contracted as he thought of her friends hearing the news that reliable Ralph had done a runner. They would all rush to support Helen and to judge him, he had no doubt. He shook himself and moved back to the kitchen to wash-up the cracked crockery he had found with the saucepans.

He had dumped his new duvet and linen on the bare mattress in the bedroom, but before he made the bed he laid out the remainder of the things he had brought with him and went to the wardrobe to hang up his jeans. The enormous wooden doors filled almost the entire wall and he took hold of the ornate brass handles and gave them a tug, but they wouldn't open. Then he saw a blackened key in a lock below the handles and he tried it. It turned and pulling the doors again they swung open, but instead of dry air and the tang of moth balls, he felt a cold evening breeze on his face and he was looking out onto the night sky. This wasn't a wardrobe, but a doorway to some sort of terrace at the back of the building.

Ralph stepped out onto a wide wooden deck, dotted with terracotta pots filled with tall bamboos and other assorted plants, many now bare and dormant in their winter hibernation. A few metres ahead of him was a long, low wall running to the left and right, with a metal handrail at waist height wound with fairy lights that sent their gentle glow towards him. Above his head strings of white bulbs criss-crossed each other to make a magical canopy. He could see that the roof terrace ran far beyond his boundary and served the flat to his left above Joe's shop and to his right, where Anna must live.

As he stepped forward he saw a makeshift bar in the far corner, built from wooden trellis panels and what looked like old fruit crates, with a thin thatched roof, edged with its own set of lights, this time in the shape of pink flamingos. Beside it were a couple of old-fashioned deckchairs and more plants in pots, the taller ones wound with their own sets of lights. Ralph smiled and looked out over the wall at the jumble of roofs that fell away down the hill below him, then up to the deep navy sky which was strung with stars that shone to match the twinkling lights that surrounded him on the roof terrace.

As he took in the view a gentle voice floated towards him, "*There are dark shadows on the earth, but its lights are stronger by the contrast.*" Ralph turned, startled not to be alone.

"Do you know Dickens?" the voice said.

Ralph looked to the other end of the terrace, where a tiny lady sat, wearing an extraordinarily large sun hat and dark glasses, at a small iron table. For a moment he thought it was another of Anna's ghosts, but he could see the orange embers of the end of a cigarette in her hand and she was gently lit by light coming through a set of glass doors behind her.

"Erm, Dickens is not really my thing," he said.

"He has been a great friend to me throughout my life. Although The Pickwick Papers are not for me generally, it's lovely, don't you think? The earth has dark shadows, but the light is always the stronger," she stubbed out her cigarette in a blue china bowl and reached for a small, stemmed glass in front of her. "Will you join me?" and she waved the glass to indicate a chair next to hers.

"Oh, thank you," Ralph moved closer and sat on the ornate iron chair.

"*Although I am an old woman, night is generally my time for walking.*"

Not quite sure how to respond, he tried, "Is it?"

"I paraphrase, of course, from Dickens...often, as a matter of fact. You'll get used to it. I'm not actually a great walker now, but every night I come up here and have my one cigarette and my one glass of sherry - my little treat. Please, help yourself," and she gestured to a small silver tray, set with another glass, a decanter of rich, brown sherry, a packet of cigarettes and a silver lighter.

Ralph had never smoked and couldn't think of the last time he had tasted sherry, if indeed he ever had, but at this moment it felt like the right thing to do - so he poured himself a glass.

He looked at the delicate little lady next to him. She sat perched like a bird on a soft cushion, perfectly balanced and relaxed. The most striking thing about her was that she looked ready for a Mediterranean cruise rather than a chilly winter evening. Her hat was pale and wide with a black band around it and as the light shone through the translucent fabric it gave a soft glow to her heart shaped face. She wore large, blue-tinted sunglasses despite the darkness around her, and a pale pink jumper with a yellow mohair blanket over her shoulders. Her pure white hair was neatly bobbed to just below her ears and he saw that her small hands were delicate, but twisted with age.

"Is everything as you expected?" She asked quietly.

Ralph looked away, "Sorry, I didn't mean to...I didn't expect to meet anyone...I didn't actually know all this was here."

"No, few do. We are creatures who hide so much."

"Dickens?"

"No, just me," she smiled. "I'm glad you found your way here, Ralph. I think you will be a very welcome member of our little club."

"Club? Joe said something about a club...wait, how did you know my name?"

She put her glass down and placed both hands neatly on her lap, "I have little gifts. Moments of colour, perhaps. Moments of revelation," she paused, turning to face him for the first time. "I also talked to Joe and Anna a little while ago."

"Oh, I see," Ralph smiled. "I thought for a moment you had special powers."

"Who is to say I don't? After a glass of sherry all sorts of visions can appear," turning back to stare ahead at the night sky, she adjusted her glasses, pushing them back up her neat little nose. "We call it a club, The Rye Rooftop Club, but it's just us. We are hidden up here, so no one is aware of us and we feel safe to just be ourselves. Do you see? I can't quite remember who came up with the name, Anna, I suppose, in one of her chatty moments. She has many of those, but do not be put off...just think of it as big, long verbal hug. That's the best way to deal with it. Have another sherry, my dear."

"No, thank you. It's nice though."

She took a deep breath and wiggled herself comfortable on her cushion. Ralph wasn't sure if he was supposed to say anything, so he waited.

"I shall be ninety-two in a few weeks' time. A ridiculous age, quite frankly, but I still find pleasure - in other people, not myself. I have too much within me that I don't care for, too many corners around which I have hidden things...regrets, memories. So, I focus on those who have enough time left to fight for things that I never did and to look up at the sky and say, 'Sod the lot of you – let me do it my way.'"

Ralph felt his heart beat faster, unnerved by his companion - was she talking about herself or him? It was as if she had taken one look and seemed to know him. He took a gulp of the sickly sherry and said, "Are you Joe's grandmother?"

"My dear Ralph, I have been called many things in my time. My given name is Evelyn. My father called me Little Evie. I became Mrs Bondolfi or Mrs B, and my husband called me Eve - the first among women – such a charming man. I have been called daughter, sister, Aunt, but never Mother or Grandmother," she paused, pulling the blanket a little closer around her shoulders. "Although I am Joe's actual aunt, all those I consider my children call me Auntie B. They are the special ones who are a part of the Rooftop Club, which tonight you have joined by simply discovering our little haven above the town. We are a small group, but we are family. A family of friends. Like all families, we fight, we laugh, we cry, but we love who we wish and we protect each other. So, you *will* call me Auntie B, won't you Ralph? Promise me that you will."

"Yes, thank you. I'd like that."

"But, Ralph," Auntie B said, reaching her hand out to touch his arm. "*Never be mean in anything; never be false; never be cruel. Avoid those three vices and I can always be hopeful of you.* Dickens and I shall always be hopeful of you, Ralph."

He swallowed and turned to the sky to hide his face from her, but he was sure that this strange old lady did not need to see it to see deep inside him. He had never wanted to be false, but the lies had grown over the years. He knew he was not a mean man, but marrying Helen might certainly be called both false and cruel.

Auntie B squeezed his arm and then released it, "It's alright, Ralph, all you need is air. This rooftop is a place where everyone is allowed to simply breath their own air. Does that appeal, my dear?"

Ralph whispered, "You have no idea how much."

"I can see that you are a man who has built walls, Ralph. Remember, walls that have taken a lifetime to build cannot be taken down overnight. Be patient with yourself. When you can breathe freely you will open your heart, bit by bit, and you will find your way."

"But everything will change."

Auntie B shook her head, "I doubt it, my dear."

The two new friends, separated by two generations, sat quietly together, protected by the moonlight and the silence of the rooftops. Ralph breathed out and his shoulders dropped. He was so tired that he let his guard down and a tear rolled down his cheek. Once started he couldn't stop and the tears ran unchecked, until he felt one of Auntie B's tiny velvet slippers move to nestle gently against his foot. She said no more and made no attempt to stem his tears, but that simple action was enough to provide comfort and encouragement for him to begin to release whatever was inside him into the night.

Eventually the tears dried and Ralph knew that Auntie B was right, he was able to breath better. His lungs filled deeply with clean, fresh air and he felt as he had never done before - that here he might finally begin to tell the truth.

CHAPTER 5

The Butterfly Bar, Ginger Rogers
and a long-eared visitor.

J oe kicked the bottom of a paint tin until it was lined up perfectly with the other three against the step in the middle of The Bookery.

Ralph rubbed his hands together, "This is great, I can't wait to get started. So, where did you go after Vietnam?"

Joe leant against one of the old shelves, "Ah, now we get to the serious stuff. No world tour is complete for any young guy without a trip to Bangkok, and I can tell you it was certainly a trip," he shook his head and let out a long whistle.

They'd been chatting while Ralph collected the paint and equipment he'd ordered from Let's Screw, and Joe had started to reveal a brief history of his expulsion from his parents' home in Canada for smoking pot, his days living in a squat in Quebec and then his time hitchhiking around the globe.

"Bangkok is quite a place, I had never seen anything like it. After three days I was stony broke, not a dollar to my name. So, I got a waiting job at The Butterfly Bar, this cabaret place, packed to the ceiling fans with beautiful people. It was *the* place to hang out. I waited tables for a week, but I could see that the real money was to be made on stage."

"You performed?" Ralph asked.

"Sure did, that's where six years as a junior at the Tabatha Turner School of Dance came in real handy," Joe grinned. "They were making twice what I was and the tips were huge. So as soon as an opening came up I auditioned and I was in. Everyone in the show, all the acts, wore a butterfly, that was the gimmick."

"Nice."

"Just a butterfly."

Ralph's jaw dropped, "You mean, *just* a butterfly?"

Joe shrugged his shoulders, "Some were bigger than others, obviously." He ran his fingers through his well-trimmed beard, then rested a hand on Ralph's shoulder, "You look a little brighter today, it suits you. You were wound up pretty tight when you first got here."

Ralph was getting used to Joe's directness, but he still found it hard to be as open in return, "Thanks, but it's complicated," he said, stepping away from Joe's warm touch. "I know I've got to be more...me, I suppose, but I'm still working on who that is. I do feel better though. I had a good chat with Auntie B on Saturday night, until I made a complete idiot of myself. I suppose she told you?"

"Not a word. She's very protective, she holds secrets like a clam shell – shut tight. We wondered why she refused to let me go get you when we had a birthday drink on the roof for Anna."

"She seemed to be able to look right inside my head and, believe me, that is not a great place to be right now."

"Yeah, she does that. Sits all quiet, like a nice, innocent old lady, quoting her Dickens at you, then bam – cranks open your brain and has a damn good stomp around inside. Don't know how she does it, but she's got better at it since she went blind."

Ralph looked at Joe in shock, "What? Wait, she can't see?"

"Nope, she'd been losing her sight for about two years, but she lost it completely about six months ago. I really thought it would be the end of her when she wouldn't be able to paint. That was her life for so long after all, but she has adjusted real well, or at least that's the side she shows us. You should see her paintings, they're crazy," Joe started towards the door. "Let's get the rest of your paint, I'll have to open up soon."

Ralph followed Joe back to Let's Screw, admiring once again the bright yellow exterior of the shop, "There is no way anyone could pass this place without noticing it, is there? The colour and the name. I still can't believe you called it that."

"You'll never forget it, though, will you? First rule of marketing – brand recognition," Joe said as he headed down the neat rows of shelves that filled the shop. "Oh, the smaller paint brushes you wanted arrived too, I'll just grab them. Help yourself to some coffee."

Ralph went behind the counter by the window, at the end of which was a large pot of steaming coffee keeping warm on a filter machine. He found a mug under the counter and filled it before he noticed the slogan written across the front; 'I am hot, I am wet, I am delicious!'. He was still getting used to Joe's potent sexuality everywhere, but he tried to relax as he looked out of the window at the deserted street. It was Monday morning and still too early for anyone to be about. He turned as he heard Joe returning from the back of the shop.

"Two more cans of blue paint and your brushes. Is that it?"

Ralph took them from him and set them down by the door, "Yes, that's brilliant, thanks. Coffee?"

"Definitely."

Ralph grabbed another mug for Joe, "So, what made you want to do dance lessons in the first place?"

Joe leant across the counter, "It was my Mom's idea, she was named after Ginger Rogers, the old film star who danced with Fred Astaire."

"Wow, so your mum was a dancer," Ralph said, handing him the coffee.

"Nope, couldn't dance a step..." Joe was interrupted by a loud knock on the shop window behind him. They both turned and saw a stunning woman in a tight black coat, her blonde hair tied fiercely on top of her head. She stared angrily at Joe, her breath steaming wildly in the cold, then flipped him her middle finger before stalking off down the street. Joe watched the early morning sun bounce off the garden tools in the window display for a moment and then turned back to Ralph, "My Mom's actual name was Virginia, but everyone called her Ginger..."

"Wait, wait," Ralph pointed after the angry figure. "Who was that?"

"Hm? Oh, that was...erm. She was...Friday, no Saturday. No, Friday."

"Are you serious? You don't even know her name?"

"No, and I bet she can't remember mine either," he said and paused for a moment. "But do you think she expected me to call her over the weekend?"

"Well, maybe."

"Look, do you wanna hear about my family tree or not?"

"Yes, sorry."

"So, where was I? Oh, yeah, my mom, Ginger, was born here. She was the youngest of six children and Auntie B was the eldest. They were actually real close, as Auntie B was old enough to help raise her. I think she was devastated when Mom eloped in secret with my Pop and moved to Canada."

"So, if you were born in Canada, how did you end up here?"

Joe took a long sip of his coffee, "I had always had a vague idea of coming to the UK to see the family I'd never met, but when The Butterfly bar burnt down – don't ask, but all I will say is that little can prepare you for running through the Bangkok red light district at two in the morning with nothing but a slightly singed paper butterfly to cover el chorizo! Anyway, I contacted Auntie B and she wired me the money to pay for a flight to get me here."

Joe checked the time and went to the door and flipped the sign to 'Open' before he continued, "I worked for her and Uncle Cliff for a while to pay her back. Did you know this place used to be Auntie B's bakery, well, her and her husband's? The ovens were out back. The shop wasn't doing so well by then, though. They'd had a good run over the years and made enough to buy the other two shops in the block, yours and Anna's, with the apartments above. But the supermarkets had come along and people stopped buying from independent bake shops. I got here just as things changed, they struggled on for a few more years, but in the end they'd had enough."

"How come you didn't finish your travels or go back to Canada?"

"Not sure, really. I guess, I decided it was maybe time to grow up," Joe said.

"Really?" Ralph said, as he pointed at Joe's mug, which read 'World's Greatest Farter'.

Joe laughed, "Well, grow up *a bit*. Uncle Cliff sold the other two shops, but I persuaded him to keep this one for a while. I wanted to turn it into a hardware store that had a real personal service for people. Somehow I made the shop work, bought it off them in the end and I'm still here," Joe started emptying small bags of change into the till.

"How long have you been here?"

Joe paused over a bag of pound coins, "I was twenty-five when I got here, so nearly ten years, I guess. I'd already decided that going home to my parents wasn't really an option. Rye is a pretty cool place and Auntie B needed me when Uncle Cliff died, so..."

Joe turned as a customer came through the door of the shop, "Good morning, Mrs Hemstalk, come along in. You just yell if you need me." The elderly lady giggled a little and Ralph thought she had tried to flutter her eye lashes at them, but it could have just been a twitch.

"I'd better get going. Loads to do," Ralph picked up the tins of paint and made his way to the door. "Thanks again."

Joe went behind the counter as Mrs Hemstalk approached with a pair of pink gardening gloves in her hand, "Wait, Ralph, you've not heard today's joke," he leant over the counter to the old lady, giving her the full benefit of his blue eyes. "You'll love this one too, Mrs H. OK, what do you call a fish with no eyes? Anyone? Nope? A Fsh!"

Mrs Hemstalk looked at Joe then at Ralph, not quite sure what was happening, but they were such nice-looking young men that she really didn't care. Ralph groaned as he struggled next door with his load, while Joe continued to entrance the twitching, giggling old lady.

This morning Ralph had already been for a run and created signs from large cardboard boxes, cut into the silhouettes of open books. He had hung them in the windows announcing the grand reopening of The Bookery on Monday the 17th November - just two weeks-time. It was a risk going public with a date, but he was feeling confident that he would be ready – he couldn't afford not to be. After his embarrassing melt down with Auntie B on Saturday night, he had started to attack the shop on Sunday morning with a vigour and energy that surprised him. Ploughing on solidly throughout the day, in a strange way he had found it rewarding as he sanded and scrubbed The Bookery back to life. A little like himself, the shop was slowly starting to show the world what had been hidden for so long and he was pinning his hopes on people liking it. There was still a lot of work to do however, and today was going to be another long day.

* * *

Anna saw Ralph behind the book-shaped signs in the window. He was up a ladder painting some of the shelves and she paused for a moment to admire the sight of his snug jogging bottoms, paint covered vest, toned arms...then she remembered that anyone might see her ogling him and set off quickly to the door.

"Morning! Oof, shit...not again," she had not even considered that the door would be locked and had walked straight into it, crushing two cups of coffee this time. She stood back, milk foam dripping over her hands, holding them out to avoid it staining her pink kimono and leopard print fur-lined boots.

Ralph hurried to the door, opening it quickly, "Sorry," he said. "I didn't think anyone would be coming in."

"No, no, my fault, I'm an idiot - award winning, in fact," she paused, remembering not to push too hard and startle him, like last time. "Can I come in?"

"Sure, can I take something?" he stepped back into the shop allowing her room to pass.

"Yes, here, they're coffees. Well, two half-cups of coffee now and I've brought lunch. Today's baked bean and sausage pie and some apple turnovers. Mind you, I did feel at least one of them crunch between my knee and the door, so it may have to be apple crumble instead. Hope that's OK."

He took the crushed cups from her, putting them down on the step in the middle of the shop, "Yes, of course, thanks. You really didn't have to."

"It's no problem, Monday's a quiet day. Irene's having fun taunting some vegans at the moment, so she won't even notice I'm gone," and she plonked herself down on the step and gazed around the shop, taking in the new colours, partially sketched out murals and paintings and a collection of junkshop pieces he had picked up in local charity shops and antique centres. "Well, you're not wasting any time, are you?"

"I've only given myself two weeks to do a revamp and re-open, so I can't hang about. I've got loads of stuff I want to do."

"I bet, well, if you need any help or guidance in that department just let me know. Colours are my thing," she wafted a pink kimono sleeve at him. "Oh, who's this?"

Ralph turned as a soft brown head with two huge floppy ears, large eyes, a pink tongue and damp nose appeared around the bottom of the open door. A moment later the rest of a mucky beagle dog trotted happily into the shop.

"Now, look, you can't come in here," Ralph said, getting to his feet. In response the little dog dumped his bottom on the floor and looked at him with shining eyes. "You don't have a collar, but someone must be missing you. Hang on," he headed out onto the street, but couldn't see anyone who might have lost him. When he returned the dog was wolfing down the last of Anna's pies.

"Sorry, he was starving. Whose is he?"

"No, idea. Now listen, fella, you have to go home," Ralph said as he knelt scratching the dog's head. The beagle responded by happily rolling over and looking back up at Ralph, large eyes rounder than ever. Ralph obliged, scratching and stroking the dog's stomach, "He's certainly on the skinny side. Perhaps he's run away or got lost. Who are you, little one, eh?" To which question, the dog simply flipped back onto his feet, barked once, trotted out of the door and went on his way to wherever he was going before his impromptu lunch stop.

Anna watched him go, "So cute, but it looks like it's just half a cold coffee and crushed apple pastries for lunch then."

Ralph remained where he was and reached out for his coffee, "We used to have a couple of dogs on the farm. They were working dogs and didn't live in the house, but they were my best friends as a kid."

"Where was that?" Anna asked.

"The Peak District, my parents had a sheep farm there. They're retired now."

"You didn't fancy the life of a farmer, then?"

"No, never. My Dad always wanted me to take over. I mean, I understood why he wanted to keep it in the family, as his dad and grandad had farmed there before him. But, well...it just wasn't for me."

"Of course not," Anna said, jumping up. "Just look at this place, you have an altogether more creative side. You couldn't spend time shaving sheep or whatever you do to them. It's not finished yet, but I can see you've got a good eye. Now, you've used quite soft colours as your palate, but don't you think it's maybe a wee bit feminine?"

"Well, I..." started Ralph.

Anna was peering at the paint cans and colours, fingering fabric and poking around in the antique shop finds, "I know you've had a go, but honestly what are you going to do with these old suitcases?"

Ralph mumbled, "I was going to line them with the

fabric and then use them as browse boxes for people to pick up the latest reads or..."

"Hm, girly again. Not sure. I'd just pile them on top of some of the shelves, perhaps the travel section. Are you having a travel section? I would."

Ralph's jaws were now tightly clenched, "Of course, I'm..."

"I see you've sketched out a painting here of a castle. Nice, but a fairy castle? Really? A bit girly again. Now, what you need..."

"...WHAT I NEED..." Ralph's raised voice shocked them both. "...Is to get back to work."

"Sorry, I just thought...well, that I could help."

"Help?" An old fear had gripped him and he couldn't stop himself, "I've come here to do things my way...even if it is too girly or feminine. So, thanks for lunch, but, please go away." His neck had a deep red blush as he stepped to the door and held it open for her. He kept his eyes to the floor not able to meet hers or to show her the tears that were burning there.

Anna wrapped her kimono around herself, collected the cups and bags in a mortified silence, tucked her copper curls behind her ears and left the shop without uttering a word. She didn't look back as she heard the door thunder into its frame behind her and the two bolts shoot fiercely into place.

CHAPTER 6

The postman, a pickled egg and rooftop tales.

A nna plonked a large cake on Auntie B's little iron table on the roof terrace, produced forks from her voluminous yellow 1950's swing coat and threw them down beside it with a clatter.

Joe looked at the cake, "Oh, dear."

"What is it?" Auntie B said, quietly, sitting beside him.

"It's Anna," he said.

"I didn't say who, I said, what? I can smell cinnamon."

"It's an enormous carrot cake, with an enormous amount of cream cheese frosting."

"Oh, dear," she said.

Ralph frowned from the other side of the table, wrapped like the others in his coat and a blanket against the chill of the night, "Why 'oh dear'? It looks pretty good to me."

Anna was now slumped low in a deckchair, chewing an enormous piece of cake she had carved off with a fork. Joe looked at her, "Anna had a date tonight."

"Oh, dear," Ralph said, catching on.

"Don't you start," Anna mumbled through a mouthful of cream cheese.

"I didn't know you had a date," he said. "Mind you, I haven't really seen you since Monday."

"Please don't drag that up again. Irene won't let it drop, she keeps saying I was showing-off in front of boys again and got what I deserved."

"I thought you guys had patched things up?" Joe said, picking off a mini marzipan carrot from the top of the cake.

"We have," Ralph said. "Anna apologised to me for...well..."

"...showing off?" Auntie B asked.

"Aaarrgh," Anna moaned, ladling another big pile of cake into her mouth.

"Well, I was going to say, for being over enthusiastic and I apologised for being over-sensitive," Ralph said. "So, it's done with, but I think she's been hiding from me for the last two days."

Auntie B tutted, "Yes, she does that."

"I am here you know, while you all gang up on me, when I've had the worst day of my life," Anna wrapped her coat closer around her.

"All I meant was that I haven't seen you, so I didn't know about this date. Having a date is nice," Ralph said, looking around. "Isn't it?"

"Well, the signs are not good," Joe said. "Judging by the size of the cake."

"It was all Dew-drop Dobson's fault," Anna said loudly, waving her fork and spiralling crumbs into the air.

* * *

It had all started earlier that afternoon when Irene had scuttled into the back of the kitchen declaring, "I'm bleaching tea pots. You can sort him out," and refused to budge.

Anna took off her apron and went into the café only to come face to face with the familiar pinched features of her nemesis, Mr Dobson. "Oh, hello," she said, attempting a sweet smile.

"Good afternoon, Miss Rose."

"What can I do for you, Mr Dobson? A cup of tea is it?" She tried her best not to stare at the large droplet swinging enthusiastically from the end of his monstrous nose.

"Hardly. No, I am here to make a simple request," he flicked an imaginary piece of dust off his stained cuffs.

Anna muttered, "Oh, yes." She had been familiar with his simple requests, ever since she stopped supplying pies and cakes to his tea shop, The Copper Kettle, and opened The Cookery in direct competition.

"I believe that you have been advertising as the...and I quote...'premier pie shop in town'. Do you deny it?"

"No, no, I don't deny it. I did have an advert in the local paper last week."

"Ah ha, as I thought! Well, Miss Rose, the dictionary definition of premier states its meaning as...and I quote...'The first in importance, order or position.' As you are well aware, The Copper Kettle has been established in this town for more than forty-years and if any provider of the pie can claim the title of 'premier' it is surely me, not your little...place." He managed to pour enough sourness onto the final word that it made Anna shiver.

"Well, yes, but as I have won the best tea shop or café award from the local paper for the last two years, I don't really think I am misleading anyone."

Mr Dobson sniffed and the dew-drop bounced wildly, "Arbitrary awards mean nothing. My point remains a simple one - kindly refrain from overstating your modest business. It remains a little fish in a very large pond and the big fish are swimming around amongst the giant lily pads, which, I may add, are laden with greedy frogs let alone the dragon flies who may well...erm...may indeed..." but he had lost himself and was swiftly drowning in the metaphorical pond of his own making. "...The dragon flies may, erm...fly over and, indeed, past your tiny fish one day...and that, young lady, will be a fishy end for you." He finished with a loud sniff causing the droplet to disappear from whence it had come, then turned on his soft, rubber soled shoes and strode out.

The postman, a cheerful, ruddy faced man with bright ginger hair, had to step aside as Mr Dobson charged past him.

"Blimey, old Dew-drop was in a hurry. Has he had the curry pie again?" He chortled, enjoying his own joke as he made his way through the chairs and tables and plopped some letters onto the counter.

"Thanks, Jay," Anna said, still a little stunned as she always was after a visit from her old client.

"Mon pless-ear, madam," Jay said. "So, this date you owe me - I'm free tonight, if that's any good." Not expecting a reply to his daily quip, he turned and weaved his way back to the door.

"Pardon?" Anna said.

"Come on, you can't blame a chap for trying. Two years I've been bringing in your post and two years I've been offering my undying love and maybe a bit of lust on mother's second-best eiderdown."

"Are you married?"

He blinked at her, "Me? No one has yet been so lucky," he held up an empty wedding finger as if to prove it. "Why?"

"Then, yes, you can have a date tonight. I mean, *we* can have a date tonight. Why not?" She couldn't believe she had said it, but Dew-drop Dobson had made her mad and Irene would not let her forget her consistent failure with men, yet here was a man who wanted her - even if the man in question was Jay, the ginger postman.

"Oh, right, I see. Well, good. Blimey! Tonight then," he seemed considerably surprised at his own success. "We'll get something to eat, then, shall we? My treat, obvs. I'll pick you up at seven. Mother will be settled in front of the telly by then. Plus, I don't like to eat late. It sits on me - right here," he punched the middle of his chest to release a healthy bit of trapped wind and went off to finish his round.

Anna returned to the kitchen where Irene sat on a stool, frozen with her hand inside an emu-shaped tea pot.

"What?" Anna said.

"Ginger Jay?"

"There is nothing wrong with ginger, I mean, red

hair. Look at mine."

"Yeah, but *Ginger Jay?*"

"Don't call him that. Anyway, what's wrong with him? He's got a good job. Regular hours. His own uniform. He must be fit to walk as far as he does every day. He's good to his mother. What's not to like?"

Irene shook her head and went back to scrubbing the emu with extra vigour, "I'd be taking some of this bleach with me before I put any part of me on his eiderdown. Ginger Jay!"

* * *

Anna speared another large piece of carrot cake, "I don't know what I was thinking, Dew-drop Dobson just got under my skin - again. I'd made a fool of myself with a man – again. Plus, I swear I'd seen that shadowy woman in grey across the road this morning."

"Not that again," Joe groaned.

"What was she doing?" Auntie B asked.

"Nothing, just standing there. She always stands in the shade or a shadow, so I can't see her face – if she has one. By the time I've got to the window or opened the door she's vanished."

Auntie B shifted uncomfortably, "Oh dear, I am sure it is nothing, just the shadow of a cloud perhaps. Has anyone else seen her?"

Joe and Ralph both shook their heads.

"I am not making it up," Anna said.

"Let's forget about the imaginary ghost woman. I want to hear about your date," Joe said.

"So, hang on, who is Dobson?" Ralph was trying his

best to keep up.

"Anna used to provide Dew-drop...now you've got me doing it," Auntie B said. "I mean, Henry Dobson, with some of her delicious pies and cakes at The Copper Kettle before she opened The Cookery. Let's just say that old Henry Dobson was not best pleased when she left and his business suffered as a result. Most people simply followed the food with their feet down the hill."

"He's had it in for me ever since," Anna said with a mouth full of icing. "He is very influential in the town, god knows why, but he is on this committee and in that society. He probably rolls his trouser leg up and skips round the woods beating the Rotary Club on the bottom with pig's bladders, for all we know. So, don't get on the wrong side of him."

"OK, got it," Ralph said. "He sounds like a dick...Oh sorry, Auntie B."

"My dear, don't be sorry. Henry Dobson was a dick when he was a grubby little boy and remains so now that he is a grubby little man," Auntie B smiled, drawing delicately on today's cigarette.

"So, you had a bust-up with Dew-drop Dobson and made an idiot of yourself with Ralph," Joe said, bringing everyone back to the point. "As a result you decided these were valid reasons to go on a date with the only man in town no one wants to touch?"

"Oooooh," Anna groaned and buried her head in her hands.

"Well, hang on," said Ralph. "That seems a bit unfair, he seems like a nice enough guy. He's always cheerful anyway, from what I've seen."

"Exactly, thank you, Ralph," Anna raised her head and stuck her tongue out at Joe. "He is nice, was nice.

I mean, he picked me up on time. He'd had a wash – I think."

"Where did he take you, my dear?" asked Auntie B.

"Erm... the Chippy Chipper. I know, I know, Joe, before you say it, but he had brought his own little wooden forks, so he'd made an effort. We had a portion of chips and a pickled egg, because he said it was a special occasion. Then we stood under the old lamppost by the post office to eat them."

"Well, the old lamppost sounds kind of romantic," Ralph offered.

"The one by the supermarket bins?" asked Joe with a smirk, receiving a smack on his arm from Auntie B.

Anna grimaced, "Until my dying day I shall never forget the sight of him eating a pickled egg speared on the end of a wooden fork...and the noise. Oh, dear god, the noise!"

There was a moment's silence as all four of them pictured the scene and the sound, then Joe and Ralph could hold it no longer and they both snorted with laughter.

"Boys," warned Auntie B, before she started to giggle herself, picking up her sherry glass to try and hide behind.

Anna stared at them all, yet another fork full of cake halfway to her mouth, "Well, thank you all very much. What if he'd been a pervert? You wouldn't have been laughing then," which only seemed to make them all worse, as Joe and Ralph were now howling, holding their sides and Auntie B had gone quite red. Anna knew she couldn't hold out for long as the corners of her mouth started to twitch and she soon joined in with the laughter.

As things started to calm down, between gulps of

air, Ralph was able to ask, "How did you escape?"

Anna, bright red and laying full length on her deck chair, simply answered, "His pickled egg got stuck in his throat and he started choking..."

Joe moaned at this, "Oh, please, no more..."

"No, it's true. He was properly choking. I smashed him on the back a few times and the bit of egg flew out and bounced off the bins...but so did a couple of his teeth! Turns out his front teeth are false. Got knocked out by an Alsatian called Linda, he said. He...he...had to get down in amongst the bins to find them."

"An Alsatian called Linda?" wheezed Ralph with tears rolling down his cheeks.

"He found them eventually, but they weren't looking their best. He just picked them up and ran away."

It was nearly a full five minutes later that the laughter had subsided and they were all able to catch their breath. Auntie B took a last swig of her sherry, stubbed out her cigarette and got to her feet, "Anna, you are a tonic. You survived as you always will to fight another day, *Never use your failure today as an excuse not to try again tomorrow.*"

"Good old Dickens," Joe said.

"Not this time, dear - Facebook. Good night, little ones."

"Good night, Auntie B," Ralph and Anna said together.

Joe got up and Auntie B took his arm as he led her back into her flat, "Night all," he said over his shoulder.

"Night, Joe," Ralph said, watching them make their slow journey. "How can she read Facebook?" He whispered to Anna.

"One of us reads it to her. She loves it, can't get

enough of what she calls the greed, need and cheese."

Ralph nodded, licking his fork clean, "Where does Joe live, somewhere in town?"

"No," Anna said. "A few years ago he and Auntie B swapped houses. She had a house on the beach at Camber Sands, a few miles up the coast, and he was living here above the shop. When her eyesight started to fail, she wanted to be closer to everything and have people around her. He says he likes the peace out there by the beach. I reckon he gets less attention there – in other words, his conquests can't find him quite so easily as they used to here."

"Does he really have that many?"

"Conquests? Oh, yes, loads. Now he's moved it's hard to tell how many, but I reckon it's pretty much a revolving door situation."

"Well, being that good looking helps, I suppose," Ralph said, trying to ignore the images of paper butterflies that were floating around his head.

"Oh, yes, I mean that's partly why the shop has done so well. Who knew so many old ladies needed to replace their gardening gloves so often, not to mention, how many screwdrivers can some men own?"

"Men? Really?"

"Oh yes. He's not bothered, as long as he can flirt with them and they buy stuff. He's the world's biggest flirt, don't say you haven't noticed him trying it with you? I know you're not interested, but I sometimes think he enjoys the chase more than the end result."

Ralph got up to move to the railings beside them.

"Not that I'm judging," Anna said, continuing to tuck into her cake. "Joe's just...well, he's just...Joe. He's a hard nut to crack – not a euphemism, as he would say.

I'm still not quite sure who the real Joe is. But Auntie B would be lost without him. Are you OK?"

"Yes, I'm fine."

"I'm not saying he's had any men. I don't *think* he has. Women are definitely his thing, but he once said that men are the ultimate challenge. Tell me about it, I said," she appeared beside Ralph who was looking out over the town. "Honestly, I sometimes wish I was into women. Surely, we are so much less complicated than men? Well, the men *I've* dated anyway. Take this bloke I dated once, for instance, now he..."

Ralph let out a small groan and leant forward over the rail, dislodging a couple of the twinkling fairy lights, "Are you OK?" she asked.

"Sorry. It's just that...I don't mean to be rude, but..."

"...I talk too much. Is that what you want to say?"

"Well..."

"I do, I know I do. I hate silence. Sorry," she looked at him for a moment and could see the tiredness around his eyes. "Would you like me to be quiet for a few minutes? Or go away?"

"Yes...I mean, no. Don't go away, but it's such a lovely night and I'm pretty tired, so perhaps we could enjoy the peace and quiet?"

"Sure. I can do that. Right. Silencio. Here I go..." She pinched her lips together and leant on the railing next to him.

Ralph looked out over the shadowy streets below and the red roofs scattered under the dark night skies. He thought about his new companions, the other members of the Rooftop Club. None of them were really like anyone he had met before, they seemed to live with an openness that he could only dream of. He longed to be as confident as they were at sharing their lives and accepting each other for who they were. He knew he had to learn from them. Perhaps it was time to take a few bricks out of the wall that was still firmly in place inside him?

Next to him Anna let out a tiny squeak, "Eeeeek."

He turned to her as she stifled another noise by putting both hands over her mouth. He laughed, "This is really hard for you, isn't it?"

"Mm," she nodded.

"OK, you can speak now," Ralph smiled at his small, noisy, overpowering new friend. "Thank you for trying, it was very brave of you."

"Wasn't it? I was holding on so tight I thought my pelvic floor was going to come out of my ears at one point."

"I really appreciate it. I guess I'm just not used to all this."

"What? Noise? Other people? Have you been in a monastery? I knew there was something odd about you. Has your hair grown back? You know, the little bald bit in the middle?"

"Anna, shut up," he laughed. "I was not a monk. If you want to know, I've come here to do some thinking and hopefully some changing. That all takes time and, well, a bit of peace and quiet. That's all."

"Oh, right, I see. That's good. I'm glad you weren't a monk. That would have been a bit weird, wouldn't it?" She paused and looked out over the rooftops, "I see John and Julia have had another fight."

"Who?"

"John and Julia," she pointed to a narrow roof over to their right that was slightly crooked and seemed to stand above the others. "Can you see, both rooms are lit upstairs? They've had a fight so they are in separate rooms tonight."

"Do you know them?" he asked.

"Nope, I've no idea who lives there. I have stood here so many times that I feel I know each individual building and I've started to make-up imaginary lives for people inside them. You see that house there, with the missing slates? Well, that belongs to Gregor, the Russian drug smuggler. He lives next door to Sheila, the elephant trainer."

"Elephant trainer?"

"Yes, her back door is enormously wide, can't you see? You pick one."

"Me?" Ralph felt embarrassed.

"Go on. Just pick a roof, any roof, don't show me, just put it back in the pack when you're done. Only kidding. Go on just pick a roof...for me."

Ralph scanned the roofs of Rye in the darkness and settled on one, a little to their left, that looked small and simple. He pointed it out to Anna, "That one."

"Great," she linked her arm through his unselfconsciously. "So, what's going on there?"

Ralph felt uncomfortable, he had never been a great talker, finding it easier to let others do it all, but he was learning that perhaps he should go wherever his new family might lead and see what happened.

"Well," he thought for a moment. "They've just made some soup."

"Nice."

"They've got it on trays in front of the fire."

"And?"

"Well, they've got a chunk of bread each, with loads

of butter on it. And a glass of wine. Red wine."

"Brilliant. What else?" Anna was watching Ralph and she saw a much softer, almost boyish face appear as the tension that always seemed to be under the surface fell away. She smiled to think that he was comfortable enough to start to let go a little from whatever was haunting him.

"There's music playing, cheesy '80's pop, and they are both singing along as they eat. There's not much light from that window, do you see? Just a really warm glow. They've only got a couple of lamps on and the fire is lit."

"It sounds really lovely."

"It is."

"What are they called?"

Ralph hesitated and she noted a tense pulse return to his temple, "I don't know. Does it matter?"

"No, not really. I dream of evenings like that, someone to feel so comfortable with that soup and slippers are all you need."

Ralph shifted and turned around to lean his back against the railing, "Me too."

He looked around the beautiful, long terrace, illuminated by tiny lights and bulbs strung above their heads that threw out a warm white glow - he suddenly felt at home. He looked at Anna, a beacon in her shocking yellow coat, enhanced by the lights around them and smiled, "What's your issue with silence, then?"

The question surprised her, "What do you mean?"

"Well, you said you hate silence. Up until just then you have filled every second we've spent together with chatter or noise or, well, something. I played your game, now it's your turn. What's your issue?"

She looked back out over the rooftops, "I don't know, I'm just a chatterbox, always have been. Mum said it. Dad, well – I'm not sure really, he may have done. I don't remember him that well, he died when I was a child," Anna shivered, pulling her coat collar up around her ears.

"I'm sorry," Ralph said, taking the blanket from his shoulders and wrapping it round her.

"Oh, ta. It's OK, it was a long time ago. Blimey, after he went it was awful. I was an only child you see, no one else but me and Mum. There was a lot of silence then in the house. I just tried to keep things going I suppose, talk for both of us. To cover Mum's drinking, maybe? She was a maudlin drunk. She just sort of shrank when she drank - oh, that rhymes. Sorry."

"To keep the pain away?" He asked quietly.

"Yes, maybe. Blimey, this is getting deep, isn't it?" She laughed a little. "She married again, of course. Derek, 'The Dalek'. She stopped drinking for a while, but to be honest Derek was enough to drive anyone to the crème de menthe frappe, he was soooo boring. I kept talking so *he* couldn't - self-preservation for all of us. Still, it all led to The Cookery. Despite the booze and The Dalek, the one good thing Mum did was to hold on to some of Dad's life insurance money for me. I used it to buy The Cookery in the end, you see. So, that's my story. Old news. What's yours?" She looked at Ralph, hoping that the moment of honesty between them would allow her to finally find out what he was running from.

"Another time," he lent down and kissed the top of her head. "I'm glad we're friends again. 'Night."

"'Night."

Both friends went to bed knowing that they had

ended the evening a long way from where they had started it - a little happier and a little more connected, but with so much more to say.

CHAPTER 7

The beagle hunt, Rye Fawkes and the mad monk.

T he next few days were busy ones for Ralph, sourcing materials, meeting suppliers, ordering stock and finishing the artwork around the shelves as the clock ticked towards The Bookery's opening date. However, he did not work alone. Around lunchtime every day, a small damp nose would appear in the glass of the shop door and the sound of a tapping paw heralded the arrival of the scruffy beagle. Ralph would let him in and he would trot around the room inspecting progress, give his approval with a happy woof and then settle down to a bowl of water and one of yesterday's left-over pies.

Ralph rang all the local vets and animal charities, but no one seemed to have reported a missing beagle. A beagle who was becoming increasingly settled, arriving a little earlier each day and staying a little later. Finally,

Ralph decided he needed to know once and for all if he really was lost or just taking advantage of the hospitality on offer. Late one afternoon, after they'd shared a pleasant few hours together in the shop, Ralph opened the door and away the dog went, his tail high in the air as he marched down the High Street. Ralph set off in pursuit. The dog travelled at a leisurely pace so was either in no hurry to get where he was going or he knew that Ralph was following along behind.

Finally, they arrived at the quay and Ralph held back as he watched the dog disappear into a narrow passage between two of the larger warehouses that housed antique shops and cafes. Ralph followed quietly and stood with his back against the bleached wood-cladding of the wall, then he stuck his head around the corner. Peering into the gloom, he could just make out what he thought were the white patches of the dog's back-end disappearing under the building halfway down the cramped alley. He crept slowly into the gap, trying not to make a noise. After a few steps his eyes adjusted to the darkness and he could make out a hole in the cladding just about big enough for a dog to get through. He knelt down, wishing for the first time that he still had his mobile phone to use as a torch. Instead, he put his eye against the hole and squinted into the darkness.

Suddenly he got a wet smack across his face and shot back, crashing against the wall behind. As he scrambled onto his knees, out of the hole in the wall popped the cheerful face of the beagle, with his pink tongue waving enthusiastically.

"For heaven's sake," Ralph panted, dusting himself off. "Did you have to lick me? I nearly died of shock."

The dog barked, not as a warning, but as a welcome.

He squeezed himself back out of the hole and danced around Ralph, excited to see his new lunch companion again so soon.

"Stop, stop, you're dribbling all over me," Ralph pushed him away and tried to get to his feet, but was knocked back again as the dog enjoyed the game. "Get off. Go on, get down!" With the magic words the dog stepped back obediently and sat down, smiling at him.

"Oh, so you're trained then? Good boy. Right, well, it looks like you are officially homeless, but you haven't always been if you know how to sit to command. What am I going to do with you? You can't stay here on your own, dog."

"Woof," the dog answered in agreement, looking up at him with round, blameless eyes.

"Fine. Well, yes, I suppose that's the answer. You're alone. I'm alone. We might as well be alone together, eh?" He tickled the soft brown ears. "Come on then, time to make this a permanent arrangement."

They set off together back up the hill, the little dog trotting quite happily beside his new friend. They stopped off to buy essentials at a pet shop, including a soft bed, a collar, harness, dog food and Ralph's main concern, some shampoo to make sure the dog didn't infest his new home with any other unexpected visitors. The dog took to the collar and harness as if he had worn them all his life, and Ralph wondered how anyone could give up such a friendly dog?

Back at The Bookery, Ralph settled him in with a bowl of proper dog food and sat at the counter, watching as it disappeared in a few noisy mouthfuls.

"It seems like we both get a new start, dog. So, what's your name, eh? What can we call you?"

The beagle was now working his way around the shop, sniffing at boxes and checking out the curious shapes and smells of objects hidden under paint splattered dust sheets.

"What would suit you? A beagle...Eagle? Eagle, the beagle? Nope, ridiculous. Patch? Boring."

The dog had stopped by one of the old radiators and was snuffling around from one side to the other, trying to get at something that he couldn't reach. He tried with his paw, then his nose, but with no luck.

"What are you after? Leave it," Ralph called, but the dog kept on fussing around the radiator. "Hang on, hang on. What have you found?" The dog was now lying on his side pulling at something with his teeth. Ralph pushed the dog out of the way and pulled out a dusty paperback with bent pages and new teeth marks in its cover.

"Flat Stanley? Hah, I used to love these books as a kid. Oy..." Ralph said as the dog snatched the book from his hands, pottered away to the front of the shop and hopped up into the window display, where his new bed lay in the perfect spot to catch the afternoon sunshine. He proceeded to circle three times and then flop down, with the book under his chin – clearly claiming it as finders-keepers. "Fine, it's yours. You saw it first. You like Stanley, do you?"

The dog raised his head and barked once, before settling down again.

Watching him curled up in the warmth of the winter sun with his prized book, Ralph smiled, "Stanley. Yes, that seems just about right. What do you think, Stanley?" But the dog really couldn't be bothered to respond with more than a quizzical raise of an eyebrow, as he was already halfway to a peaceful snooze in this warm place, that smelt good and felt safe.

* * *

By Saturday night the town was buzzing with activity and colour as it readied itself for what had become known as Rye Fawkes Night. The local area had provided some of the raw ingredients for gun powder to the navy during Henry VIII's reign, so as the rest of the country celebrated Guy Fawkes' failed attempt to warm the bottoms of parliamentarians with a barrel of gun powder, Rye commemorated the town's history with fire and explosives. During that time many boats left port to raid France and were then burnt to prevent them being stolen by French raiding parties in return. So, on Bonfire Night a burning boat was towed through the narrow medieval streets and placed on the enormous town bonfire, before a giant firework display lit up the skies.

Ralph learnt all of this from Anna and Joe as they took him out, accompanied by Stanley, to experience the brilliant colour and chaos of the night as the town filled with locals and tourists alike. Anna was wrapped in a giant green poncho with purple fur edging and, to top it off, a bright pink woollen beanie hat with what Ralph said must have been the world's largest pom-pom.

"It's not the largest actually," Anna said, linking her arm through his as they walked through the old marketplace behind a crowd of elderly revellers in matching striped jumpers. "The world's largest pom-

pom was made by school children in Poland and was over two meters high."

"How, the heck, do you know that?"

"I looked it up," she said, proudly. "I knew one of you would have to say something rotten about my hat, so I just wanted to be ready for you."

"She knows us too well," Ralph laughed, turning as Joe caught-up with them. "Where have you been?"

"Just met someone on the way, as you do," Joe said, winking at him and then laying his arm loosely round Ralph's shoulders as they moved forward with the crowd.

"Animal, vegetable or mineral?" Anna shouted above the noise of the music from the hot dog vans and cries of passing helium balloon sellers.

"They were called Paulette…or Pauline…or it could have been Paul, hard to tell with all this noise and flames and stuff. I guess I'll find out later," he grinned as he waved his phone at them. "I have their number."

"How do you do it?" Ralph couldn't believe how easy it seemed to be for Joe to connect with whoever he wanted.

"Closely guarded secret, my friend. If I told you, I'd have to kill you."

Anna waved at a miserable looking girl in her late teens, dressed entirely in black, "Hi, Rosie!"

The girl paused in front of them, but kept chewing her way through an enormous cloud of candyfloss which she held in her black gloved hands. "This is Rosie, she works at The Cookery on Saturdays," Anna said.

"Hi," Ralph said and her panda-black eyes lurking behind a heavy black fringe flicked to him briefly, but displayed little interest. She tore off another great lump of candyfloss with her teeth, nodded at Anna and trudged off trying to lever the pink sugar fluff into her black rimmed mouth with her tongue. "She seemed nice," he added.

"Yes, she has confidence issues. We're working on it. Anyone want a toffee apple? I'm getting one..." but she was already gone, separated from them by a wave of children dressed as skeletons running at full speed pursued by a red-faced woman shouting, "Jeremy, Jeremy...Shin splints! Shin splints!"

"She's not the only one with confidence issues, is she Stan, my man?" Joe said, ruffling the dog's head. "Honestly, Ralph, look at you. You're a hot guy, good looking, fit. A man of few words, but a decent personality – assuming you are not a serial killer, which I haven't ruled out by the way. Just get out there, I mean, you should be fighting them off. What's holding you back?"

"Nothing. It's complicated..." Ralph could say no more as someone knocked roughly into him. "Ow, careful."

The man snapped back, "Watch out," as Ralph straightened himself.

"Sorry," Ralph said, even though he had been the one bumped into. He looked up into the face of a tall, slim man, in his early thirties with a stubbled chin and piercing green eyes half hidden under the peak of a grey baseball cap. Ralph recognised him or the cap from somewhere, "Oh, hi, erm...?"

"What?" the tall man said, looking annoyed, pulling the cap lower over his forehead and sticking his chin out in a gesture of arrogance. "You need to take care in these crowds, I could have dropped these," he held up three small foil food trays he was carrying in his gloved hands.

Joe stepped up to them, "You OK, Ralph? I see you've met Sam."

"Hey, Joe, how's it going?" The man, now identified as Sam, shifted the trays and reached round to give Joe a brief hug, forcing Ralph off balance again.

"Do you know each other?" Ralph looked from one to the other, trying hard not to take an instant dislike to Sam.

"Of course," Sam said, abruptly, then bent down to Stanley.

"Sam is in charge of meals on wheels for Auntie B, aren't you?" Joe said.

Sam grunted and stood up, "Something like that."

"Your face looks really familiar," Ralph said.

Sam turned away, "Really?" the arrogant chin tensing forward again in profile.

"Ah, now, that's an interesting thing..." Joe said.

Sam spun round and said, "...Joe," as if warning him. "Look..."

"I know! You run in the mornings, don't you? I've passed you, round by the quay? I pass you almost every day," Ralph had begun to recognise most of the early day dog walkers and joggers around the town, exchanging brief 'hello's' and grumbles about the weather - except for Sam who never made eye contact, refusing to allow any kind of connection.

"Oh, right, yes, maybe," Sam said, shuffling his feet, clearly anxious to be somewhere else.

Joe looked at Ralph, then at Sam, "I guess this is where I make a joke about you not recognising each other with your clothes on, right?"

Ralph blushed, but Sam frowned, "I don't think it is."

"OK, but I've got a special bonfire joke for you. It's a doozy, wait 'til you hear it..."

Waving the foil trays at them, Sam abruptly set-off through the crowd, "Sorry, I don't have time now. I need to deliver these to Auntie B before they get cold. Good to see you, Joe and...erm...Ralph."

"Wait," Joe shouted. "I'm great at firework displays - I've got a flare for it! Sam? Oh, well, I'll save it for next year."

Just then Anna appeared, elbowing people out of her way, "Can you believe it? No toffee apples. Health and safety, apparently. Some kids used them as weapons last year and broke the Mayor's nose. Was that Sam I saw? He normally avoids nights like this."

"He was delivering Auntie B's dinner," Joe said.

Ralph scowled as he watched Sam's cap bobbing through the crowd, "I hope he's more cheerful when he meets the old people on his round."

Anna laughed, "Oh, he's alright, he's probably a bit spooked by these crowds, he doesn't usually show himself for this sort of thing. It puts the wind up him. Joe, what are you doing?"

Joe was kneeling on the cobbles next to Stanley as the crowd pushed and shoved to get past the group, "I think Stan is a bit overwhelmed by everything, aren't you fella?"

Ralph looked down and saw Stanley sitting on the pavement with his tail hidden under him, quivering slightly, "Oh, Stan, I'm sorry." He bent and picked the frightened dog up into his arms, "I'd better get him back home. He's not really going to like the fireworks anyway, is he? You guys have a great night, though. I'll see you later."

78

"Lunch tomorrow?" Anna shouted to him, as he made his way back against the flow of the crowd.

"Great, see you tomorrow," Ralph said over his shoulder, before being swallowed by the crowd.

Anna looked at Joe, "Shall we get a hot dog or something?"

Joe offered her his arm, "Come on then, I like fine dining. I can't be long though, I have a date remember."

They followed the throng down the street and joined the queue at a brightly coloured catering van.

"You always have a date," Anna said, miserably. "It's not fair. I mean, it's not like you care about any of them."

Joe shrugged, "Not true. For the time we are together, I care enormously."

"Yeah, about twenty minutes, you mean. Don't you ever want some sort of commitment? Love, even?"

"Not yet. Do you want onions on yours?" he stood up on his toes to see over the heads of the others in the queue and nearly fell sideways as Anna grabbed his hand and started pulling him away.

"Quick, there, look," she said, pointing down a crooked little lane ahead of them.

"What?" he said as she started to run, dragging him behind her.

"It's her, the grey woman, I saw her," Anna dropped Joe's hand and started pushing people out of the way, forcing herself towards her ghost.

"I can't see anything," he shouted, then as he drew up beside her he gasped as they watched a tall, shadowy figure hurrying down the narrow lane. "Shit, what is that?"

"You can see her?" Anna whispered.

"Yes, she's...it's...I don't know, it's so dark down

there, but it was definitely something or someone," he walked slowly forwards, just as the distant figure seemed to dissolve into the mist ahead of them. "They've gone."

Anna came up behind him and held tightly to his arm, "That was her, the ghost woman I see outside The Cookery. I saw her through the crowd back there, just a glimpse. She was in the shadows at the entrance to the lane so I couldn't see her face, but she was watching me, I know it."

"If you couldn't see her face, you can't have known she was watching you."

"She looked angry, didn't she? Don't you think?"

Joe turned to her, "Anna, you are over thinking this. She wasn't angry, maybe she wanted a hotdog too and decided the queue was too long. She was just in a hurry."

"No, no, it was the grey ghost and ghosts don't eat hotdogs. Why does she keep appearing outside my shop and why does she seem familiar? Do you think I knew her in another life?"

Joe started guiding Anna back towards the bonfire night activity, "Perhaps she's on a diet or has a gluten intolerance and is plucking up courage to come inside. There is no such thing as ghosts, Anna. Trust me."

"There is, everyone knows there is, especially in Rye. There are loads; Allen Grebell murdered by a butcher, and the mad monk bricked up for trying to elope – you can still hear him in Turkey Cock Lane..."

Joe laughed, "You're just making that up."

"It's true, ask Auntie B. It's called Turkey Cock Lane because the sounds of the mad monk behind his wattle and dottle wall, or whatever you call it, were just like a gobbling turkey. It's a well-known fact, but the point is, she scares me."

Joe looked down at Anna who was quite a bit shorter than him, but at this moment looked tiny as she hugged herself and leaned in against him. He sighed, "OK, OK, how about we stick together tonight? Paula can wait for all her dreams to come true another time."

"Really? That would be amazing, I think I'd be too scared to stay out here on my own."

"Come on crazy lady, let's get that hotdog. I've got a bonfire joke for you too," he led her back to the van.

"Wasn't her name Pauline?"

"Probably," Joe said with a grin and put his arm around her.

As they stood in the queue and Anna returned to her habitual complaints about his casual attitude to the women he hooked up with, Joe looked back to where he had seen the grey lady disappearing into the distance. He didn't believe in ghosts and certainly not this one, especially when he had smelt the faint, unmistakable scent of Chanel No. 5 as she ran from them. But who was she and what was her interest in Anna?

CHAPTER 8

The man in the cap, a Sumo wrestler
and being alive.

O nce Ralph had fought his way back through the crowded streets, he settled Stanley onto the sofa in the living room, closed the curtains and put a football match on the TV to muffle the sound of fireworks outside. He then made his way up to the roof terrace with a mug of coffee.

"Ralph?" Auntie B called, hearing his footsteps.

"Yes, only me. Are you OK?"

"I'm just fine, dear. Just fine."

Ralph came round a large potted conifer tree to find Auntie B in her usual place at her little iron table. She was wrapped up in soft blankets and a pale blue scarf, still with her large summer hat on her head. However, she was not alone. Sitting opposite her at the table with his back to Ralph was a man with floppy, sandy hair. As the man turned he saw that it was Sam without his cap.

Ralph felt himself tense, "Oh, it's you," recognising the haughty jaw andintense green eyes from earlier. "Sorry, I didn't think you'd still be here."

Sam put his cap back on, tucking his hair inside, "I'm just off."

"No need to rush, Sam," Auntie B said. "Have you met our newest club member, Ralph?"

"Yes, we just met in town," Sam said, not looking at him. "Anyway, enjoy your dinner. See you later in the week." He went round to Auntie B, gave her a quick peck on the cheek, then looked briefly back at Ralph without meeting his eyes, "See you," and disappeared through the doors into Auntie B's flat.

"What is his problem?" Ralph said, taking his place at the table.

"Oh, dear, didn't you hit it off?"

"He's not the friendliest person I've met so far, let's put it like that."

"Oh, he's a sweet boy really, when you get to know him," Auntie B said. "But that can take a little while, obviously."

"Has he been bringing you your food for long?"

"Oh, yes, a little while now. It's always delicious. He worries about me not eating proper hot dinners, so he makes sure I get some of my favourites. Fish pie tonight. He's really very kind and so handsome, just like a film star, don't you think?"

"Hmm," Ralph said, Sam certainly had the pretension and affectation to be a film star. "Are you warm enough? It's a really cold night."

"Yes, I'm all wrapped up - I feel a little like a sumo wrestler. How are things out on the street?"

Ralph warmed his hands around his coffee mug,

"Chaotic, the place is heaving. For a small town it's certainly popular."

"That's why it's great for shops like yours. I know you are going to be a huge success. I can't wait to come down and visit."

"And I can't wait to show you around. Actually, I had a favour to ask you."

"*When we have done our very, very best and that is not enough, then I think the right time must have come for asking help of others*," she turned to him with an apologetic smile. "Isn't it annoying that Dickens has a quote for everything? I'm sorry, I really can't seem to help myself. I spent a long time learning these little titbits, so I might as well make use of them while I still can, don't you think? Anyway, Dickens and I digress. How may I help?"

"Well, the shop is taking shape, but I'm running out of time. I have a wall beside the art and craft section that I need to fill. As well as the books I'd like something local and unique that draws people in."

"I see, is that where I come in? Being both local and unique. Should I come down and sit on a shelf during opening hours?" She raised a delicate white eyebrow as she reached out and her fingers found the stem of her sherry glass.

Ralph laughed, "I hadn't thought of that, but if you were free I'm sure you'd be a big draw. What I was actually thinking of was some of your paintings. Joe told me that you were...I mean, are...an amazing artist. I'd love to show some of your work, if you'd let me."

"But you have never seen any of my work. They're just daubs, dear, daubs."

"Well, that's not what Joe says or Anna. May I see some of them?"

For the first time since he had known her Auntie B seemed unsure, "Of course, if they are private then I quite understand," he said.

"No dear, they are not private. I painted them to be seen. I had quite a few exhibitions at one time, but it is a part of my life that I have left behind, that's all."

"I'm sorry, I didn't think..."

"...and nor should you," she said, placing her glass firmly on the table. "No, you must see them. Come on, help the old girl up. Let's tiptoe down memory lane."

Ralph moved around the table and gave Auntie B his arm as she rose from her chair. He took the blanket that covered her knees and held it as they walked together toward the lit room behind them. As he guided her down the steps from the roof terrace, through large glass doors, he found himself in a warm, elegant living room.

"Thank you, Ralph, I can take it from here. Give me the blanket."

He passed it to her and she made her way carefully across the room to the door beyond, gently feeling her way between the furniture, "Back in a tick. Make yourself at home."

While he waited Ralph wandered slowly around the room. The furniture was minimal, but extremely stylish. Everything was designed with simple clean lines, pale woods and upholstery in modern takes on classic 1950's and '60's designs. The walls were white and dotted here and there were large, white-framed canvases of what, he assumed, were Auntie B's paintings. Joe had been right, they were crazy, but they were also amazing. Subtle colour washes of pale pinks and purples formed backdrops on the canvases, then wild, extraordinary plants and grasses sprang up across them. He recognised a few of the flowers on the tips of the green stems that shot over the paintings, but many were clearly from her imagination in bold colours and eccentric shapes. He didn't know what he was expecting - perhaps something restrained and delicate, like Auntie B. However, these paintings were bold and energetic, alive with their swirling colour. No wonder Joe thought Auntie B might fade away when she lost her sight if this was how she saw the world when she was painting.

He jumped as a voice just behind him said, "Our friend Mr Dickens told us, *Nature gives to every time and season some beauties of its own.* Well, I tried to give nature a little something extra of *my* own, if that's not too grand."

"They are amazing, I love them."

"Really? You are kind, but you are also polite so I would expect a sensitive young man to say that, but thank you anyway. Shall we go back out and you can describe the fireworks to me?"

"I'm not being polite...well, not *just* being polite. I love them, genuinely. People should see these; please may I have some to put in the shop? Do you have many? Can we sell them or are these the only ones you have?"

"You really like them? Don't you think others will find them a bit dated?"

"Dated? No. These could never get old or go out of style, they are so alive. I really want them in the shop. I had wanted to try painting some of my own, but I just don't have time and these are way better than anything I could do."

"Well, if you are sure, you are welcome to take what you wish. I have more in the other room. Come back in the morning and take whatever you want. Just not that one," she pointed towards a small painting that hung above the fireplace. "That is Ginger's picture and it stays with me."

Ralph went across the room to look more closely. The frame was simple and white like the others, but the painting was smaller. It had a soft yellow background, like a hot summer haze over a meadow or cornfield. The stems and grasses that grew from the bottom of the picture were pale lime and delicate sage greens with flowers or tips painted in gold leaf, which shone and caught the light.

"This is incredible," Ralph said, almost to himself.

"Thank you, dear. I painted it for Ginger. She was incredible too."

"Your sister? Joe's mother?"

"Yes, Joe's mother. She died in Canada. She never saw the painting, but...well, it is very personal."

"Of course. I'm sorry about your sister. She was the youngest of the family, wasn't she?"

"She was the baby, yes. She was rather unexpected. With five of us already, a sixth mouth to feed was difficult, but we managed. She was worth it."

"Are you the last of the brothers and sisters?"

"Yes, I was the first and now I am the last. Come on, I can hear the fireworks starting, let's go back out."

Ralph tore himself away from the beautiful little painting and let Auntie B take his arm as he led them back out onto the roof.

"What about you? Are you from a large family, Ralph?"

"No, just me. My parents never really talked about it to me, but I heard them sometimes when they thought I wasn't listening, and I'm pretty sure that I had a brother or sister who died."

"How awful for them. Losing a child is the worst pain possible, but to love a child even for a short while is the best gift we can be given."

"It must be."

"Have you ever loved someone fully, my dear?"

Ralph's breath caught in his throat; Auntie B's seemingly innocent questions were aimed so carefully that he was sure that she knew the answers long before she asked them. They had reached the edge of the terrace and the bangs and cracks of fireworks were filling the air. He looked up at the explosions racing in front of them.

"No, I haven't loved anyone. Not fully, not really. I might as well tell you - I had a wife...*have* a wife, Helen. I've left her. It wasn't, well, it didn't...I couldn't stay. I need to let her get on with her life. I need to begin mine."

"I see....and has it begun, your new life?"

"Yes, I think it has. A little, but I need to be braver."

Auntie B laid her hand on his arm, "Of course you do and you will. Be patient with yourself, it takes as long as it takes." She tucked her hand under his arm and they stood together as the firework display reached its peak and then fell still, leaving echoes of light and fury.

"I remember as a child feeling that I never wanted fireworks to end. I was so sad when they were gone, I always cried," Auntie B said, then turned to Ralph. "We all have to know loss and we all have to know love at some point, it is part of who we are. We can't be whole until we have known both, don't you think?"

"I don't know really," Ralph sighed. "I seem to have spent my whole life hiding from it...from love. So, I've had nothing except the loss part, without any of the benefits of loving someone first. It's ridiculous. I'M ridiculous," his voice began to rise in the night air as he gripped the rail tightly. "What am I AFRAID OF? What am I WAITING FOR? What is so wrong with being GAY?" He gasped as the words floated out of his reach, away over the rooftops.

Ralph stood frozen. He had heard the words as if they belonged to someone else, but he knew they were his. He knew that the wall he hid behind had fractured.

"Nothing is wrong with it, that I'm aware of," Auntie B said gently, reaching to find his hand and taking it in hers. "Nothing in this world could be so *right*, in my opinion, Ralph. The majority of us love with very little effort on our part and have the instant approval of the world around us. However, you and those like you have to *fight* to love who you choose and, too often, you have to do it alone. It seems so unfair and yet I often wonder, when you do find love, if it is a much richer reward because you have had to fight so hard for it? You have earned it in so many more ways than people like me will ever know."

"Do you think so? Really? I've always been afraid. The humiliation, the prejudice, feeling less than others."

"Why should you feel less than anyone else?" Auntie B said, releasing his hand. "That's *your* prejudice, Ralph, not other people's. Yes, some people will judge you for who you love – but for goodness sake don't judge yourself for it."

"Don't you care?" he asked. "Genuinely, doesn't it change who I am to you?"

"Ralph, dear, I am still getting to know you and

everything new I learn makes me like you more, not less. The more we reveal, the better friends we will be. The big task for us all is to unpick which bits of our friends are truly them and which bits they have just built to protect themselves."

Ralph looked at her, was the version of himself that he had played all of his life about to step aside? "Thank you. You are...very kind and wise and..."

"...and very old, very tired and freezing my tits off, to quote Anna rather than Dickens on this occasion. Take me in, Ralph," she turned and waited for him to guide her. As they reached the glass doors she stopped and turned to him, "Don't stay in hiding any longer. Let that wall come down. I waited too long." With that she turned and stepped lightly down the steps, her hands on the wall to guide her, and shut the doors leaving Ralph alone.

He slowly walked back to look down over the roos as Rye settled back to its usual quiet pace, but nothing seemed the same. Every tile seemed to be redder, every star brighter - at the age of twenty-seven he was, finally, more alive than he had ever been.

CHAPTER 9

The cover up, baked beans and The
Ceiling of Curious Things.

Sunday morning arrived with clear skies and a sharp frost to douse any smouldering bonfires from the night before. Joe stood naked at the large glass windows of his bedroom, looking out beyond his beach-side garden to the horizon, where the iron-grey sea met the winter sky.

He wasn't really given to soul searching, he'd always just taken the next move that presented itself; his parents told him to leave home, so he did; the squat he ended up in was raided by the police, so he left. He hitch-hiked wherever his ride was going and came to the UK when he had no money left to go anywhere else. He wasn't quite sure why a rickety corner of these damp islands had held him for so long. Lately he had begun to feel unsettled and started to worry that he should be moving on. He had no desire to start again, but he knew something was changing - he just couldn't figure out what it was.

Before he could think further his phone rang and the screen told him who it was and he swiped up, "Morning, Auntie B, everything OK?"

"Yes, dear," she said on the other end of the line. "How are you?"

"Good, thanks."

"Are you...alone?"

Joe sighed, "Yes, Auntie B, I'm alone."

"Excellent. Are you wearing trousers?" she asked.

"Good god, how do you do that?"

"Put some trousers on, Joe, I cannot speak to you until you do."

Joe scrabbled to grab some shorts and pulled them on, "I mean, you are super spooky, you know that?"

Auntie B laughed down the phone, "I just know you, Joe, that's all."

"Right, everything is now under cover, satisfied?"

"Good, now what is wrong?"

"What do you mean? You called *me*."

"I have already told you, Joe, I know you. You didn't ring me last night and Anna told me that when you dropped her off you were going home to bed...alone. So, I repeat, what is wrong?"

"She had a fright, that's all. So, I made sure she was OK and then I came home for a quiet night."

"Ah, yes, the grey ghost that is haunting her, she mentioned it."

"Yup, we saw her last night."

Joe heard scuffling noises on the other end of the phone as if Auntie B was changing position, "You saw her?" she said.

"Oh, yes, we followed her but she ran off. I didn't see much, just her back..."

"But you didn't see her face?" Auntie B's question was urgent.

"No, just her back in the distance."

"Good."

Joe sat on the edge of his bed, "What do you mean, good? What do you know that you aren't telling me?"

Auntie B laughed, "Joe, there is a great deal I know that you don't. Too much, perhaps."

Joe lay back, scrubbing his face with his hand, "Isn't it exhausting to be the holder of so many secrets?"

There was silence from Auntie B for a moment, "It can be, but I have been used to it for so long. They are not my tales to tell...well, not all of them. There is a right moment for everyone to reveal what they struggle to face and it is up to them to reach that moment alone. It's like a key turning in a lock. *A very little key will open a very heavy door,* Mr Charles Dickens said in one of his plays, did you know...?"

"Auntie B, please don't change the subject. I'm worried about Anna, that ghost is no spook. I smelt her perfume, I doubt even Chanel is for sale on the other side even with their level of marketing. She's as real as you and I, so she must be following or spying on Anna."

"Oh dear, that is unfortunate."

Joe started pacing the room in frustration, "*Unfortunate?* Are you kidding? What's going on, Auntie B? And don't fob me off with one of your mysterious quotes."

"Joe, that woman is no danger to Anna. I will speak to her, there will be no more sightings of the grey lady."

Joe's pacing stopped, "You know her? Who is she?"

"I can't tell you and you must say nothing to Anna. It

is nothing sinister, I promise you. You just need to trust me."

"Auntie B..."

"Joe, please don't say anything to Anna. The ghost will disappear into the ether as they are prone to do and she will forget all about it. Let that be an end to it."

"You can't just..." but Joe was speaking to a dead line as Auntie B had gone.

✳ ✳ ✳

"Sorry, sorry, sorry. Damned alarm didn't go off," Anna said, as she flew into the café at the train station, which was deserted except for Ralph already at a table with a coffee in front of him.

"Where's Stanley? Oh, there he is. Hello, Stan, how are you?" she stroked the dog's head as he came out from under the table to greet her. "What are you having?"

"Full English, I think, I'm starving," Ralph pushed the chalk board menu across the table as she struggled out of the copious folds of her poncho.

"Hmm, well, I'm out for dinner tonight on a date, so better not have too much. I'm hoping he's paying and I want to make the most of it. So, just a stack of pancakes and some bacon, I think."

"Something light then," smirked Ralph.

"It says they're light and fluffy - a little like me," she shook her copper curls at him and tried to pout, just as the young waitress came to take their order.

"Yes?"

"Oh, sorry, I'll have the special pancakes please. No

94

maple syrup though. A cappuccino too, please."

"And what do you fancy, sir?" the girl said, moving closer to Ralph and producing a far superior pout for him.

"Full English, please, and another black coffee. Thanks."

"Coming right up," she said with a wink.

"Hey," Anna leaned in to get her attention. "I will have the maple syrup after all. We mature women can take it," she added venomously as the girl retreated to the kitchen with a distinct wiggle of the hips.

"What's the matter with you? She was only doing her job," Ralph laughed.

"Yeah, if she was a spider sizing you up for lunch."

"She was just being nice."

"Whatever. You have no idea the effect you have on women, do you?" she sat back and crossed her arms.

"What's got into you? All I said was, *Full English*."

"Yes, I know, sorry. It's me," Anna slumped in her chair. "Look, let's just be friends, shall we?"

"I thought we were. Are you sure you're OK?" He reached across the table and took her hand, "Has anything happened?"

Anna looked down at their joined hands, "Not for want of trying," she felt him tense. "I'm kidding. It's just that friendship seems to be about the limit for me. I've dated umpteen guys, well, probably several umpteen, to be honest, and all they really want is some rumpy-pumpy and a fried egg breakfast. I'm only seeing this bloke tonight because Irene wound me up. She kept going on about how I'll never find a man and how I should chuck my eggs next to the frozen peas in the freezer for safe keeping, all that sort of stuff. Then this guy came in for a coffee and - bam! - I'd wangled a date, but I really don't want to go."

"Then don't."

"He's bald. He's got nice eyes, but no hair. I mean, I know it's wrong, I'm usually a completely open person, but I can't cope with shiny heads."

"Anna, just cancel. I don't know why you have this pathological need to date men you have absolutely no attraction to."

"Look, I wouldn't have to go on anymore rubbish dates if you were interested in me, would I?" Anna took a sharp intake of breath. "Damn, there I go again. Sorry, we're just friends, I know that. I'm happy with that. Honestly....Unless?" She looked at him coyly.

"Anna, look..."

"I know, I know I'm not your type," she released his hand and began to tear a paper napkin apart. "You're into blondes or bigger girls or smaller girls or just girls that aren't me. I know, don't worry, I get it."

"Wait, Anna, you don't get it. Look, erm..." he coughed.

"Oh, my god, you're dying. You've got something terminal."

"What? No, no, I'm just gay. I'm not dying," for the second time in as many days the words were out of his mouth before he knew it, as naturally as if he'd been saying them aloud all his life.

"You're gay? Oh, thank god," Anna exclaimed just as the waitress returned with the drinks. Anna gave her a triumphant smile, "Thank you, young lady."

After the waitress had withdrawn with less of a wiggle in her step this time, Anna continued, "I thought you had cancer, I'm such a bad hospital visitor. I never know what to say, as hard as that is to believe, so I end up eating everyone's fruit and then have to go out and buy them some more. It costs me a fortune."

"No, I'm fit and well, but I am gay. Sorry."

"Oh, don't apologise, that's brilliant."

Ralph was astounded, "Is it?"

"Of course it is. It means it's nothing to do with me, doesn't it? Except I've got a dangly bit missing. Well, I've got two great big extra dangly bits as well, but you know what I mean. It's a shame though because you are gorgeous, but isn't that always the way? You're not in love with Joe are you? Please don't be, everyone else is, but he's not right for you," she took a sip of her cappuccino leaving a foam moustache above her lip.

Ralph looked at her and picked up his napkin and wiped the milk froth away.

"You see, if that had been Joe, as a straight bloke he would have left it so I would walk around with it all day and make a compete tit of myself - pardon my tit. You on the other hand, being gay, have rescued me straight away."

Ralph laughed, "I'm glad I'm useful to you for something. And no, for the record, I'm not in love with Joe. I'm not quite sure who is right for me, but I don't think it's Joe."

"Well, at least you've got me on your side now," she said. "We can find love together. I'll find you yours, if you find me mine."

"Deal," Ralph said, as their plates of food arrived and were dumped unceremoniously between them. Ralph smiled at the waitress, but just got a sullen nod in return, "So, you didn't know then?"

"Well, there were some signs that you were and

some that you weren't. Honestly, I think I go a bit man-blind when one comes along that's single, has all his own teeth and some hair. I do, honestly, I need help."

Ralph fed a piece of sausage to Stanley under the table, "You need to spend more time getting to know people, that's all. Didn't your mum teach you that? More haste less speed, mine used to say."

"Mine used to talk to the bottom of her wine glass mostly. Anyway, she's not around anymore. So, it's you, me and the Rooftop Club."

"I'm sorry, I didn't realise she was..."

"It's fine, she's been gone a while. Talking of being gone, does your wife know about you? Helen, was it?"

Ralph pushed a pile of baked beans around on his plate, "No, she doesn't, I didn't tell her. I just left her a note to say I couldn't stay."

"Oh dear, poor girl. Sorry, I know you're my new gay best friend and everything, but that's rough."

"I know, I know, I just didn't have the words. I came here to sort my head out and see if I could live without lying. To see if I could be me and not feel ashamed," his voice grew thick with emotion as his journey of the last few weeks started to overwhelm him.

Anna reached out to him, "Well, your plan seems to be working. You're not lying to anyone and I can't see anything to be ashamed of. Not here, we're the Rooftop Club, we're a family. We take each other for just who we are - faults, fowl-ups and other things beginning with F. Who you choose to fall in love with is no one's business but your own. Oh, and mine, because I want to know all about it, but you know what I mean. Come here you," Anna struggled to get up from her chair as it was pushed tightly under the table and losing her balance she put her hand firmly in Ralph's baked beans. "Oh, bugger, I wanted to give you a hug, but in my head it was going to be a lovely moment. Now I'm sloshing around in your breakfast."

Ralph looked at his new friend as she wiped herself clean, "Thank you," he said.

She took hold of his face gently with both hands, "You are very welcome, Ralph Wright. I feel like I'm looking at a new man...and I like what I see."

"I feel like a new man, thanks to you and the rooftop and The Bookery and Stanley..."

"Can't forget, Stanley."

"How could I? This place is magical, a little bit unhinged too, but special, and I don't know what would have happened to me if I hadn't found Rye and the Rooftop Club. Right now, I feel like whatever happens next - I'm ready for it."

"Bring it on," Anna shouted, waving her pot of maple syrup in the air. "By the way, you've got a baked bean on your cheek."

✽ ✽ ✽

Anna spent the rest of the afternoon working with Ralph in The Bookery, both feeling relaxed and enjoying their work. He concentrated on finishing the painted castle in the children's section, which now had a dragon flying over its turrets, knights hacking back thorn bushes on its walls while a dynamic princess escaped under her own steam down knotted bed sheets to a moped waiting at the bottom for her. Anna set to work on the bric-a-brac pieces that were to be used to encourage people to explore the rest of the shop.

She nipped back to her flat and rummaged in the back of cupboards to pull together several boxes of other interesting objects that she had gathered over the years, but never used. She laid them all out on the shop floor, fighting off Stanley who was intent on borrowing the most delicious smelling items. She suggested to Ralph that instead of using them to take up valuable space that he could use for books and other sales stock, she could instead create a flying display by suspending a lot of the curios and smaller pieces from the ceiling. It would be unique and would definitely get people talking. She was relieved that Ralph loved her idea, so she spent a couple of very happy hours running up and down step ladders hanging Victorian dolls, copper kettles, unusual glass bottles, rubber ducks, wartime comics, an old fox fur wrap complete with head and glass eyes, a Cilla Black vinyl LP and a complete replica of the Star Ship Enterprise made from hair grips.

Eventually, with her face red and hair looking wilder than usual, Anna stood back to admire her work, "There you are, I give to you - The Ceiling of Curious Things."

Ralph came from the back of the shop wiping his paint covered hands on a rag, "It's absolutely brilliant, I love it! I would never have thought of that and it's got something for everyone. It's amazing - you're amazing! Thank you so much," he pulled into a warm hug.

"The feeling is mutual my clever new friend. I am very glad you found us."

"Me too," he said. "Me too."

* * *

As the days flew by towards the opening Ralph worked from dawn to dusk without caring about the hours or the hard work. He was the happiest he thought he had ever been, experiencing a new sense of freedom and confidence. Another joy was that Stanley was always at his side, supervising the work, the deliveries and a photo session with a local newspaper, in which he took pride of place, of course, at his best friend's feet.

Ralph organised and re-organised the lay-out of books on the shelves, the installation of a new till and stock-management system, not to mention a brand-new website that utilised all of his skills from his previous career. Auntie B let Ralph select and hang paintings from her extensive collection. Joe and Anna shared their experience of running shops, along with advice on managing stock levels and cash flows, which made his head swim. Then, finally, on Sunday - the eve of opening, they worked together through the night. Fuelled by laughter and a crate of beer they filled the two front windows with spellbinding displays of books amid more than a dozen different vintage reading lights - gathered by Anna from online auction sites for next to nothing - all lit with coloured bulbs. Ralph painted the words, 'Let your adventure begin...' along the bottom of the window glass and finally The Bookery was ready, its transformation complete.

"Damn, that looks good," Joe declared as the three of them stood outside the shop admiring their work.

"I can't quite believe we've done it," Ralph said, wiping the last smear off the shining windows.

"*You've* done it, my friend," Joe said. "We were merely the Gromit to your Wallace, the Ant to your Dec, the wind beneath your...."

"Yes, alright, Pam Ayres," Anna said, flicking a cleaning cloth at him. "We were happy to help a bit, that's all. What time is it anyway?"

Joe checked his watch and yawned, "Three-fifteen."

Ralph turned to them, "You're joking? I'm so sorry, I've kept you up all night."

"Not quite, there are still a few hours left for wild abandonment before the new day dawns," Joe said.

"The only thing I'll be abandoning is consciousness, the moment my head hits the pillow," Anna said, kissing first Joe then Ralph. "Good night, my fine young gentlemen." They watched her wave over her shoulder at them as she shuffled next door to her flat and the cosy embrace of her bed, but as she turned into her doorway she let out a piercing scream. Both men immediately ran to find her.

She was standing frozen at her front door, "What?" Ralph shouted.

"I thought it was her," she gasped. "The ghost."

"Not again," Joe said, stepping out to look up and down the road.

"It wasn't though. I was opening my door and then I just saw a shadow behind me, but it was Stanley going past."

"Jeez, woman," Joe said. "That little dog is nothing like the grey woman. He's got a tail for a start!"

"I know, I know, sorry. She hasn't appeared for a while, but I'm always conscious that she could pop up at any moment."

Joe clapped his hands in front of Anna, "For the last time, there is no such thing as ghosts. You imagined it. Just forget it."

"OK, OK, I'll try, sorry. Goodnight," and Anna closed

the door behind her.

"She's really spooked by that ghost," Ralph said.

Joe shook his head, "Ralph, there is no ghost. I don't know who she was, but she's gone now."

"You mean she's not seeing things?"

"Nope, I saw her too, on bonfire night. Look, I don't know the full story, but Auntie B put a stop to it and swore me not to tell Anna. So you can't say anything."

"How did Auntie B get involved?"

"I have no idea, she's like the Mafia Godmother of Rye. Nothing happens here without her knowing about it, apparently. So, it's better just to let her do her thing and we won't wake up next to a dead horse from the kids' riding stables, if you know what I mean."

"Aren't you just a bit curious about who the woman is though, if she was stalking Anna?"

"Sure, trust me, if she shows up again I won't let her get away so easily, but as long Anna is safe then it's better just to drop it or she'll just be freaked-out the whole time."

As they returned to The Bookery Ralph rubbed his eyes, "I think there are a couple of beers left if you want one more for the road."

"Why not?" Joe said. "I used to know a joke about beer...but I can't remember it. Do you think that's a sign of ageing?"

Ralph handed him a bottle, "No, I just think it's a sign that it's quarter past three in the morning."

"True, true. This place is so great, I hope you are proud of yourself."

"To be honest, I think I am," Ralph said as they sat on the step in the middle of the shop.

"You've worked hard to make this happen in so

many ways. I can only stand back and admire every-thing you've achieved since you got here. Arriving with nothing, then the coming out thing, fitting into the Club as if you'd always belonged and this place...you are a pretty cool guy, my book-loving friend."

Ralph looked at Joe, hunched forward with his arms resting on his knees, "Thanks, but it's no more of an achievement than you've created next door. You started here with nothing too - apart from a small butterfly."

Joe snorted, "It wasn't that small! Anyway, I didn't have to use my brain or guts like you; Auntie B bailed me out, then I flashed my teeth and tits and everything fell into place. I don't think it compares really."

"Blimey, are you always this cheerful after mid-night?"

Joe sat up, flexing his shoulders, "Sorry, ignore me. It's been a strange few weeks, that's all. Here's to your success," he held up his bottle and Ralph struck his against it.

"I haven't known you for long, but I've never seen you down. It's kind of reassuring."

Joe frowned, "Reassuring?"

"That you're not perfect and that even charming, potent Joe has his bad days."

"Potent? Really? I like that."

Ralph laughed, "Don't let it go to your head."

"Can I ask you a question?"

"Sure."

"Do you know where you're going?"

Ralph paused, "Down my own path, I suppose. I have no idea what's at the end of it, but it'll be the path I choose."

"Good answer," Joe said, picking at the label on his

bottle.

"And you? Where are you going?"

Joe stayed still for a few moments, then smiled and stood up slowly, "Home."

"You're going back to Canada?"

"No, I'm getting on my bike and riding home to bed," he finished his beer and handed it back to Ralph, then bent down and kissed him gently on the cheek. "Good work, Ralph. Sleep well."

Joe then picked up his jacket and walked back to Let's Screw. He let himself into the shop, wheeled out his bike and set off for the twenty-minute ride back to his beach house. As he cycled through the empty streets, he hoped that the cold wind and exercise would shake off the nagging feeling that just as Ralph was finding everything he needed to move forward, Joe himself still had something missing from his life and was going nowhere until he could work out what the hell it was.

CHAPTER 10

*The green apron, Shakespeare
and a touch of tartan.*

A few hours later Ralph and Stanley were back in the shop checking that everything was set for their first day of trading. Once he was satisfied that there really was nothing more he could do, Ralph went outside and stood by the same lamppost he had shivered under on the night of his arrival in Rye. The cold air, edged with the tang of the sea, nestled in around him as he looked at The Bookery. Stanley sat at his feet waiting to see what would happen next, but Ralph just stood and stared.

His mind whirled through the events of the last two weeks; his hurried flight from Yorkshire, the train depositing him in this freezing Sussex town, the dizzying climb up the hill with Anna chattering away at his side, the first sighting of The Bookery shrouded in gloom, his new family of friends bursting into his life, tearing away the old Ralph and releasing the new one who stood here now - exhilarated, proud and whole. So much had happened that he should be exhausted and yet he felt more awake than ever.

Stanley pawed his leg gently, reminding him that not only was he new in his life too, but that breakfast was long overdue, "Come on then, Stan," he said and led the way back inside.

As he got to the doorway he paused as Stanley's ears pricked up, and a second later he too heard the unmistakable sound of what could only be a heavy object being dragged along the ground. He stepped into the road, the light still dim through an early mist, but he saw nothing that could be making the noise. As quickly as it had started the sound stopped and was replaced by a familiar hollow rattle, just as he had heard on his first night in Rye. He had started to move up the road towards the noise, when suddenly out of an alley came a tall figure shrouded in a long dark coat with grey hair flowing from under what looked like a tartan hat. Ralph froze as the forlorn figure looked directly at him, its eyes hollow in the half light, before turning and scurrying back into the alleyway.

"Good morning, good morning," Anna sang from behind him, as she sailed up the street with her arms full of cake boxes. "What are you doing in the middle of the road? There's no good ending it all now, there are going to be hundreds of people wanting to buy books off you today."

"Did you hear anything just then or see...well... something?" he asked.

She stopped, "No, what was it?"

Ralph shook his head, remembering Joe's warning

about not wanting to spook her, "Nothing, I think I'm just over tired." He took the boxes from her and brought them inside The Bookery, hoping the ghostly figure was not some sort of omen for his opening day.

Anna stood in the middle of the shop and turned a slow circle, "This is amazing, just amazing. What you have done in only two weeks is amazing. Would you like me to say amazing again? You should be really proud...and you look fabulous, if I might add."

Ralph was dressed in a crisp white shirt and smart jeans, with an old-fashioned green shop-keeper's apron, that Anna had persuaded him would add an air of class and character. He smiled and looked around, he had loved every minute of his time creating this unique place he now called home, but it needed to start to pay him back or the debts would soon mount up.

"Let's hope it's all worthwhile," he said as nerves gripped his stomach.

"It can't fail," Anna said, giving him a hug.

"I can't afford for it to fail."

"It won't, you'll see. Come on, help me unpack the cakes," she went back to the boxes and revealed lavishly iced cup-cakes, each with a tiny fondant-icing book on top, "I know you only asked for thirty, but I've done fifty. I have a feeling you are going to have a busy day."

"They're beautiful, thank you so much."

"You are very welcome. Oh, here's Irene, she's bringing the trays to put them on."

Irene marched into the shop with three silver trays under her arm, "Since when have I done outside catering?" she demanded. "I'm café staff."

Anna looked at her in surprise, "Irene, it's only next door and it's for Ralph."

She slammed the trays down, "Hasn't he got legs? I've got things to do, you know, and with my kidneys I have limited time to do them."

Irene turned to stalk back to The Cookery, but paused, reversed and looked at Ralph. With a barely imperceptible softening of her features she took a step towards him and reached out a scrawny hand, making him flinch slightly. She ignored his reaction and adjusted the collar of his shirt, which had caught on his apron, "Good luck, young man. May the force be with you." Then off she went back along the pavement to start work in The Cookery.

"I think Star Wars was on the telly last night," Anna said. "She's as soft as anything underneath, you know."

"I know, but she still frightens the life out of me," Ralph sighed.

"Room for a little one?" Joe asked as he arrived at the shop door with Auntie B on his arm. He guided her inside, where Ralph took her hand.

"Morning Auntie B, you didn't have to get up early, you could have come down anytime," he said.

"I know, dear, but it's a special day and I wanted to be the first to see the shop. Patrick left it in such a mess, I believe, all the fault of the lady circus performer, of course. I believe she was an aerial specialist who could contort herself in the most extraordinary ways."

"So, I've heard," said Ralph.

"Yes, I imagine you have, my dear," Auntie B said, smiling.

Ralph looked at Joe, "How are you? Everything OK?"

"Always, always," Joe said with a smile that gave away nothing of his mood from last night.

"So, are you going to show me around, Ralph?"

Auntie B said.

"Of course."

While Anna unpacked a pile of bacon sandwiches she had made for them all, plus a few sausages for Stanley, Ralph took Auntie B on a guided tour of the shop describing each section to her. She felt her way around many of the objects displayed here and there, until finally he led her to the wall where he had displayed half a dozen of her paintings, "And last, but not least, here we have some incredibly important art works by a hugely respected local artist – Evelyn Bondolfi. You might know her."

"I think I may," she said. "Do they look alright here?"

"They look wonderful," Anna said, finishing off the display of cakes.

"They're fantastic," Joe added, swiftly moving out of Anna's reach with a bacon sandwich and a stolen cake.

"Well, as long as Ralph makes some money from them and someone enjoys them, then I will be happy."

Ralph looked at her, "Me? No, if I sell any the money is yours."

She patted his hand, "Good heavens, no, I gave them to you. I don't need anything except to know that they have gone to a good home."

"Well, I'll take a small commission for selling them, but the rest is yours."

"Ralph, I won't hear of it. Take the money, keep it, use it to make this new life for yourself. They are a gift," she paused, tapping his hand with her finger. "I'm trying to think of a Dickens quote, there must be something...all I can think of is, *What greater gift than the love of a cat,* but that won't do at all."

"How about a joke, while the old girl thinks?" Joe

offered.

"No," all three of them said at the same time.

"Well, shoot a man for trying to bring a little joy into your lives, why don't you? I've been saving this one for today, it's special. It's a bookstore joke."

Ralph shrugged, "Go on then, I suppose I owe you for all your help, but just today."

Joe put his breakfast down and rubbed his hands together, "Great, OK, so, this guy goes into a bookstore and says, 'Can I have a book by Shakespeare please?' and the bookstore owner says, 'Sure, which one?', so, the customer says, 'William'." He grinned expectantly at the others.

"I need to get on," Ralph said, heading for the counter.

"I'll get back to The Cookery. You need to eat something," Anna said, putting a bacon sandwich in Ralph's hands.

"Guys, guys, it wasn't that bad. It had a bookstore and Shakespeare in it, that's worth something, surely? Auntie B?"

"Time to take me home, Joe. Good luck, Ralph, I know it will be a great success."

"OK, OK, I'll come up with another one tomorrow. Have fun, Ralph," he called, as he guided Auntie B out of the shop. "Rocking the apron look by the way. Makes your ass look great."

Anna, letting them pass ahead of her, agreed, "Yes, it does. I thought that."

"Such a shame I can't see it then," Auntie B added with a chuckle.

Ralph came out from behind the counter laughing, "Clear off the lot of you and leave my arse out of it," just as a tall figure appeared outside the shop.

"Oh, hi, everyone," Sam said, his usual cap pulled low over his forehead. "Did I hear someone shout 'arse'?"

"Ass, actually," Joe said and pointed to Ralph. "He said, arse, the Brit."

Sam looked briefly at Ralph, "Oh, right, hi."

"Morning," Ralph said, stiffly.

"We were talking about Ralph's rear and how his apron enhances it," Anna said. "Any thoughts?"

"What, me?" Sam stuttered. "No."

"Shame," Anna said with a grin, handing him a bacon sandwich, as she skipped off back to The Cookery, blowing a kiss to Ralph.

Auntie B came to Sam and Ralph's rescue, "Do you have something lovely for my tea, Sam?"

"Oh, yes, it's just a few left-overs from yesterday, I'm afraid, but I know how you like to pick at things. It's a bit of a mini buffet."

"Perfect, bring them up. Joe, you stay here and help Ralph, Sam can take me from here. Good luck, Ralph."

Joe sauntered back into the shop, "Anything you need doing?"

Ralph dug his hands deep into his pockets, "What's going on? Why is he giving Auntie B left-overs?"

"Sam? Oh, he often brings them over instead of a full meal."

"But that's disgusting. It's not right, how can you let that happen? You should get on to the council."

"Council? What's the council got to do with it?"

"Well, whoever Sam works for, the meals on wheels people."

Joe laughed, "He's not really from meals on wheels.

He's a chef, he runs the best restaurant in town. Some would say the best in Sussex. It's called Cinque! Not like the kitchen sink, but the French number five - Cinque. I made that mistake first time. Apparently, Rye was one of five medieval seaports used to defend you Brits from the French – called the Cinque Ports. They made a bit of a hash of it in 1066, if you ask me, but they still seem proud of it. Anyway, the restaurant is also at number five West Street. He paid some big marketing firm from London to come up with a name and they earned a fortune for, 'Cinque'. Can you believe it?"

"So, why does he deliver food?"

"Because he's a good guy, I guess. When he was setting the restaurant up I gave him a hand with some of the interior work. You should have seen the designs he got from so-called professionals for the refurb. One looked like the inside of a tart's handbag and another one could only be described as Telly Tubby chic. So, he and I worked it out together. He got to know Auntie B up on the rooftop when we were doing some planning and became an honorary member of the Rooftop Club. Ever since then he's brought over a couple of dishes a week for her and they chat for hours."

"Oh, I thought he was...well, a bit of a git, to be honest."

Joe hovered by the cake table, "Oh, he can be," he said, laughing. "But he takes time to get to know people, for obvious reasons."

"People keep saying that - 'for obvious reasons'. What is so obvious? What am I missing?" Ralph could see all the reasons why he disliked Sam, but, apart from providing Auntie B with some occasional leftovers, he still couldn't see what all the fuss was about.

"You really don't know, do you? You don't recognise him?" Joe pulled himself away from the food and started to leave.

"What? Who is he?" Ralph called after him.

"It's not for us to tell, that's down to him. It's good you don't know, he'll like that," Joe said as he turned right out of the door and went to get Let's Screw ready for another week's trade.

"Wait," Ralph jogged out after him. "I don't get it, who is he?"

As he stood on the pavement the door to Auntie B's flat opened and Sam appeared putting his ever-present cap back on his head.

"Oh," they both said as they came face to face.

Ralph, determined not to be put into a bad mood, turned and went back into The Bookery. Sam hesitated in the door of the shop watching Ralph stomp up to the counter, "Erm, it's today you open, isn't it?"

"Yes," Ralph said, refusing to turn around.

"Right, well, good luck," Sam said, taking a brief look inside without actually going in. "They were right, by the way, it looks great."

Ralph relaxed his frown and looked again at the transformation, "Thanks, glad you like it."

"I didn't mean the shop," Sam said and quickly disappeared back up the street.

Ralph stood in shock, unconsciously putting his hands in the back pockets of his jeans. What was the big secret around Sam and was he now deliberately trying to wind him up? He didn't have much time to worry about it as he checked his watch and opening time was rapidly approaching. He rubbed his face with his hand, smoothed his new apron and turned the sign on the door to 'Open'.

CHAPTER 11

*The green-eyed chef, Rye's rovers
and soft-soled shoes.*

Ralph had no idea how the day would go and after opening the shop there was a tense half hour in which nothing happened. Ralph hopped nervously from his seat at the counter to the window, then to a shelf to fiddle with a book that didn't need fiddling with and then back again. Stanley sat patiently in the window as usual, snoozing. Then, at last, a customer wandered in. An impressive man dressed head to toe in tweed, began a slow browse around the shop. He tipped his smart tweed hat to Ralph, who attempted to look busy sorting out pens at the counter. After what seemed like a lifetime the customer returned to the front door, grunted, looked at Ralph and declared, "Excellent. I shall bring the good lady wife," before leaving empty handed. Ralph breathed out and realised that he had been so tense that he had forgotten to offer him a cake.

Soon he had plenty of other opportunities to give them away as the shop was quickly buzzing with shoppers. They chatted with him enthusiastically about how they loved the place, its artwork, the little curios on the ceiling, the interesting choice of books and Stanley, who made it a point of greeting everyone personally. Ralph was amazed that most people bought at least one book each and he soon relaxed.

By lunchtime Ralph was in his stride and trade was brisk. It was as if Rye had been waiting for its bookshop to re-open and most people saw it as quite an event, with many making a special visit into town to come and see what The Bookery had to offer. At closing time the day seemed to have flown by, all Anna's cakes had gone and he already needed to restock a few titles. Most importantly, the day's takings were way more than Ralph had anticipated.

Much to his relief the rest of the week continued to follow the same pattern as word spread about the shop and curious locals and passing tourists were all drawn in to explore the unusual interior. Two of Auntie B's paintings had sold to the owner of a local guest house and he had to make a quick visit upstairs for more to fill the gaps on the wall.

By the time Friday arrived Ralph had a healthy sales sheet, aching feet and the feeling of having had one of the best weeks that he could remember. Although he'd started with just a wish that he might make a go of The Bookery as a means of funding a new life for himself, he knew that he had actually created something special - not just for the people of Rye but for himself.

As the clock ticked towards lunchtime shops like The Bookery started to empty and the tea shops and cafes of Rye filled up. Ralph took the lull in proceedings as an opportunity to put his feet up behind the counter and eat an apple, while Stanley had his lunch in a bowl beside him. He watched the good people of Sussex pass his windows until Stanley sat to attention, ears alert, listening hard. Ralph was immediately on edge following the recent ghostly activity. A few seconds later he heard what sounded like a ball bouncing down the pavement and Stanley took off, barking and jumping at the window.

Ralph opened the door, holding an excited Stanley back by his collar, to find a football rolling past. He stuck out his foot and expertly hooked the ball up into the air and caught it with one hand. He looked up the street and saw what seemed to be a massive net bag of footballs struggling towards him. As they got closer, his heart sank as a familiar, annoying baseball cap appeared above them.

Sam dumped the net of balls on the pavement in front of The Bookery, "I don't suppose you've seen any stray footballs, have you?"

Ralph held out the ball in his hand.

"Great, I think I've sprung a leak. I nearly lost them all back there," Sam leant forward and tried to take it from Ralph, nearly losing more balls in the process.

"Careful or they are going to go everywhere," Ralph snapped.

"I'll be fine," Sam wrestled with the net, as another ball found its way out and into the gutter. "Damn."

Ralph shoved Stanley back into the shop and shut the door on him, then hopped into the road and deftly chipped the ball up into his other hand, "You'll cause an accident if you don't fix that net, bring it inside," he then opened the door with his elbow and held it wide for Sam to pass.

"If you say so," Sam said, reluctantly, dragging the troublesome net behind him.

Sam pulled the net to one side, leaving enough space for customers to get past. After a struggle, Ralph got Stanley back to his bed, where he lay sulking at missing out on all the fun. Then Ralph returned to Sam with the escapee balls and they both bent down to the net, nearly crashing heads, "Sorry," Ralph said and Sam tutted.

"I'm just trying to help," Ralph had really had enough of Sam's superior attitude.

"I know, I wasn't tutting at you, I'm annoyed with this bloody net."

"Right, well, I'm sure it's not doing it deliberately."

In silence they felt their way around the net checking its knots to find where the hole might be. Eventually Sam identified a gap and was able to tie the loose ends back together.

"That should hold it," he said, pushing the cap back on his head. "Thanks for your help. Bloody things, I can't believe I've been landed with them."

Ralph stood and looked at Sam properly for the first time, he had caught a glimpse of the electric green eyes before, but now he saw how they fitted into a clean-cut, astonishingly handsome face. He fought to focus and stammered, "Are the footballs...for the restaurant?"

Sam looked at Ralph and frowned, "Well, no. It's a restaurant."

Ralph could have hit his head against the wall for being so dumb, but he'd been distracted, "Of course, it is. You sell dinner, not footballs. It's a restaurant. You said that. I know that. *Idiot!*"

"What?"

"Not you, I didn't mean you. I was talking to myself," Ralph's face had turned a deep red.

Sam laughed at him, "If you say so. Anyway, the balls are for the Rye Rovers. Have you heard of them?"

"No."

"No, I forgot you're new here," Sam said, getting to his feet as Ralph tried not to take offence again. "They're the local under-ten's football team. I sponsor them, well, Cinque does. You see? The balls have our logo on them, as do their shirts. It's not much, but it helps them cover their costs so anyone can join the team never mind the financial situation of the family."

"You help the poor kids then," Ralph said, feeling that Sam was now patronising the disadvantaged of Rye as well as him. "While promoting your high-end restaurant?"

Sam's jaw clenched and extended slightly as he looked at Ralph, "Well, that's not how I'd put it."

"I bet."

"What is the matter with you?"

"Me? Nothing, I'm fine," Ralph straightened his shoulders and put his hands in the pocket of his apron. Why did this man wind him up so easily and so often? What was his problem? Why did he have to be so good looking and yet so unpleasant?

Before he could say anything Sam started to gather up the net of balls, "Anyway, it was Joe that got me into it all. He knew the coach and helped out at training and matches, but he got himself entangled with one of the team's Mums and has had to keep a low profile for a while. Then the old coach had a heart attack a few weeks ago, he should be OK, but he's got to take it easy and won't be back. So, for the time being it's down to me. They'll have to fold, I reckon."

Ralph smiled as he thought how karma had come back to strike Sam and his ego, "Do you know anything about coaching football?"

"Nope, I can blow a whistle and give the kit a quick rinse, but that's about it. Oh, hang on, damn!"

The net appeared to have sprung a second leak with the strain of Sam humping it up onto his shoulder and another ball had escaped and bounced across the floor of the shop. Like a brown and white bullet from a well-oiled gun, Stanley appeared from the window display and went into attack before the ball had time to get its bearings. Giving it a good bash with his nose he gave chase around the shop. Ralph set off as well, trying to get hold of either Stanley or the ball, but the little dog had not finished working through his full repertoire of ball handling skills and would not be put off. Ralph was dashing past the display of recommended books for Christmas when a customer loomed in the doorway and announced his presence with a loud sniff.

"Mr Dobson," Sam said, trying to hold the remainder of the balls in his net. "How are you?"

Dew-drop Dobson ignored Sam and looked at the game of rough and tumble that Ralph was pursuing with Stanley. Ralph had now managed to get to the ball and was trying to control it with his feet, but every time he paused to pick it up Stanley would tackle him and knock the ball back into play.

"Stan, pack it in," Ralph yelled as he managed to take possession again and dribbled the ball with some skill away from the dog and into a tight corner by the window display, where he was able to hook it up with his right foot and into his arms out of the dog's reach.

"Stanley, ENOUGH! Calm down, go to your bed. Bed, NOW."

Deciding that he'd shown the young ball everything he needed to know, Stanley agreed to settle down in the window and take a nap after his exertions.

"I'm so sorry. Please come in, just a bit of an accident," Ralph puffed.

"Really? It looked not unlike an extraordinary breach of health and safety regulations to me. Wild animals allowed to run free. Ball sports being played in a confined space," Dobson sniffed again, the droplet on the end of his nose vanishing at speed. "As a long-standing senior member and former chair of the Rye Independent Traders Association..."

"Oh, yes, RITA. You were voted out last year, weren't you, Mr Dobson? That must have been awful for you," Sam said, looking him straight in the eye.

"My term of office came to an end, you are quite correct, Mr Ross. However, I was very happy to hand over the onerous duties to a new Chair. I was very pleased to be able to concentrate on my other business interests. It was time for a new broom to sweep RITA forward, and I was happy to allow the brush and not to say the handle also to be in new hands." He sniffed as he addressed Ralph, "On this occasion I may overlook this moment of madness, let us call it, but it will not be tolerated in the long term."

"Quite," Sam smirked. "Not tolerated until a new broom is purchased."

"Quite...what?" Dobson turned away from Sam and pointed a grubby hand at Ralph. "Anyway, I believe you are the new proprietor and I would like to know if you have in stock the biography of Rudyard Kipling? It is entitled, 'Rudyard Kipling'."

"Didn't he make cakes?" asked Sam, innocently.

"I don't think I have it, Mr Dobson, but I can always order a copy for you?"

"Please, don't bother. I would have thought a local independent book shop of any quality should have an edition at all times. A book celebrating the life of this country's greatest writer, not to mention a Sussex resident."

"Does he still live locally?"

"Sam, you are not helping," hissed Ralph.

Dobson turned to Sam, smoothing down the front of his stained raincoat, "Indeed, you are not, Samuel. You are perfectly well aware that Rudyard Kipling died many years ago, just as you are aware that he does...or rather did...not make cakes of any kind. Your parents, despite their apparent notoriety, clearly failed in your classical education. However, if this is what passes as humour in your world, Mr Ross, then I dread to think of the quality of the ambience at your little eatery. Good morning, gentlemen," with that he turned on his soft-soled shoes and crept silently out.

There was a moment's pause before Sam let out a long breath, "Dew-drop Dobson, I haven't seen him for months. It's always nice to chat with him. Ow! What was that for?" Ralph had launched the ball at him, hitting a perfect strike in the centre of his stomach.

Ralph shook his head, all tension seeming to have temporarily vanished between them as they faced a common enemy, "For winding him up."

"Oh well, it keeps him on his little rubber-shoed toes. Talking of which, you are pretty good at handling a ball. Do you play?"

"I did before I came down here. Every week, rain or shine, in a local league team," he picked up a couple of books that had become dislodged during his tussle with Stanley. "Look, I did some courses on coaching football for kids and helped with a local little league for a while. So, well, I'd be happy to help out, just until you find someone else."

"Really? Erm, right," Sam pulled the peak of his cap back down over his forehead and adjusted it from side to side. "They have a practice every Wednesday night and a match every Sunday during the season, so we need someone pretty committed."

"Oh, well, if you don't want my help..."

"No, no, it's not that. Look, we have a match this Sunday morning at nine. You don't open here until eleven on Sundays, do you?" Sam said, checking the opening times on the door. "So, you'll be back in plenty of time. It's only twenty-five minutes each end, as they are so young."

"That's fine, I'll be there, but I'll need to know a bit more about the team and how it all works."

"Oh, right, of course. What are you doing tomorrow night?"

"Saturday? Well...."

"Come to the restaurant at about nine. I'm cooking, but most people will have their desserts by then – they tend to eat early around here or it messes with their regime of pills. We can have a drink and plan what needs to be planned," Sam stuffed the football back into the net and tied up the extra hole that had set it free.

"Fine," Ralph said, not sure how he'd gone from being ready to swing for this guy, who had been nothing but smug and surly since they'd met, to now having to spend time having a drink with him. "So, what did Dobson mean about your notorious parents? Should I...?"

Sam threw the footballs back over his shoulder, his head and cap down again, "See you later. Oh, and don't eat before you come, I can feed you, if you want."

Ralph watched as Sam shot out of the shop, not sure whether the feeling of breathlessness he was left with was caused by Stanley and the football, his first run-in with Dew-drop Dobson, or Sam, the most annoying green-eyed chef in Sussex? However, he had little time to think about any of them as new customers arrived and threw him into another busy afternoon.

As he closed the shop at five thirty, his confidence was higher than it had been for years. It really felt like he had found his place in the world, he could be himself and put all of the fears and frustrations of his previous life behind him. However, as he stood in the doorway to turn the door sign to 'Closed', he looked down the street to see a very large part of his past turn the corner and start walking towards him.

CHAPTER 12

The Mermaid Inn, scampi and Princess Anne.

J im Scattergood was a big man; size twelve shoes, long legs, a barrel chest and a round face with frenzied afro hair. Having his extensive frame crammed into a straining grey suit and a car seat all the way from Barnsley, meant he found the walk up the steep cobbled street tough going until his joints slowly eased their way back to their rightful positions. His mobile phone guided him through the town to his destination and his head was down as he turned the corner at the top of Conduit Hill into the High Street. So he didn't see his old friend hesitate in the door of his shop or his face fall as he recognised him.

Jim stopped to get his bearings, looked up and scanned the street ahead of him, his eyes eventually locking onto Ralph's. Both men froze, then Jim raised his hand and phone in the air, "Ralph!".

Ralph disappeared back into the shop as Jim headed down the street covering the short distance in long, loping strides. Ralph's heart was thumping in his chest as he struggled to remove his shop apron with shaking hands. He laid it across the counter stool and turned just as Jim arrived at the door.

"Jesus," Jim stopped to catch his breath, steadying himself against the door frame. "This place is designed to kill you. Have you seen those bloody hills? I nearly tipped over backwards and tobogganed all the way back down on me arse." He stepped into the shop and took a long look at Ralph, "Well, you're not dead then."

Forcing a smile, Ralph stepped out from behind the counter, "Nope, still alive. Unlike you, by the looks of things. Pint?"

Jim nodded slowly, "OK, pint," and stood back sweeping his arm towards the door, letting Ralph lead the way.

* * *

The Mermaid Inn was a short walk from The Bookery and its six-hundred-year history of timbered beams, giant fireplaces, smugglers, hauntings and hidden priest holes was legendary.

Ralph took them in through the old courtyard to the Giant's Fireplace Bar, Jim having to duck as he went through the crooked wooden door. While Ralph went to the bar Jim looked around the room, which had a sloping ceiling and creaking floor, but was entirely dominated by the largest fireplace he had ever seen. What looked like several large trees had been chopped and stacked on the enormous hearth either side of a roaring fire. A great oak beam ran across the top of the fireplace from wall to wall, with four vicious-looking medieval pikes hanging above it. One wall of the room had narrow, lopsided lattice windows, which showed the date 1420 etched into them, and against the opposite wall rested an ancient grandfather clock that peacefully ticked and tocked its time away.

He chose a corner table by the fire, pleased to find that the large, upholstered chairs would fit him easily. He nodded to an elderly couple at the next table who were finishing crosswords while they waited for their dinner, the husband already anticipating its arrival with a paper napkin tucked into his smart V-necked jumper. Ralph arrived with two pints of local Harvey's Sussex bitter, removed his jacket and sat opposite Jim.

Jim swallowed a large gulp of dark, rich beer, "Hey, that's not bad. You'd never know it was a southern brew."

A brief silence fell between them.

"Still, it can't beat a good old pint of Theakston's Old Peculiar in the student union bar, can it? Remember them days? When we were mates? Students together. Us against the world. Looking out for each other. Nothing..."

"OK, OK. I'm sorry, alright, I'm sorry," Ralph looked down into his pint, his hands turning the glass slowly.

Jim leaned across the table, "What the hell happened? We've been worried sick. No one knew where you were, what had gone on, I mean, if you were even alive!"

"How did you find me?"

"Well, it wasn't easy, I can tell you," Jim said, scratching his head. "We rang everyone we could think of. I mean, your phone that you left behind was no good, seeing how you'd wiped all your contacts. In the end I tracked down your parents and your Mum told me all she knew was that you'd gone down south somewhere. So we had nothing else to go on. Bloody hell, Helen spent a night driving round looking in gutters and under hedgerows for your body, mate. What were you thinking?"

"I'm so sorry, I never thought you'd think I'd...well, died or...I never thought."

"No, you didn't, did you? All the way down here I changed from wanting to rip your head off to hugging you to death," he paused, sipping his drink in an attempt to remain calm. "Anyway, eventually, I found some shitty little local paper online that had an article about this bookshop with a new owner who had your name - and there was a photo with your ugly mug in it."

Ralph nodded slowly, still staring deep into his drink, "Is Helen with you?"

"No. Actually, she doesn't know I'm here."

Ralph looked up, "Really?"

"She's my sister and I don't like lying to her, but I wanted to know what we were dealing with before I told her. Bloody hell, mate, we'd thought all sorts. I mean, you could have had six children with a Vietnamese nail girl hidden away down here, or lung cancer or...anything."

"How is she?"

"Well, she got a torn bit of cardboard from some biscuits, with a scribble on it saying her husband had left her and vanished into thin air, so, she went out and bought a new hat after having her bikini line waxed –

what do you think?"

For a moment neither man spoke. The old couple next to them got their food, two plates of scampi, chips and garden peas, while the logs in the fire cracked and shifted in the heat.

"To be honest," Jim said, in a quieter tone. "She said she could cope with you leaving. She actually said that she knew it would happen one day, but I think she was just saying that to be brave, you know. But the worst thing was not knowing you were alright. I think she thought you'd killed yourself."

"Oh, god," Ralph said with a sigh. "I never meant her to think that. I just needed to get away, to find...to find...well, just to get away."

"But why, mate? Why didn't you talk to me? We've known each other from that first day at uni, from before you and Helen, before Beckham had tattoos."

Ralph took a sip of his drink and looked at the couple next to them as they chased peas around their plates in contented marital harmony, "The thing is," he said. "I don't know how we ended up married. It wasn't right for either of us. When we finished university all our friends were talking about marriage and planning their weddings, you remember, we seemed to spend our lives at hen do's or stag weekends. Then, suddenly, we were married too."

"Well, that's what happens," Jim said, looking confused. "That's the natural order of things, isn't it? Then you become parents and are sleep deprived and stony broke for the rest of your days. The natural circle of life."

"But we should never have done it. The life we found ourselves in, through no apparent thought or planning of our own, well, it made us miserable. We were both unhappy, but for different reasons."

"OK, you and Helen may have been having problems, but it's nothing that can't be fixed. You don't have to hide away down here in this shit-hole. Come back with me, we can work it out."

"No. It's not like that and this isn't a shit-hole. It's amazing, I love it here. I can be myself, at last. I've found...I've found..."

"What, mate? What have you found? You keep saying you came here to find something, but what? You had everything. A good job, mates, the footie team – you had a great wife, a house. What else do you need to find?" Jim looked at Ralph, his eyes wide, genuinely not knowing what to make of his friend of so many years. "What else is there?"

"Truth? Honesty? Love, maybe, if I'm lucky."

Jim sat back and rubbed his fingers through his hair, making it even more extraordinary than it was before, "You're not making sense, mate. Honestly, I think you need to see someone, get some help. I don't get it."

"I know, sorry, it's hard. It's been really hard for me, for years. But I'm happier now than I've ever been. You see, I'm..."

"...Happy? Here? In a pissy little bookshop? You had a wife – I know she's my sister and everything, but she's pretty hot. You had a nice job, a great house, a *really* good car - that's what we're all looking for, isn't it? You'd got it all. You just had to settle in, maybe move jobs if you were bored. Buy a bigger house. That's what we wanted, what we worked for. Come back, Ralph, it's all still there. Just do a bit of crawling, lots of flowers, chocolates, whatever. Say you had a melt-down, a mid-life crisis."

"NO!" Ralph said loudly enough to make the lady at the next table drop a scampi into her glass of tonic in shock. "Sorry," he said, lowering his voice. "I didn't have it all, I didn't have anything. You don't understand. The plastic house, the flash car, designing boring websites for boring people, it was never...*will* never be enough. I love The Bookery. I love the creativity, the risk of my own business standing or falling with me. I haven't been here long, but I love this mad, tiny, creaky little town. I've met amazing people who have taken me for who I am, for what I am, and they don't care. We laugh and we look at roofs and we fight and we drink sherry and I've got Stanley and...Oh, my god, Stanley!"

As Ralph leapt to his feet, the sudden movement sent another piece of scampi skyrocketing up into the air next to them just as the first piece had been fished out of the drink.

"I'm so sorry about that," Ralph said as he grabbed his jacket from the back of his chair and hauled Jim out of his seat. "Come on, we have to get back."

As they marched back up the hill to the old church square Jim stumbled along behind Ralph, "Wait, wait. What the hell are you talking about? This is crazy stuff. Who looks at roofs and when did you start to drink sherry? What are you, gay?"

Without turning or breaking his stride Ralph said "Yes, I am actually."

"Yeah, right," panted Jim, trying to keep up as they went round the edge of the churchyard and came out at the top of yet another hill leading down to the High Street. "Course you are and I'm Princess Anne. Look, it's nothing to be ashamed of, you've had a bit of a melt-down. Mental health is very popular now. I've seen it on the telly, even the royals are doing it. You don't need to be ashamed."

Ralph suddenly stopped and Jim very nearly bowled into the back of him, "But that's the point, I'm not ashamed, not anymore. Not here. But back there, back at home, I was, and I was scared." He set off again, pointing to a café on their left as they headed down the hill, "That's The Copper Kettle, Anna used to work there until she opened The Cookery, which is next to The Bookery. Dew-drop Dobson runs it and we hate him, he's a creep, with a nose like a leaky tap, so we don't go in there. Irene would cut your balls off anyway if you did, so I wouldn't bother."

Jim's hair was blowing in the wind as he staggered onwards, his fine leather shoes slipping on the icy cobbles, "Have I gone mad? Is it me? Cookery, Bookery, Irene, Anna - I mean, are these people in your head? Are they imaginary? Who is Dew-Drop Dobson when he's washed? I'm Googling how to get someone sectioned, there has to be some way to stop you. And who the hell is Stanley?"

"That is Stanley," Ralph said, pointing to the dog who had spotted them coming down the hill. Stanley was up on his hind legs, paws resting on the glass of the shop window, barking with delight to see Ralph back again, knowing he hadn't been abandoned and, more importantly, that dinner was in the offing. Ralph let himself into the shop and Stanley leapt out of the window display, circling and barking loudly to welcome him home.

"Right, well, at least he's real and not one of your imaginary friends," Jim mumbled as he sat on the step in the middle of the shop.

"Oh, thank god you are back," Anna said as she charged in, lilac silk flying around her below the yellow beret that sat on top of the copper-coloured pigtails she had forced her curls into. "Poor Stanley's been barking and whining for ages. You have to get a mobile so I can get hold of you if you go wandering off, with... with...", she waved toward Jim. "Hello, who are you? Oh, shit! Pardon my language, but have I interrupted something?" Her hands flew to her face, "Are you two? Wow, you don't waste much time, do you?" She giggled and put her arm around Ralph's waist, "I'll leave you to...well, whatever..."

"Anna, stop it, calm down. This is Jim, my old mate from university. "Jim, this is Anna. I was telling you about her."

Jim was looking confused and running his hands through his hair again, "Were you? I mean, is she the one who is going to cut my balls off?"

"No, that was Irene," Ralph said.

"Oh yes, she would," Anna nodded in agreement. "Why though? What have you done?"

"Me?" said Jim in panic. "Nothing. In fact, I have no idea what the hell is going on or what anyone is talking about. It's like being down the bloody rabbit hole with flaming Alice in this place."

"I know, brilliant isn't it?" Anna laughed. "Come on, 'Jim, the mate from university'," she picked him up from the step, taking his hands gently from his head. "You need to give your hair a break, it looks like it's about to make a run for it. Let's go upstairs for a drink and you can meet the Rooftop Club."

"I have no idea what is happening, but you have nice hands and I'm sure you said the word, drink, so I'm going with it," Jim said.

"That's the doozy, come on. Ralph, you sort Stanley out then come up," Anna said as she led Jim away.

CHAPTER 13

The Lager Bellini, lattes and a Yorkshire
lawn mower.

By the time Stanley had popped out to catch up on the latest news from the local lampposts,been fed and was snuggled on the bed in the flat, Ralph found the Rooftop Club all wrapped up against the cold night air around Auntie B's table. Jim, despite his size, had somehow fitted into a deckchair, his crumpled grey suit now covered by a large purple quilt for warmth. He sat with a drink in a pint glass topped by a small green cocktail umbrella and a red and white striped straw.

"What are you drinking?" Ralph asked as he approached the group.

"No idea, I asked for a lager then this appeared," Jim said, eying the glass with suspicion.

Anna, who was sitting next to him, pushed out an empty chair for Ralph, "It's a Lager Bellini. I made it, well, I just made it *up* actually, but I think it'll catch on, don't you, Jim? Lager and prosecco with a hint of fruit? I couldn't find any lemons though."

"Dear god, there could be anything in there if she made it. Let me get you a proper drink, my friend," Joe said, starting to get up.

"No, no," gulped Jim, successfully navigating a mouthful via the straw. "I'll give it a go. When in Rome and all that," and he winked at Anna, who giggled tossing a pigtail over her shoulder.

"So, Jim, have you known Ralph for long?" asked Auntie B.

Jim was momentarily distracted by a slice of banana floating across the surface of his drink, then said, "Yes, we started university at the same time. We were on different courses, I was doing accountancy, but we both joined the football team and we've been best mates ever since. He even married my sister," Jim laughed as he took another suck on the straw.

There was silence from the group as they absorbed this information and reassessed how to proceed from here. The quiet, broken only by Jim blowing down the straw to dislodge a raisin that had swum up the shaft, was broken by Ralp, "Jim was in goal. Long arms and legs, you see. But it was his hair that stopped most of the balls," he attempted a laugh and Anna squeezed his hand.

"I never really got the hang of soccer until I moved here," Joe said. "Well, to be honest it still doesn't float my boat, men and little balls and all that."

"If that is leading to a joke, think again, Joseph Gordon Wells," Auntie B said, firmly.

"It wasn't, but now you come to mention it..."

"I think Jim is struggling enough with that drink

without inflicting any further damage on him just now," Ralph cut in. "Besides, it's Friday night, don't tell me you are staying in? No date?"

"Of course, fear not, my little Barnsley bookworm. An evening of good conversation, soft music, fine wine and a good long..."

"Joseph," said Auntie B.

"...walk along the beach," Joe looked at Auntie B with mock disgust. "Get out of the gutter, old lady."

"Just go," she replied. "Have fun, be good and if you can't be good..."

"...Give them a false name," the club members all chorused, raising their glasses.

"OK, OK, night all. Nice to meet you, Jim, any friend of Ralph's is a friend of ours. And let me leave you with this thought folks, friends are like condoms, they protect you when things get hard."

There was a collective groan as Joe waved his hand at them and headed off back through Auntie B's flat.

Anna called after him, "Who is it tonight? Anyone we know or care about?"

"Don't think so, she's called Dale, I think, or Hills? Something to do with the countryside," then he was gone.

"He's funny," Jim said, chuckling and sinking further into his deckchair with his knees now up around the level of his head.

"What brings you to Rye, Jim?" Auntie B asked gently.

Jim pointed at Ralph, "He does! It took me forever to find him. Like Miss Marple I was, trying to track him down. I'm here to bring him home."

"Are you indeed? I rather thought that Ralph had

made his home here, *Every traveller has a home of his own, and he learns to appreciate it more from his wanderings.*"

"Right, that's, erm...poetic," Jim said.

"Isn't it? A Christmas Carol, Charles Dickens."

Ralph leant over to Jim, "She does that a lot."

Anna turned to Ralph, a look of confusion on her face, "You're not leaving, are you? Not now you've finally..."

"No," said Ralph, quickly. "I'm not going back."

"Phew, that's good. I'm working on a bit of a date for you. I know exactly who, just need to sort-out the how and the when."

"Hang on, hang on," Jim waving his feet in the air as he struggled to sit up. "Let's not get into dates, he's still married to my sister. Helen is his wife. He has a house and a job and a car and...and...and a lawn mower waiting for him back in Yorkshire."

Auntie B deftly picked up her sherry glass, "A lawn mower? Goodness, you'd better hurry back, Ralph."

"No, well, not a lawn mower...well, he does have a lawn mower...but I just meant...it doesn't make any sense. His whole life is back up north, everything he needs is there. It just seems so stupid to throw away everything he's worked for and always wanted."

Auntie B turned her eyes on Jim and, although unseeing behind her dark glasses, they seemed to bore into him like lasers, "*There is a wisdom of the head, and a wisdom of the heart.*"

"Is there? Erm, Dickens is it? I don't... I mean, head and heart, I get that, but...Ralph, aren't you going to say anything?"

All three heads turned to Ralph, who sat with his

head bowed and his hands clasped tightly between his legs, "Jim, I know you think I've gone nuts, but I haven't. I was slowly driving myself crazy before, but now, my head is clear for the first time in ages. There's something you should know."

"We should go in and leave you two boys to talk," said Auntie B, starting to unwrap the blanket from her legs.

"No, stay, please. It's not a secret anymore, thanks to you. It's not something I'm ashamed of either," Ralph looked across at Jim. "I don't know whether you'll understand it or like it or whether it will just freak you out. God knows, I didn't really understand it myself, but the thing is, I'm gay. That's why I had to leave. That's why I can't go back to Helen."

Jim's round face flushed and his hand shot up to rifle through his hair. He didn't say anything, but, after a brief pause, he started to try to escape from the quilt and get up from his deckchair. Anna leapt forward, "Let me help, honey, it's not a one-man job," she took his pint glass and helped haul him up until he was on his feet.

"Thanks," Jim said, before turning and walking to the back of the terrace, looking over the scattered houses below.

Anna turned to Ralph, "Upsy-daisy."

"What?"

"Up. You," she hissed. "Go talk to him."

"Oh, yes, right."

Ralph crossed the terrace and stood beside his friend. Knowing Jim well enough to realise that he would need a bit of time to process this news, he waited, leaning silently against the railing looking out at the sky, tonight like a purple bruise spreading from west to east.

"How long have you...I mean, is it a new thing?" Jim asked.

"I think I've known all my life. Well, since I was a kid anyway. I always felt different to other boys, I guess, but I've never actually named it until I came here. I was scared, Jim, I knew it would change everything."

"But why did you marry Helen, if you knew?"

"I'm not sure."

Jim turned to him, anger in his eyes, "Yes, you are. Why?"

"You're right. The thing was, I guess I didn't want to be on the outside - the one people pointed at, the freak. I just wanted to belong. Helen was brilliant, funny and we had a great time together. Things just, kind of progressed and it was easy to to fit in. I did love her, Jim, in my way. I know that might seem crazy, but I did. She was...is...amazing. I tried so hard, but it was making me ill. I couldn't do it anymore. I just couldn't carry on lying, it wasn't fair – especially to her."

"I can't believe I didn't see it, that I didn't know. I mean, all those years."

"I'm sorry I didn't tell you before, I just couldn't. I needed time to work out if I could really live this life - my real life - and I can. I really appreciate you coming to find me, but I'm not going back. This is my home and this is me."

Jim took a deep breath and turned back to Ralph, "Actually, you don't look quite as, well, stressed as you used to. Maybe you do look happier. It might take me some time to get used to it, but it shouldn't change anything, should it?"

"I hope not."

"But you have to tell Helen, I can't do it. She'll think I'm winding her up."

"I know. I will, soon, I promise."

"Good."

The two friends looked at each other as a new dynamic settle between them. Anna quietly slipped in between them, putting an arm around each of their waists, tears in her eyes.

"You two are brilliant. I think you should have a hug now, don't you?"

"Oh, well..." Ralph said.

Jim stammered, "Erm, well..."

"Too soon?" asked Anna.

They both nodded, "Too soon," and they fumbled an awkward fist bump.

"Men," sighed Anna. "Useless. You haven't finished your drink, Jim, do you want me to get it?"

"No," Jim said, quickly. "I mean, no thanks. It's been kind of a long day, I should be heading back, I've got a long journey."

Anna grabbed his arm, "Back? Not to Barnsley?"

"Yeah, I'd only planned to come down for one day, find Ralph and then we'd drive back together."

"No, you can't do that," Ralph said. "Stay, at least until tomorrow or Sunday even. Ring Carol."

"Who?" Jim was looking at Anna's hand on his arm.

"Carol, your wife."

"Oh, her, yes, Carol, of course. Yes, then I'll find a hotel."

"Don't be daft, you can stay with me, come on. 'Night, Auntie B."

"Good night, dear. Another brick out of the wall, well done you," she smiled.

"Night, Jim," Anna called as they disappeared into Ralph's flat.

Jim turned back, "Good night, thanks for the drink and everything. Banana and lager? Wow, it's been a night of firsts for me. Really nice to meet you as well, Mrs B."

Auntie B raised her glass to him, "*Sleep tight, rest easy and come out fighting!*"

Jim pointed at her, "Ah...*The mark of a true killer!* I know that one, from 'All About Eve', Joan Crawford."

"Close, Bette Davis, actually, but I'm impressed, young man."

* * *

The next morning was Ralph's first Saturday of trading in The Bookery and he was up early, but Jim had still not surfaced after he had come back from his run with Stanley, showered and got dressed for the day. If he was honest, he was relieved as it avoided the possibility of an awkward breakfast conversation. On the other hand, now Jim knew, he felt even better about really moving forward and the worst was over in terms of telling people. Except Helen, of course. That was the next big hurdle he had to face, that and the date that Anna had threatened to organise. Then there was having to meet Sam for a drink tonight to discuss the Rye Rovers, something he was sure was a big mistake. He didn't know why, but he had a bad feeling about it.

All of this passed from his mind as he and Stanley were preoccupied with a rush of early customers. It was mid-morning when Jim appeared through the pass door from the flat with two cups of coffee in his hands.

"Morning, mate, I've brought you a coffee. Not sure how you drink it, now you're gay. Wasn't sure if you were a latte man now?"

Ralph groaned as he took the coffee and said, "Is this how it's going to be now? Gay jokes?"

"Pretty much, for a while anyway," Jim grinned at him. "Nowt you can do about it, you've just got to let me get them out of my system. Morning, young Stanley." He bent down and fussed the little dog who was doing his rounds, having just spent ten minutes helping a brother and sister select the best children's books for the festive season.

Ralph served a couple of customers while Jim explored the shop with Stanley hovering at his side ready for any questions he may have. When the shop was briefly empty again he said, "Nice place, was it like this when you got it?"

"No," Ralph said. "Nothing like this. It was pretty knackered to be honest. The guy who ran it was distracted by a lady acrobat who could put her lipstick on with her left foot apparently, so it was pretty run down."

"It would be."

"I spent a couple of weeks paiting it and doing it up. "

"You painted these pictures? The castle and the sea pictures and everything? Mate, I never knew you could paint," he let out a whistle and said to Stanley, "Who knew there was so much hidden in such skinny fella, eh, Stan?"

Ralph sipped his coffee, "Well, we all have our secrets and our hidden talents."

"Not me, what you see is what you get. Mind you, I

suppose I might have some hidden talents...the problem is they are so well hidden under all this, I can't find the buggers," he patted his stomach.

"Morning, team," Anna chirped as she poked her head into the shop. "Jim, have you had any breakfast yet?"

"No, not yet, that bed and breakfast place upstairs is pretty poor to be honest. Lots of doilies and avocadoes, but no bacon and eggs."

"Doilies?"

"Don't worry, Jim's just hopped on to the hilarious stereotype bus this morning."

"Oh, I see, right," she laughed. "Just pop next door, Jim, when you're ready, I'll give you something. I've got eggs to spare, if you know what I mean? Got to head back, I've got a double-entendre taxi waiting for me. Bye"

Jim turned to Ralph as more customers arrived, "She's funny - pretty too. Is she single?"

"What do you care? You're married."

"So are you, my friend, so are you," Jim said as he sauntered off into the street and towards The Cookery, with a smile on his face.

CHAPTER 14

*The Mediterranean Couscous, motherhood
and iced missiles.*

"Who's got you all of a dither?" Irene said as she appeared in the kitchen, waving a plate at Anna. "They wanted Mediterranean couscous with their pies, not peas. Why anyone would want them bits of sawdust with their dinner I will never know, but that's what they ordered."

"Sorry, sorry. Hang on, I'll change it."

Irene stood with her arms folded, shifting her bra into a more comfortable position, "I need to stop putting tablets in here to remind me to take them. I keep forgetting and they get all crushed up, it's like Brighton beach in there sometimes."

"Has Jim finished his breakfast?" Anna asked, passing Irene back the plate while trying to look over her shoulder.

"That big thing? All legs and hair? Not yet." Irene

poked the Saturday girl, who was leaning against the counter flicking black nail varnish from her thumbs, "Here, Rosie, take this to them two in the window and say sorry for the mistake."

Rosie sighed and Irene watched her plod off with the plate, "I bet her mother regrets calling her Rosie, that is certainly one thing she is not. Who is he anyway, the big fella?"

"He's an old friend of Ralph's, come down to visit."

"So, what's your interest in him?"

"None. No interest. Just want to be welcoming."

"Yeah, right. Oy, Rosie, shall we try something new and exciting? It's called clearing tables. Give me strength," and she shot off round the counter with a tray.

Anna fluffed her hair and made a couple of coffees before heading out into the café, which was thinning out ahead of the lunchtime rush.

"Phew," she said as she plonked herself and the drinks down at Jim's table. "How is it?"

"Great," Jim said with a mouthful of sausage. "I needed this."

"You're welcome. So, you're an accountant? That must be so hard, I'm rubbish at numbers - can't even remember my own age."

"Thirty-three," Irene said as she swung past the table on her way to the ketchup.

Anna pulled a face, "Why I keep her on, I don't know."

"I know where the bodies are buried," Irene answered with a dark face as she returned with a bottle of sauce in her hand.

"She's a character, reminds me of my nan," Jim

chuckled as he put his knife and fork down and pushed the empty plate away from him.

"Yes, so, numbers are not my thing. I'm a cook really and a creative. Everything you see is my creation. Not Irene obviously, I think she was Dr Frankenstein's doing."

"Do you make all the food yourself?"

"Yes, dawn until dusk, I'm here. I don't get a chance to go out much. You know, what with the baking, the wages and the marketing, the accounts and everything. I suppose that's why I'm still young, free and single."

"Well, two out of three, anyway," Irene chipped in again as she returned for sauce for another customer.

"Well, look, I've decided not to head back until to-morrow. If you wanted me to take a look at your books, I'd be happy to. That way maybe you'd have a bit of spare time tonight and I could buy you a drink, in return for breakfast."

"Oh, I couldn't let you do that."

"Why not? You've done less for a pickled egg re-cently," Irene had the tiniest smirk on her normally dead-pan face as she past by again.

Anna flushed at the memory, "It's hard to talk here, everything's up in my flat. If you really mean it, you are welcome to come up and I'll show you. When things are quiet later today we can have a drink then, but if you get bored you must say."

"No, I won't get bored. I love business and figures and it looks like you're doing well on both counts," Jim grinned.

Anna laughed, "I hope you're better with a calcula-tor than you are with those corny lines. Come on, Mr Ac-countant, let's see what you're made of."

* * *

Ralph and Stanley made their way through the quiet streets at the end of the day, when the shoppers had headed off for the warmth of food and a fire at home or in one of the many cosy pubs across Rye. As they turned back into the deserted High Street there was a dim glow from the back of The Cookery and Ralph peered inside as he knocked on the glass door.

Anna's head shot up in a cloud of flour from behind the coffee machine, "You frightened the hell out of me," she said, looking frazzled as she opened the door. "What time is it?"

"About quarter past six. Got any leftovers for Stan?"

"Yes, there's a couple of sausages over there he can have. Help yourself, I need to get on."

Ralph headed into the kitchen and found the sausages, feeding one to an eager Stanley, "Ta. What's going on?"

"This bastard," she gestured to a large two-tiered cake she was circling with an icing bag in her hand as if she were about to assassinate rather than decorate it. "I completely forgot, what with...well, everything. It's for a baby-shower-thing tomorrow morning. I mean, who has a baby shower on a Sunday? They should be thinking about the baby Jesus, not their own spawn. Ridiculous."

Ralph took a bite out of the other sausage, "Any excuse for a party, I suppose. Besides, if you are going to go through the excruciating pain of childbirth, then having a bit of cake and champers beforehand seems the least you deserve."

"What do you know? Anyway, why does everyone want a baby all of a sudden? Just to get some useless presents, like tiny pumps to drag milk out of your boobs until they are down round your knees, or miniature Doc Martins that'll get worn twice before they grow out of them."

"Whoa, whoa, Mother Theresa, what's given you the hump? Wait, you're not, are you?"

"No, no, I'm not. Yuk, motherhood is a mental illness if you ask me."

Ralph reached out and took the piping bag out of her hands, "Stop, stop. Little angry lady, calm down. What's going on? This isn't like you," he turned her until she was looking up into his face. "What's happened?"

"Oh, I don't know. Nothing, really," Anna's shoulders slumped and Ralph let her slide gently to the floor with her back against the kitchen cupboards.

"Spill, lady," he said as he joined her on the floor.

"Well, Josie rang about an hour ago and she's all; 'Just checking the *gaw-geous* little cake of yours is going to be ready to pick up at ten tomorrow. Can't wait to see it, I just know it's going to be *sooooo* pretty.'"

"OK, annoying, but not really worth going all Pontius Pilate and killing small babies for."

Anna twisted her apron in her hands, "King Herod had the babies killed actually. Pontius Pilate had Jesus done in."

"I stand...or sit, corrected. So, who is Josie?"

"Josie Shaw. She's lovely, too bloody lovely. Perfect. I mean, she probably farts in Marks and Spencers when no one is looking like the rest of us, but I bet hers smell of bergamot and wild orchids..."

"You digress…"

"What? Oh yes, anyway, we went to school together and, like everyone I knew then, she's got married, got a perfect husband, got a perfect life and now got a perfect sticky-outy belly button with a baby stuffed in behind it and she just annoyed me, that's all. I've made cakes for her and all the others for their happy life events and no-one's made one for me, ever," she wiped her nose on some kitchen roll and blinked back the threatening tears.

Stanley shuffled across the kitchen and laid his head in her lap, looking up at her with his best puppy eyes. Ralph settled for taking hold of her hand, unable to compete with Stanley.

"Did your Mum never bake you a cake when she was alive?"

Anna snorted, "Once or twice, if the drinks cabinet was locked. But that was years ago…and she's not dead. Why did you think she was dead?"

"You said she wasn't around anymore and I just assumed."

"No, she's still very much alive. Well, I think she is. I haven't spoken to her for about six years. She's a very sad drunk. I tried everything, but in the end it has to be her decision to stop. She was bringing me down with her and I had to get away. So I did and I haven't seen her since."

Ralph squeezed her hand, "I'll make you a cake. It'll be a crap cake, but I'll make you one."

"Thanks, hon," she sniffed. "It's not really about the cake or my mother or Josie-perfect-tits-Shaw. What I mean is, I've never had anything significant enough to have a cake for. No engagement, no wedding, no baby-shower, no christening, no divorce..."

"OK, OK, I get it, but your time will come. Don't you think that some of those women,who seem to have everything look at you and think that *you* may be the lucky one? Perhaps their marriages aren't everything they seem to be from a few carefully edited Facebook photos? Maybe their kids are a nightmare or serial killers in training? Maybe they haven't slept since 2010? Maybe they are angry at giving up careers or missing out on promotions because of the choices they had to make? Maybe they'd have loved to just follow their hearts and run their own business, like you do? Perhaps they want to do what they love every day and not have some walloping, great, flat-footed fella buggering about in the background, getting in the way of their dreams?"

"Well..."

"Hm? Maybe?"

"Yes, well, maybe...", she wiped her wet cheeks with the corner of her apron.

"Talking of great flat feet, is Jim still upstairs going over your accounts? He's been gone hours."

Anna started to scramble to her feet, "Oh, no, I completely forgot about him."

"Wait, wait, settle down," he pulled her back to the floor. "Are you OK?"

"Yes, sorry. Just a bout of self-pity blown in with the sea breeze. That blooming ghost lady always appearing started it all, she freaked me out and everything seems to have been a bit strange since then."

"I thought Auntie B had dealt with her?"

"Auntie B? What do you mean?"

Ralph gulped, "Oh, nothing, I thought you meant...you know...something else..."

Anna looked at him, "What's Auntie B got to do with the ghost?"

"Nothing," Ralph squirmed awkwardly. "You know what she's like...erm...she just said that ghosts like that come and go, you know."

"At first she was there all the time, then suddenly she was gone. Just like that. What's that all about? It's put me on edge and made me think about all sorts of strange stuff, but I'll be fine. Besides, there's always Jim."

"Jim? No, no, there is *not* 'always Jim'. He's my mate and so is his wife, Carol. Don't start on him."

Anna got to her feet, brushing the flour from her purple and blue palazzo pants, "That's up to him, don't you think? As someone recently said, maybe people's marriages aren't everything they are cracked up to be."

"I'm thinking of you...and Carol. Look, you can't keep chasing after people who just aren't right for you, or that aren't even available," Ralph said, getting up from the floor. "Why can't you just wait until the proper Mr Right comes along? He has to be out there somewhere; I need someone to take you off my hands at some point."

"Charming," she took the piping bag back from Ralph and started working tiny pink roses around the edge of the cake. "I like him, that's all. He seems quite normal – and, just at the moment, normal seems like a really good thing. What will be, will be. Besides, you still have a wife and you didn't object when I said I was setting you up on a blind date."

"That's different and you know it. Anyway, I wanted to talk to you about that."

"Oh, no, mister, you are not backing out now," she waved the icing bag at him, a tiny piece flying off the end of the nozzle and landing just above Stanley's left eye, which he pursued with a tongue that was just a fraction too short for the task. "I have selected the candidate carefully... actually, it was the obvious choice."

"The thing is, I'm not sure I'm quite ready yet. I wouldn't know where to start, what to say?"

"Rubbish, you'll be fine. Come out with me and Jim tonight, you can practice on us."

"Damn, that's what I needed to talk to you about. I'm meeting someone for a drink tonight, so I'll have to abandon Jim for a while, can you entertain him – without causing a divorce, that is?

"Bingo!" Anna cried, dancing a little jig and startling Stanley, who moved into the café to continue to locate the icing that was setting hard amongst his eyebrows. "You've got yourself a date. Tell, tell, tell."

"It is most definitely NOT a date, trust me. Mind you, it started just like one of your recent disasters, it was Dew-drop Dobson's fault."

Ralph then recounted his run in with the footballs, Dobson and Sam, resulting in his being caught off guard and volunteering to coach the Rye Rovers in the absence of anyone else.

"But this is amaze-balls - Sam was who I was going to set you up with! He's perfect," Anna gave Ralph a big floury hug.

"Sam's gay?" Ralph asked, his breath being forced out of him by Anna and the news.

"Oh, as a goose. The whole world knows that...except you, obviously. Where have you been for the last twenty years? So, what are you wearing? Don't wear that old grey sweatshirt will you, there's retro and then there's past-it..."

"Wait, it is NOT a date. I didn't even know he was gay. We wanted to meet to discuss the football, that's all."

"Yes, over a drink and dinner - of course it's a date. You need to think of it as a date. Dress for a date. Do your hair for a date. Smell like a date. You do have some sort of scent to put on, don't you? I know you've been living as a straight guy, but now you are on the Yellow Brick Road you need a proper aftershave..."

"Yes, yes...I'm not a complete Neanderthal. I think I'll be OK to make myself presentable...except now you've completely freaked me out. We don't even like each other, I'm only doing it for the kids."

"Listen, Michael Jackson, you'll be fine. You just have to get to know him and he has to get to know you. He's kind of private, but because you don't know anything about his past it'll make things so much easier."

"What is it with his past? I'd talked myself into a calm place, but now it feels like this huge, big thing."

"It *is* a huge, big thing," Anna paused, thoughtfully massaging the icing in the bag between her fingers. "Love is just around the corner for both of us. I can feel it and you know I'm sensitive to these things. How about that? How would it be if we both found the right man at the same time – thank goodness it's not the same man, can you imagine?"

"Anna, Jim is *not* the right man, not for you, I know him. Why can't you wait for someone who is free, without flaws and a car boot full of baggage? You are completely strong and self-sufficient on your own, why do you need some mixed-up bloke to hang on to?"

Anna turned on him, eyes blazing, "Some friend you are – to Jim and to me. You are no great shining example of how to choose the perfect partner, are you? You married a *woman*, didn't you? Have you ever dated a man? Hm? Do you even know your type, I mean, beyond David Beckham, Brad Pitt and other fantasy men?"

Ralph stared at her, "No, I don't. I have no idea what I'm doing," then walked quickly through and out of the café.

Anna stood in the kitchen watching him slam out, then she grabbed the nearest object to her, an iced bun, and threw it with all her might. It hit the large front window, sticky side to the glass, and stayed there quivering for a moment. A few seconds later Ralph reappeared and called, "Stanley, come," which the little beagle did without any need for a second request and they both shot out of the door and back to The Bookery, as the bun slowly slid down the glass.

CHAPTER 15

The green eyes, a hidden cupboard
and a glass of mouthwash.

After a long shower and a bottle of beer, Ralph was not feeling much calmer. Stanley, on the other hand, after a chunky duck and venison dinner was ready to settle in for the night on the sofa with BBC Radio 4 for company. Ralph was not sure he would ever be ready for an evening in Sam's company, but he had dressed in a black button-down shirt, smart, well-fitting Levi's and his best, dark trainers. He didn't want to look over-dressed and definitely not like he was going on a date, but, somehow, he also wanted to look his best. Maybe it was a layer of armour to protect his nerves. He ran his hand through his hair for the last time, gave an extra squirt of Dior's Savage to spite Anna and he was ready.

"Wish me luck, Stan," he said as he looked in on him before leaving, but all he got was a drowsy twitch of an eyebrow. "That'll do. I won't be late."

* * *

As Ralph stood outside the restaurant part of him wished that his walk had taken a lot longer than it actually had. Two bay trees in stainless steel pots stood sentinel on either side of the entrance, lit from above by subtle lighting. The name 'Cinque' was hand-painted in deep red on the sandblasted brickwork above the door and had its own spotlight. A rich, golden glow came from the large sash windows that showed happy people tucking into their dinners. He hesitated, looked down at the pavement and took a deep breath, *"Don't be an idiot!"* he warned himself, then took a step forward and looked up into Sam's amused eyes as he stood in the doorway.

Ralph felt himself blush instantly, "Oh, not again!"

"Yep," Sam smirked. "You said it out-loud again."

"Crap."

"You know, normally you have to work people out by subtext and body language. Whereas you just say whatever is in your head. It's so simple, I don't know why no one thought of it before?"

"Well, it's new, you know. It's something I'm trying out for the Christmas season."

"How's it going for you?"

"Not so well," Ralph stamped his feet. "It's freezing out here, any chance you are going to let me in?"

Sam stepped back and threw open the door for him, "Be my guest."

Ralph moved into the warmth of an open foyer and started to unwind his scarf. Sam stood to one side in his chef's whites, with another cap on his head, this time dark red and worn back to front. "I've just got a few things to finish-off in the kitchen, so Dawa will look after you," Sam turned and disappeared through a set of double swing doors as a large shadow fell across Ralph from behind.

"Good evening, sir," said a voice so deep that Ralph felt it reverberate in his chest. He turned to find an enormous man in a light grey suit, with a white shirt and a silver tie standing behind a slim reception desk. He had an extensive beard and matching eyebrows underneath an impeccable, tight grey turban, "My name is Dawa Singh, welcome to Cinque. May I take your coat?"

"Hi, yes, thanks."

Dawa took Ralph's jacket and handed it to one of the hovering waiters and took him through the brick arches of the old warehouse, that had been sympathetically transformed into a relaxed but tasteful space, full of small corners and tucked away tables, that meant no diner ever felt overlooked or overheard.

"Sam has saved you a table in the bar, I hope that's alright?"

"Fine with me," Ralph said, sliding into a leather seat that formed a half circle around a marble topped table in the far corner of the bar. "This place is great."

"Thank you, sir. Is this your first visit?"

"Yes, I've not been in Rye long. Please, call me Ralph."

"Welcome to this strange little corner of our country, Ralph," Dawa said with a genuine smile. "I'll get your drinks. Sam had chosen a white Spanish Albariño. He has been looking for a good one for some time, I trust that is acceptable."

"Has he?" Typically pretentious behaviour from

Sam, Ralph thought. "Yes, fine. I'm more of a beer man myself, but I'll have some wine, if you think it's good."

"Good for you," Dawa said as he went off to the bar.

Ralph picked up a cocktail menu from the table and flicked through it while he waited, trying to calm his nerves and ease the annoyance he already felt with Sam's behaviour so far. Dawa returned with the bottle of wine in a terracotta cooler and two glasses, which he placed on the table in front of Ralph.

"I'm sorry it's a little noisy in here tonight," he said as he poured the pale golden wine into Ralph's glass. "We have a hen party that have been enjoying the cocktails. They're now having some food, which we hope will soak up some of the excess alcohol. I hope they won't disturb you."

"It's fine, don't worry. We're only talking about football; I probably won't be here long."

"Football? How stimulating. Excuse me, Ralph, I have some new arrivals."

Ralph watched the elegant man glide back to the reception and greet a young couple, both blushing and awkward, clearly on their first date together. He felt the leather cushion beneath him ripple and Sam was easing in beside him.

"Sorry about that, we are busier than I had thought," he said.

Taking the opportunity Ralph said, "Oh, well, if you need to postpone, that's fine, I can go."

"No, you're alright. The hen party were late to their table, too much Sex on the Beach at the bar, but it's all under control now."

Ralph tried to restart things on a positive note, "I was just saying to Dawa that the restaurant looks great,"

"Thanks. It took me long enough to get it right."

There was a pause as if neither of them knew where to go from here.

"How's the wine?" Sam said as he poured himself a glass.

"OK. I was saying, I'm more of a beer man myself."

Another pause, during which both sipped their wine and looked deep into their glasses.

"I've been looking for a good Albariño for some time."

"Yes, Dawa said. You must be very pleased with yourself."

The next pause seemed to qualify more as a silence and dragged on and on, as both men sat taking stock of their next move.

"Look..."

"Listen..."

They said together.

"What is your problem...?"

"Why have you got such a...?"

But before either could finish their sentence a scream rang out from the end of the bar as one of the hen party, wearing a bright pink boob-tube and penis earrings, stared across at them, "Oh, my god...Big Rachel, Big Rachel...come quick, see who it is," and she minced back into the restaurant to presumably bring forth Big Rachel.

"Shit," Sam said, sinking down into his seat.

Before Ralph had time to react, Dawa Singh appeared at Sam's elbow and lifted him out of his seat, he then reached across to Ralph and dragged him from behind the table, "This way," he thundered, pulling them both with him away from where Big Rachel's friend had been standing. He wrenched open a door that Ralph had not seen as it was disguised to match the wall around it, and more or less threw them both inside.

Ralph hit the floor first, sprawling across hard concrete, then Sam came in behind him tripping over Ralph's feet and landing on top of him. The door was then slammed shut and all sounds and light from the restaurant were cut off.

"What the hell?" Ralph yelled. "Get off me."

"Stop flailing about and I might be able to. Stay still. It's too bloody dark, I can't see anything."

"No shit, Sherlock. You've got my legs pinned down, I can't move them."

"Good, keep still then and I can get up and find the light."

Ralph gave in and lay still, the weight of what must have been Sam's chest lying on his, as he felt Sam's breath on his cheek.

"I just need to feel where I am, there's a desk on one side and some shelves on the other."

"I don't need a guided tour, just get the light on."

Sam was squirming about feeling both sides of him until he located the leg of the desk, "Right, got it. Hang on." Ralph felt Sam twist to one side and then their bodies separated as Sam was able to clamber on to his knees and stood up using the desk to help him. The next minute they both blinked in the light of a desk lamp that had snapped on. Sam leant back against the desk, catching his breath, "Shit, I should have known that would happen with that lot."

"Don't mind me," Ralph said from the floor. "I'll just sort myself out."

"Here," Sam said, offering him his hand, but Ralph

batted it away.

"I can do it," he rolled over on to all fours, got to his feet and immediately started towards the door.

"Wait," Sam said. "You can't..."

"I can do what I bloody well like," Ralph snapped, turning the door handle, but it wouldn't budge. "What the...is it locked?"

"Yes, probably. Dawa will have locked it from the outside."

Ralph turned on Sam, "Now look, this is not funny. What the hell is going on?"

"We just have to wait until they've gone, that's all. It shouldn't be too long. They'll be onto their desserts soon and then Dawa will move them out."

"No, no, no," Ralph began to pace up and down, which didn't take him long as they were in a thin room, with a narrow desk filling one long wall and a set of shelves on the other, full of binders and folders marked with 'Invoices' and 'Orders'. "This is mad, why are we locked in a cupboard?"

"It's my office, if you don't mind," Sam said, sitting on the desk with his back against the wall, drawing his legs up and hugging them with his arms. "I'm sorry if we dirtied your nice trainers, but it can't be helped."

Ralph rattled the door again, "You need to let me out, this is crazy."

"Yup, welcome to my world," Sam reached down and pulled open a drawer in the desk, he scrabbled inside and came out with a small bottle and then two glasses. "Drink?"

"No," Ralph said, crossing his arms and leaning heavily against the door. Sam ignored him and poured two large glasses of scotch and held one out. "I said, no thanks."

"Oh, stop being so pious all the time, take it," he waved the glass at Ralph.

"Pious? Me?" Ralph was stung, but took the glass. "Fine, if you'll wind in your ego and tell me what the hell is going on," he took a swig of the drink, instantly regretting it as the harsh liquid bounced off the back of his throat and took his breath away. "Jesus," he gasped. "What's that, the cooking brandy?"

"It's actually an eighteen-year-old Lagavulin single malt."

"Well, I hope it's very happy with itself. It still took the skin off the back of my throat."

"That's because you are not supposed to chuck it down like mouthwash."

"Listen, Sam, I know you don't like me and the feeling is mutual, believe me, so if you just tell me what is going on, I can drink my mouthwash and get out of here."

"Are you serious?" Sam looked at Ralph with genuine surprise.

"Deadly. From the moment we met you've been rude and smug and…"

"No, not that…which, by the way, is not true…but, you really don't know what this is about?"

"I wouldn't have asked you three hundred times if I knew, would I? I know there's some big secret about you, you think you're special, you're some sort of recluse creeping about with your cap always hiding your face. Everyone tells me you don't trust people for 'obvious reasons', but I'm buggered if it's obvious to me."

Sam quietly sipped his drink, then he pushed the contents of the desk to one side and shuffled up to allow room for Ralph, "Then I owe you an apology."

"Too bloody right you do."

"I don't meet many people like you, you see. Please, sit," he took off his cap and threw it in to the corner and ruffled his soft, messy hair. "I'm sorry."

Ralph looked at Sam, his face exposed and suddenly looking vulnerable, all the arrogance gone. He moved to the desk and sat on the edge, "So, what's the big secret?"

Sam sighed, "Nothing is a secret and that's the problem."

Just then the door rattled and opened part way as Dawa Singh stuck his head into the room, "Sorry about this. The hen party have just started on their desserts. I've told them the coffee machine's broken and we don't serve cocktails after nine, so they'll be gone soon. Are you OK to stay put for a little longer, gentlemen?"

Ralph looked at Sam, who's head hung down, his floppy hair grazing the top of his nose. Sam brought his green eyes up to meet Ralph's, "They're after me not you, so you are a free man...if you want."

Sam looked so sad and exposed that Ralph didn't have the heart to do anything except swirl his drink and say, "I haven't finished my eighteen-year-old mouthwash yet, so I'll hang on, if that's OK."

"Sure, fine with me," Dawa said. "I'll come back when the coast is clear." The door closed and they heard the lock turn on the other side.

CHAPTER 16

*The second most eligible bachelor, Friday's
socks and soggy chips.*

"It's a funny word, poofy," Jim said, sipping a hot chocolate and stretching his legs out in front of him, his socks proudly displaying the word, Friday, across the soles.

Anna adjusted the Judy Garland cushion between them on the sofa, "Well, the thing is that what you have your feet on is a 'pouffe'. I think it's pronounced with an 'a' at the end, not a 'y'. It's French."

"Oh, right, that makes more sense. No offence to Ralph, I didn't mean anything by it."

"Don't worry, say what you like about him, we had a fight, so it's every man for himself at the moment." Anna said, stirring her cream into her hot chocolate.

"I think it'll take some time to get used to him being, you know, like that. I had no idea."

"No, I think he'd buried it all pretty deep, so there is

no reason you would have known. And you're OK with him going out on a date tonight? I mean, leaving you alone."

"Well, I'm not really alon. If he hadn't gone out I wouldn't be here with you enjoying this delicious...what was it again?"

"Hot chocolate and horseradish."

"That's it. Blimey, it's clearing the tubes, I'll tell you that. So, he's done me a favour there, to be honest." Anna tucked a few curls back behind her ear, as he continued, "The other thing is Helen, of course. She did say she wasn't surprised when he left, but now I'm thinking about it, she didn't seem that bothered about her marriage breaking down. She just wanted to know he was alright. Perhaps they were more friends than anything else?"

"Perhaps."

"Just goes to show, you can never really know what goes on in someone else's marriage."

"Don't you start."

"What have I said?"

"Nothing, sorry, go on."

"Right, well, I suppose it's opened my eyes a bit. Thinking back to what our life was like back in Barnsley. Pub Monday, footie practice Tuesday, curry with the lads Friday, you know, it's nice and all, but it's kind of...well, tame, I suppose. Regular. No, what's the word?"

"Boring?" Anna said.

"Yes, I suppose it is. Maybe to someone like Ralph, who had this whole side of him hidden away - not even to mention his painting and stuff. Then seeing him with all of you Rooftop lot, well, he's a different man. Probably a *better* man, to be honest. I suppose, I'll be going back knowing that he's OK now."

"Are you going back soon, then?" Anna asked, edging a little closer to him.

"Have to, I'm afraid. I've got work and...well..."

"Carol?"

"Carol, yes," Jim sighed. "It seems like such a long way away when you're down here in the middle of all this. It's like another world," he waved his mug at the stuffed water vole and the trio of miniature ukuleles hanging on the wall.

"Well, it is really, isn't it? But there's no need to rush back. It'll all be there waiting for you, won't it?"

Jim stretched his long frame across the sofa, "I suppose it will, yes."

"More hot chocolate?"

"No thanks...Are you hungry?"

"A bit, yes. You?"

"Always," he patted his well-padded stomach. "A physique like this does not appear on its own, you know. We're by the sea, so I can't go home without having some fish and chips. What do you say?"

Anna dismissed a flashback to Ginger Jay and put on a brave smile, "Great idea."

* * *

Ralph choked on his drink, sending a spray of expensive scotch over Sam and jumped off the desk.

"Careful, that cost a fortune," Sam said, wiping himself down.

"Jane Scott? THE Jane Scott? Hollywood-movies-Jane-Scott, is your *mother*?"

"Yup, 'fraid so."

Ralph began to pace across the floor of the tiny cupboard once again, "The green eyes, of course! I knew they were beautiful, but now I know why - they're the same as hers."

Sam looked at him, "Beautiful?"

"...well, I didn't mean beautiful, I meant, you know...striking."

"Striking? OK, thanks," Sam blinked and looked away.

"So, that means your dad was Damien Ross?"

"He was."

"So, you're Sam Ross."

"The penny drops," Sam said sulkily.

"What? Oh, well, I don't follow a lot of celebrity stuff."

"I'm not a celebrity, I just have famous parents."

"Wasn't he going to play James Bond, your dad?"

"Yeah, but he came off his motorbike three weeks before they were due to start shooting, broke his pelvis, so they replaced him. He died eight years later, on the same bloody bike."

Ralph slowed his pacing and leant against the bookshelves, "I remember that, it must have been rough."

Sam shrugged, "I guess, but it changed a lot. I was in Copenhagen working with an amazing chef at the time, but I had to come back and look after Mum - she went a bit bonkers. Mind you, it was the making of her in the end, all the attention revived her career, made people remember her. Every cloud and all that."

"So, is that what all the cap stuff is about? Hiding in case anyone recognises you? I mean, I can understand it being a pain if you're actually with Jane Scott, I mean, your mum - even I'd recognise her, and I'm not being rude, but who'd be interested in you?"

"Blimey, I'd love to be around when you *are* being rude."

"You know what I mean."

"OK, so you want the full potted history? Here goes, when I was about seventeen, I was at school. Boarding school, because Mum and Dad were always somewhere else. I really liked this other boy, he was cute, you know, seemed really nice, not bothered that I was the son of...blah, blah. We started a sort of relationship, my first proper crush. Then after two weeks I was all across the tabloid papers. Photos, letters, even bloody drawings I'd done. He'd sold it all for three hundred quid."

"Wow, that's not good."

"You reckon? Not only was I outed to the world, but to my parents, my grandparents, every boy and teacher at school, not to mention looking like such a sap, with pathetic love letters and scribbles with hearts all over them," as he spoke Sam's whole body seemed to shrink in on itself and tighten. Ralph saw his jaw clench and start to stick out, in what he had previously thought of as arrogance, but now realised was something far different: fear.

❄ ❄ ❄

The lights of a distant ship blinked through the mist, as Anna and Jim sat huddled together on a bench looking out to sea. They sat beside the Ypres Tower, or Rye Castle as the locals called it, a fort that had stood on the hill above the English Channel for over eight hundred years.

"Do you think they're having fish and chips on that boat too?" Anna asked.

"If they are, I bet they're fresher than this," Jim said, picking through a pile of batter and soggy chips with a wooden fork.

"Hm, I know, but the Chippy Chipper is the only chip shop open in town at this time of year. Still, this is way better than last time I went there."

"Really? Blimey, that must have been bad."

"Trust, me it was, I mean, would you ever call an Alsatian, Linda?"

"What?" Jim turned to her.

"Sorry, just thinking about something else."

"Come on, this seemed like a good idea at the time, but let's go to the pub," he stood up, wrapping the remains of his dinner back in the greasy paper. "The Mermaid Inn is just round the corner, isn't it? They do a decent pint."

"OK, good idea...Jim?"

"Yes, love...I mean, Anna."

"Tell me about Carol," Anna tucked a wayward curl back under her yellow beret. "Where did you meet?"

Jim hesitated, "Erm, in the pub. She was with her mates," he looked out to the lights in the distance. "She was fun. She likes cats. Works in Boots. She makes candles. That's it, not much else to say about her really. We're married."

"I see," Anna said, wrapping her poncho around her and getting up from the bench. "She sounds nice."

"Yeah, she is," Jim sighed. "I don't want to hurt her."

Anna kicked at a weed between the paving stones, "No, I know. Me neither."

"We're only having a drink. Can't do any harm," Jim said, offering her his arm.

"Just a drink," she said, nodding and linking her own arm through his. "Oh, hang on," she picked up their wrapped, partially eaten suppers and trotted down a slope towards the base of the tower. "Excuse me," she said to a pile of black bin bags. "I'll just leave these here, in case you fancied them."

"I may be wanting a bit of something later, when my roast pheasant has gone down," said a gravelly voice, from deep within the pile of bags. So, she lay the fish and chips on the ground, before turning and heading back to Jim.

"Who's that?" Jim asked as they turned towards the pub.

"I don't know, but he's been there a couple of weeks. I hate to think of him out in the cold every night."

"Well, you can't take in every waif and stray. At least wait until I've gone before you move in the next one."

"OK, I'll wait. I just hope he has better choice of socks than you."

* * *

Ralph was leaning into the corner of the tiny room, his legs crossed beneath him on the desk, watching Sam huddled next to him.

"In those days it was only professional photographers and a few gossipy magazines, plus the tabloids. Now though, everyone has a camera in their pocket and bam - two minutes later you're on social media scratching your arse or picking a piece of lettuce out of your teeth."

"But all that was so long ago, no one remembers it now, surely? Mind you, I do remember your dad dying and seeing Jane...your Mum, on the TV in lots of different black outfits."

"Jeez, her stylist was having a field day with that lot, he loved it. Widow chic, he called it. He once tried to get me into a matching outfit, until he decided he'd rather keep his teeth intact...I was pretty angry in those days."

"I'm not surprised, your dad had just died."

"Hm, not that the press seemed to be bothered by that. Not only was I the bachelor son of two of Britain's biggest movie stars, I was now 'tragic' and 'heartbroken', which somehow made me even more of a catch. I made it to number two in the most eligible bachelor list that year."

"Really? Who was number one?" Ralph said.

Sam looked at him, "Seriously?"

"Yeah, right, sorry. It must have been devastating to be number two."

Sam tensed angrily, until he saw Ralph grinning at him, "Idiot."

"Hey, that's my line," Ralph said, giving Sam a shove. Sam retaliated by shoving him back with his shoulder and they pushed back and forth for a moment, until they settled into companionable silence.

"What I don't get is, I thought the best bachelor list was aimed at teenage girls and you're not really in that market, are you?"

Sam gave a hollow laugh and hopped off the desk, "Oh, the press had put all that behind them by then. They'd done that story, so the new one was that I was back on the straight and narrow, literally. Until it all blew apart again over Steve," he banged his head against one of the cardboard files on the shelf unit.

"Steve?"

Sam threw a paper clip over his shoulder in Ralph's direction, "You really have been living under a rock, haven't you?" he turned and leant against the shelves. "Are you sitting comfortably? Right, so a few years ago, I must have been about twenty-five, I met this guy, Steve, in London. A lawyer, really nice guy, really cute, not bothered who my parents were..."

"Not again?" Ralph said, fearing a repeat of Sam's childhood exposure.

"Oh, no, this one is even better," Sam picked up the scotch bottle and topped up both of their glasses. "We were together nearly two years, I spent most of my time at his flat at the Barbican, in London. So far, so romantic. Until..." he did a drum roll on the desk with a plastic ruler and a marker pen. "Mum decided she needed a new lawyer and one of her girlfriends recommended her husband, who was the best, apparently. Are you ready? Yup, it turned out his name was Steve and he spent most of his time at their Barbican flat, while the wife lived in their country place and hated coming to London."

"Shit."

"Shit, indeed, my cute northern friend. I had no idea he was married, so I went mad. My mother took it upon herself to tell his wife everything, so she went mad. Then she took her revenge on him by going to the papers, and yes, you guessed it, *everything* went mad. 'Dead James Bond actor's son in gay affair with married man.' 'Love nest in Barbican flat number 007', while poor little wifey 'forced to live in pokey fourteen-room mansion in the country'," Sam threw back his drink and then leant on the desk, his head bowed with his now tangled hair covering most of his face.

Ralph didn't know quite what to do or say, no wonder Sam was wary of getting to know people and be recognised. The up-tight guy who always seemed to have somewhere better to be had suddenly become someone quite different.

"That sucks," Ralph said. "Is that when you came here?"

"Pretty much," Sam said, turning and sitting back on the desk. "I keep my head down and get on with cooking, which helps with my sanity. Just occasionally things get a bit crazy, like tonight, but Dawa does his thing, you know," he gestured around the locked room.

Ralph grinned, "He's good, I could do with him when Anna and I fight. She went for me with an iced bun tonight."

"Really?" Sam looked at him and smiled - a genuine smile this time, not a guarded one. Ralph held the look and saw the man with the stunning green eyes properly for the first time.

"Sorry, I've just talked about me all night and there you were having your own trauma," Sam said, casually placing his hand on Ralph's knee.

Ralph nodded, "I know, selfish. It had a cherry on it too, it could have had my eye out."

"I can see how that could be traumatic," Sam sat back on the desk, taking his warm hand away, leaving Ralph feeling relief and a hint of disappointment.

They looked at each other, both pretty sure what was coming next, but neither knowing who would make the first move. Then the sound of a lock being turned broke the moment and they both jumped, putting more space between them.

"They've gone, finally. Are you guys OK?" Dawa Singh said, holding the door open, allowing the noise and light from the restaurant to flood reality back into the room.

"Good..." Ralph said.

"Yep, good, we're good," Sam echoed, jumping down onto the floor.

"At least you had a chance to talk about football in here, didn't you," Dawa said, as he stood back to let them out of the office.

"Football? Damn, that's what we were here to sort out," Ralph said, moving into the bar and stretching his aching legs from sitting cross-legged for so long.

Sam rubbed his hands together, "Well, we can talk about that while we eat."

"Ah, yes, well that's the thing," Dawa shut the office door and turned to them. "Since you've been in there, we've had two new parties of four come in - unplanned. Sorry, but I've seated them and the kitchen have said, will you go back and help them. I thought you would have completed your business while you were in the office."

"Actually, we'd only just started," Sam said with a quick look at Ralph, who felt himself blush. "I'm so sorry, I can make you something and send it out to you."

"Look, don't worry, it's a busy night...I'll be fine. I've got a dog at home, I'll leave you to it," Ralph started to head for the reception area. "I'll see you at the match tomorrow. Half nine, wasn't it?"

Dawa went off to fetch his coat and Sam stood at the doors to the kitchen, "Yes. I am sorry," he said.

"Me too," Ralph said, putting his hands deep into the

pockets of his jeans and looking at the doormat beneath his feet.

"So, two things; one, the match is down at the Town Salts, under Hilder's Cliffe. Do you know it?"

Ralph laughed, "I didn't even understand the words you just said, but I'll find it. I'll ask Joe."

"OK, great," Sam paused, looking as if he was undecided about something.

"...and number two?" Ralph prompted.

"Number two: 'striking'? Really? Is that the best you could come up with for my eyes?"

Ralph smiled, "I'll work on it."

"Make sure you do."

Dawa returned with Ralph's coat and scarf, "Thanks, Dawa, and good to meet you."

Dawa bowed slightly, glancing between the two men, "You too, Ralph. I hope we get to see more of you, and apologies for throwing you in a cupboard on your first visit."

"Hey, how many times? That's my office, not a cupboard," Sam said.

Dawa and Ralph looked at each other, "It's a cupboard," they said in unison and as Ralph stepped out into the night he felt what he guessed was a paperclip ping off the back of his head. He turned with a smile, but Sam had already disappeared back into the kitchen.

CHAPTER 17

The Rye Rovers, King George and the terriers.

S unday morning arrived and a bright sun melted a clean, crisp frost. Ralph was already in the kitchen making toast when Jim came out of the shower. He held out a mug of steaming coffee to him.

"Morning."

"A good morning to you, Ralphie boy," Jim said, brightly. "How was your night of fine dining and football planning?"

"Hmmm, we didn't quite get to either - it's a long story. How was your evening? I shouldn't have abandoned you."

"Don't worry about it, it was good. Anna's got a great little business going there, I went through the books and made a few suggestions to maybe tighten things up a bit and watch some of her costs, but otherwise it's pretty sound. We had a decent pint in that pub, that's pretty much it."

Ralph sat on the stairs while Jim went into the spare room to get dressed, "I really appreciate you helping her. I don't suppose she mentioned anything about me at all, did she?"

"Not really. No, I don't think...wait...oh yes, you're a twat and she wished she'd thrown the coffee machine at you rather than a bun, but that was all."

"Oh, good, I'm glad she's over it then."

Jim laughed, sticking his head round the bedroom door, "Don't worry, she'll be fine. She said it was her fault as much as yours. She'll make you suffer for a while, but then it'll all be forgotten until the next time. That's what women do, isn't it?"

"You're asking the wrong man there. I'm no expert on women, clearly, and I'm not even sure I can get the hang of my own lot."

"Are we talking about that restaurant bloke? What's his problem? You said he was an arrogant git."

"I may have jumped the gun a bit there, actually. It's complicated, well, *he's* complicated, but he's not so bad."

"Well, don't tell Anna that, for god's sake, she's got you two married with six children in matching pyjamas. For some reason she thinks you are a bit of a catch - can't see it myself. Now if they wanted a *real* man, they'd need to look at someone like me, of course."

Ralph headed back to the kitchen as he heard the toaster flinging the toast out onto the worktop, "Oh, is that right?"

"Absolutely. Man of the month me, you know," Jim called, followed by "Ooff" and a loud thud.

"Yep, it's what every woman is looking for...a grown man who can't even put his own trousers on without falling over."

Jim came into the kitchen rubbing his elbow and snatched a piece of buttered toast, "That bedroom is tiny. How is anyone supposed to put their trousers on in there without hitting the ceiling and at least three walls?"

Ralph lent against the worktop, "So, you and Anna then. Anything I should know?"

"Like what?" Jim said, through a mouthful of crumbs.

"OK, fine. It's none of my business, you don't have to tell me."

"Nothing to tell, mate, honestly," and Jim took his coffee into the living room. Ralph picked up his own drink and followed him, after putting a bowl of breakfast down for Stanley.

"What plans have you got for today? I'm supposed to be at the kid's football match at nine-ish, but..."

"No, mate, I need to head back - got the marching orders from the missus. Time to face the music back at base, I suppose...for you that is."

"I told you, I'm not going back."

Jim sat forward on the sofa and put his coffee down on the floor beside him, "I know, but *I* have to go back. I'll be the one answering all the questions about what's happened to you. What am I supposed to say?"

Ralph sat down in the armchair, "Whatever you want to say, I suppose. The truth...pretty much."

"The truth? Or pretty much the truth?"

"Tell them I've started a new life, running a hugely successful bookshop, finding my feet in an amazing new town, with incredible, glamorous friends, blah, blah..."

"Right, *pretty much* the truth then."

Ralph sighed, "Tell them what you like. Tell them I miss them, that I'm sorry, but this is right for me. This is what I needed."

"And the gay thing?"

"The *gay thing*?" Ralph laughed. "Yes, tell them about the gay thing. Tell them I'm not very good at it yet, but I'm working on it. By the way, can you take this?" He put his coffee down and went out to his bedroom, returning with an envelope. "I couldn't sleep last night after...well, when I got back...so, I went down to the shop and rang Helen."

"Hell's bells, how did that go?"

"Better than I could have expected actually. I don't know why I underestimated everyone, just me being a..."

"Twat?"

"I was going to say, idiot."

Jim picked up his coffee, "Is she OK, you know, about *it*?"

"She is actually. There were tears, mostly from me, but in the end she said that she thinks it's better for her that I haven't left her for another woman. I told her how sorry I was, but you know what she said...she said..."

Jim reached out and put his hand on Ralph's knee, "It's OK, mate. It's OK."

"Sorry. I really have to stop this blubbing, it's even getting on *my* nerves now. Anyway, she was amazing and she said that if I ever needed support when I told anyone, you know, about me, she'd be proud to come and hold my hand."

"Blimey, that is pretty amazing. She's still a pain in the arse as a sister and crap at Monopoly, but that's special, I reckon."

"It is. That letter is just some other stuff I forgot to say or couldn't say last night. She'll understand. Look, Jim, I can't tell you how much it means to me that you've come here and..."

Jim scooped his towering frame out of the sofa and waved his hand at Ralph, "Right, that's it, you can stop that. I'm not having two grown men crying over each other, even if one is a bit of a crocus bulb."

"Don't you mean pansy?"

"I'll thank you not to correct to me on my own use of insults, I know what I'm saying. Oh, and by the way, that chef fella, Sam, is it? If you got it on with him imagine all the free food you'd get, so, think on."

"How have I lived without your wisdom?"

"Many have asked themselves the same question, matey boy. I have to ration myself sometimes or there'd be none of me left. Right, on that note, I've drunk your coffee, eaten your toast, shagged your women - or to be honest, had a quick look at their accounts – so, it's time to hit the road," Jim tucked the letter for Helen in his jacket pocket and went to collect his things.

* * *

By nine o'clock Jim was on his way back towards the M25 then the M1 and the North. Meanwhile, Ralph and Stanley were on their way to the Rye Rovers' under ten's match of the day. He wasn't sure what he was going to say to Sam after last night, he wasn't even sure how he felt about what nearly, but didn't quite, happen. There was definitely a connection between them, but was it just too much whisky on an empty stomach?

At least he had Stanley for a little moral support, he thought, as they came down the steep steps from Hilder's Cliffe to the salt flats that lay beside the River Rother and formed children's play areas, a bowling green and a football pitch. "Come on, Stan, let's do this," he said, taking a deep breath and crossing the road to the car park.

As Ralph neared the pitch Stanley strained on his lead seeing small people and footballs ahead, "Hang on, hang on," urged Ralph, hauling him back to heel, just as Sam emerged from his car, the grey cap firmly back on his head.

"Oh, hi," Ralph said, attempting a confidence he didn't really feel.

"Morning. Ready for this?" Sam said, getting straight down to business.

"Absolutely, can't wait."

Sam turned to open the boot, not allowing any further conversation, "Give me a hand with some of this kit, will you?"

They gathered the bag of balls and other equipment from Sam's car and then Ralph was introduced to the team as their coach for the next few weeks.

"Morning, everyone. Sam tells me it's a friendly match this morning, with the Tenterden Terriers. I hear you are brilliant, so just go out there, play how you normally play and let's see what you can do."

Eleven little faces looked up at him, some through thick plastic glasses misted in the cold air, others with lopsided hair that had only recently been having a lie in, but all nervous and a little excited.

Sam leant into Ralph and whispered, "The Tenterden lot are known to be tearaways, last time they came here two of ours had to go to A&E."

"Really?" Ralph looked at his frightened group of tiny players, releasing his grip slightly on the dog lead and Stanley took off like a rocket through the legs of the children and tackled a particularly suspicious football that was hanging around in the centre circle just looking for trouble. The kids turned, yelling and laughing as they gave chase and followed Stanley around the pitch. Eventually the delinquent ball was tamed and driven into the goal, to be met by a large cheer from the players and parents alike.

Ralph collected a panting Stanley, "Well," he said to Sam. "I think that had more effect than my team talk, don't you? I reckon the Rye Rovers are good to go."

Sam was still laughing, "I think you might be right. Stanley, you are here-by promoted to Assistant Coach." Stanley barked with pride at his new post and stood to attention watching every move of the ball throughout the first half just in case it should step out of line again.

When the referee called half time, the boys and girls of both teams headed back to the side lines and pouches of squash and juice from their parents. As Ralph called them all together, he noticed that lurking in the background was the familiar face of Dew-drop Dobson, "What's he doing here?" he asked Sam, quietly.

"He's got a grandson in the team."

"There's a Mrs Dobson and little Dobsons?"

"There is. She died ages ago...from boredom, I expect."

"Right, kids. Fantastic first half," Ralph said to his gathered group of players. "So much energy, I loved it. I'm not sure all of you need to run after the ball all the time, but we can work on that. Four–nil down is not too bad. It could have been a lot worse and it gives us something to aim for, doesn't it?" Little heads nodded as they sucked on their straws. "So, in this half, let's mix things up a bit. What's your name?" Ralph asked a round boy with excessive ears.

"George," he said, in a defensive manner.

"George, excellent. Good name, there are loads of Kings called George. Georges make good leaders. You started in defence, didn't you? Yes, so that is maybe roughly where you need to be for most of the time. Try to resist barging your own team players out of the way to get to the ball wherever it is on the pitch, especially if one of them looks like they might have a bash at scoring, OK? Now, where's our hero goalie?"

"Elliot, where are you?" Sam called.

A small child with large blue plastic specs and a good ration of freckles stepped forward, with his hand nervously held in the air.

"Ah, there you are," Ralph said. "Great work. The way you dived across the goal mouth when they scored for the second time was fantastic. Wrong direction sadly, but an amazing dive nevertheless." Ralph crouched down to be on the same eye level as Elliot. "Look," he said quietly. "Just a little tip I've learnt over the years. Try not to clean your glasses quite so often, like you were when their last goal went in. I bet you can see the players and the ball even with a bit of muck on them, can't you?"

Elliot squinted at Ralph, "You mean, concentrate on the game?"

"Well, yes, yes, that is what I mean. Exactly," Ralph patted him on the shoulder and sent the team back to finish their snacks.

"Nice," said Sam with a smile and turned to talk to some of the parents, just as the thin, hunched figure of Dew-drop Dobson crept in between them.

"A word if I may, *Coach,*" he managed to fill the single syllable of the last word with a match-winning sneer, followed by a deafening sniff as the cold had produced a nasal droplet of considerable proportions.

"Of course, Mr Dobson," Ralph said. "May I call you Henry?"

"I don't think it wise," was the response. "It's about my grandson and his unfair treatment."

"Unfair treatment? Oh dear, who by?" Ralph said, looking worriedly at Sam, who had joined the conversation, sensing trouble.

"To be specific, by you, Mr Wright, by you."

"Oh, dear. Well, which one is yours?"

"George. George Hawkins. The talented young player, whose free ranging skills you have just straight jacketed, thus hampering not only his opportunity to excel, but also the team's chance to build any level of success in this, their chosen sporting field of choice."

Sam smirked, "To be fair, the council said we could play in this field, so the kids didn't really choose it."

"Humour again, Samuel? Not your strong point, I fear. Well, Coach, I have registered my opinion to you and am sure that on reflection you may wish to amend your advice to George for the action in the second half."

"Actually, I don't think so, Mr Dobson. George is a...erm...sturdy young man, with considerable strength. So, I think he will shine even more brightly by sticking to his job as a defender. So, let's leave things as they are for now and see how we go, shall we?"

"Very well. On your head be it. Good morning."

As Dobson edged his way back to the side lines to watch the second half start, Sam patted Ralph on the shoulder, "Good for you, for sticking to your guns. That kid has always been a menace."

Ralph looked at Sam, but his attention had already been drawn away by the referee blowing her whistle to re-start the game, as both teams piled in towards the ball as it rolled freely across the centre of the pitch. Ralph quickly caught the eye of George, as he crossed his arms and stayed put outside the goal area, sulking.

Twenty-five minutes later it was all over; the Tenterden Terriers had not managed to score any more goals, Elliot had made a spectacular save by falling over his laces and landing on the ball, George had successfully booted the ball and several players away from the goal area, leaving the Rovers' strikers to score two excellent last-minute goals. They hadn't won, but for the first time in many matchesThe Rye Rovers had not been trounced by another team of marauding under tens. They were ecstatic and celebrated as if the victory had been theirs, leaping around Sam and Ralph, while Stanley barked and danced with them.

Ralph thanked the other team coach and the referee, chatted with happy but cold parents as they scurried back to the heat of their cars and Sunday dinner preparations, eventually finding himself and Stanley alone in the car park. He had missed Sam leaving in the chaos of the end of the match, or else he had simply left quietly which, Ralph thought, said enough for him to know that there would be no repeat of the near miss last night, now the effects of the single malt had worn off.

CHAPTER 18

*The joy of texts, Armageddon
and chocolate rewards.*

"I'm going to take that phone and flush it down the ladies," Irene thundered at Anna. "Ping, ping, ping, all day. My nerves are shot, my kidneys won't know where to put themselves later."

"I don't know what's the matter with you, Irene, it's just the odd text coming in," Anna said, innocently.

"Odd? *Odd*? There's been more pings on that phone than on Madonna's knicker elastic."

Anna's head was bent over her phone, "Hmm? I don't know what you mean?"

"I mean...are you even listening?" Irene grabbed Anna's phone from her hand.

"Ow, Irene, please."

"Every day this week you've had your nose in this thing, I don't know what's got into you? Are you in trouble? Is it drugs?"

"What on earth are you talking about? I've had a few texts from...a friend, that's all."

"Well, it's driving me mental."

Anna put her hand out for the phone, "What is driving you *mental* is not knowing who is sending me the texts."

"Hmm, well, I don't know why you won't spill," Irene sulked as she handed it back. "I know it's a fella, so you might as well tell me which gormless numpty you've got mixed up with this time?"

"Maybe, just maybe, I've met someone who is just as normal as you or I...actually, maybe more normal."

"That wouldn't be hard, would it?" Irene said, as the bell above the door of the café tinkled and they both looked up over the coffee machine, but they couldn't see anyone, just an open door.

"Oh, my god, the ghost," Anna whispered.

"Don't be daft, it's the wind," Irene said just as a familiar wet nose appeared around the corner of the counter, swiftly followed by the rest of Stanley himself. In his mouth he had a small cone of brown paper containing pink roses, which he dropped to the floor between them. He then rolled over onto his back and had a try at looking at them both from upside down.

"Well, would you look at that," Irene said, stepping back against a cupboard.

"Oh, Stanley, thank you," Anna said, reaching for one of yesterday's sausage rolls and breaking him off a piece, before picking up the flowers

"'How do you know they aren't for me?"

"Well, there's a note, so let's have a look," Anna said, untucking a little card from its envelope. "Please look after this dog. Tonight?" She laughed, "Oh, Stanley, it looks like we may be having a date night. Would you like that?" Stanley woofed enthusiastically, his tail beating time against Irene's legs.

"Ge'roff, you'll have me veins up, hairy great beast," she stepped into the café as Ralph looked around the door. "Oh, here's the other one...I thought you two had fallen out?"

Ralph looked confused, "Who, us? Me and Anna? We never fall out, do we?"

"Us? Never. Don't know what you mean, Irene."

Irene stood her ground between the two friends, with her hands on her hips, "I can't keep up with you two. One minute it's Armageddon then it's Thelma and Louise, you're both as bad as one another."

Anna ignored Irene, "Have you got a date tonight then?" she asked hopefully.

"Fat chance," Ralph had already filled Anna in with the broad outline of his evening in Sam's cupboard-office. Ever the romantic optimist, Anna had been positive that Sam just needed time to get to know Ralph, that all was not lost. "It's the first training night with the team," he said. "It's only for an hour or so, but Stan goes a bit mad with children and it's even worse when a ball appears. Any chance he could come and stay at yours for a bit?"

"Of course, we love having you, don't we boy," Anna fussed the little dog, who gave in to her tickles whilst still keeping a suspicious eye on Irene.

"Thanks so much. Thanks, Irene."

"Don't thank me, I'm not touching it. He'll have to go upstairs 'cos we can't have him in the cafe, not with customers – mind you, he's cleaner than half of them we get in here."

"I'll take him up," Anna said. "What time's the practice?"

"Five until six, so I'm going to close the shop a bit early on Wednesdays, just for a few weeks while I help out."

"Will Sam be there?"

"Probably, yes, I expect so, but don't get your hopes up. He's disappeared back under that cap... are you listening?"

Anna was still crouched over Stanley but was typing quickly into her phone.

"You'll get no sense out of her. She's got some mystery man on the other end of that thing pinging her every ten minutes. Why people can't just ring up and talk to each other anymore, I have no idea."

"Really? Sexting? Anna, I'm shocked," Ralph laughed, trying to look over her shoulder at the screen.

"That is not what it is at all," she said, tucking the phone into her orange dungarees. "It's perfectly above board, we are just chatting. We get on, he's nice, he thinks I'm really special, that's what he said, special. He makes me feel happy."

Ralph gave Anna a hug, "That's great."

"That's a miracle," Irene couldn't help but add. "I'm pleased for you and everything, but I have sugar to de-clump and straws to sponge dry, so if you don't mind, clear off the lot of you."

Ralph headed for the door, "Fair enough. Are you sure you are OK to have Stan? I'll be back about half past six."

"Yes, go on, get yourself ready, warm up your whistle or whatever you need to do, and talk to Sam, please. I can't bear the suspense. See you later."

Ralph shrugged, "The moment's gone. Anyway, I'm really pleased you could move on from Jim, I've got my fingers crossed for this one."

"Thanks, keep them that way. Come on Stanley, let's go up and watch some telly, shall we?" Anna opened the door from the café to the flat and Stanley headed straight out, knowing that up these stairs lay nothing but comfy cushions, biscuits and an afternoon of TV quizzes.

❋ ❋ ❋

Ralph had spent quite a bit of time planning the Rovers' first training session as their new coach. He was aware of Sam on the sidelines, but managed to stay focused on the kids. The session went well, nearly half the team were moved to a different role for their next match on Sunday, but they all seemed happy and more confident, listening carefully to Ralph and following his clear, friendly instructions. As the players left the pitch skipping and running with excitement to their parents, they got to dip into a large tin of chocolates that Ralph had brought with him, to say thank you for working so hard.

As the cars left the car park, with red faced children waving wildly to Ralph, many with tell-tale chocolate stains around their mouths, Sam put the last of the balls in the net bag, "That was such a great session, they've never had anything like that. Before it was just running around blindly being shouted at by a bloke with bad teeth. They've had a ball, if you'll excuse the pun," he said, jiggling the bag.

"You're excused. I enjoyed it, I've never really worked with kids this young, but I thought they just needed confidence and to have some fun mostly...oh, and chocolate."

Sam started to put the kit in the back of his car, "I think the chocolate was a winner. In fact, they're talking about using it to motivate the premier league next season instead of money. That way they can save the wage bill to buy heated seats and hostess trollies with a running hot buffet for the fans."

"It's the way forward," Ralph laughed.

"It'd be the only way you'd get me to go to a proper match, to be honest."

"Really? Have you never been to a match?"

Sam shut the car boot, "Nope. I'm afraid not. Standing on draughty terraces, eating dog food pies and singing rude songs hasn't ever appealed, funnily enough."

Ralph dug his hands into his jacket pockets, "I know what you mean, but it's not that bad these days, really. We'll have to go some time and you can see what it's really like," the invitation was out of his mouth before he knew it.

Sam looked down at the keys in his hand, "That'd be great. Sure, we must do that one day," he hesitated, then quickly got into the car. "Thanks again, see you Sunday."

Ralph stood and watched him drive away, giving a weak wave, not sure whether he had just taken a step forward or a step back. "*Idiot!*" he said, his breath spiralling in white puffs of vapour.

❋ ❋ ❋

The next few days sped by, and with The Bookery continuing to do steady trade Ralph enjoyed the experience of running his own business. There were times when he even managed to put Sam out of his mind, like when he managed to track down a well-known local author, renowned for her gruesome murder novels and she agreed to come and be the star of his first ever book event. However, he often found himself daydreaming about that moment when he and Sam had sat together on the desk, locked away, wondering what might have happened if Dawa had not released them at just the wrong moment. He knew that Sam's life was complicated, but no more than his, surely? He had so little experience of dating or romance that he twisted himself into all sorts of knots trying to decide what had happened and more importantly, what might happen next.

On Sunday morning, he was up and out early ready for another football match and to see Sam again. Stanley was spending the morning with Anna to prevent any mishaps at the match, so he arrived at the ground on the salt flats in plenty of time to greet both teams as they arrived. Sam was late and sped into the car park just before kick-off, full of apologies about a long night and a faulty alarm. Dew-drop Dobson and the rest of the parents waited expectantly, with thermal mugs of hot coffee held in thickly gloved hands and feet stamping on the hard, frosty ground, so there was no time for them to talk.

Ralph reminded his team of the changes he had made to the positions they would play in, but his main piece of advice was to simply go out and have fun. Win or lose, if they played as a team then victory would be theirs. The eleven little players cheered and had a group hug before dashing on to the field with an enthusiasm and determination that few of the parents had seen before.

The first half started with a newfound discipline from the Rovers, but as they began to tire this began to break down and a feeling of every child for himself returned, led by the rotund figure of young George. Mercifully, their opponents, Northiam United, were even less disciplined than the Rovers and the half-time whistle came with a nil-nil score line. As the players walked off the pitch, Dobson junior made straight for Ralph with his hand out, "Sweets after the final whistle, George, not yet," Ralph told him. "Any particular reason you chose to spend your time at the other end of the pitch today?"

"It's boring at our end."

"Well, you've got Elliot for company and at any moment you could be called on to save the game with a great piece of defending."

"Elliot's weird, I don't talk to him."

"I'm sure he feels the same way about you, but that is your position, so let's try it for the second half, eh?" Ralph sent the boy off for a drink and started to chat with a crowd of parents when he saw Mr Dobson talking to his grandson and suddenly look up with trouble in his eyes.

Ralph managed to avoid him for the break and got the game started again as quickly as possible. The second half started with orange squash fuelled energy and everyone played with a little more discipline. Then suddenly, Stanley appeared with a bark at Ralph's side, "Blimey, Stan, where did you come from?" He pushed him and his muddy paws back down on the ground as Anna appeared at the other end of the lead.

"Hi, just thought we'd come and see how it was going. Stan thought he might be needed."

"Great, just keep hold of that lead or he'll be off into the middle of it all," Ralph turned back to the action, but felt a body move up to his other side and he turned to see a shock of untamed black hair with Jim's familiar face under it.

"Morning, mate, how's it going? Won any cups yet?"

CHAPTER 19

*The gravy manager, chimpanzees
and creepy, creepy shoes.*

"What the hell are you doing here?" Ralph asked.

Jim ran his hand through his afro, "Oh, that's lovely, that is. Last week it was all water works over me coming down here, now look what I get."

"But you went home, to Barnsley. To Carol. To everyone."

Anna moved round to Jim's side, slipping her arm through his, "He's come down to see me actually. We've been talking every day, well, texting and talking, you know..."

Ralph looked from her to Jim, "You mean you two are...? You have...?"

Jim looked up with a smile, "Well, we haven't yet... but I wouldn't rule it out."

Anna punched him on the arm, "Oy, enough of that,

I'm a lady, remember."

"I'm hoping to confirm that myself later."

"Stop, stop," Ralph put his hands over his ears. "Enough, for god's sake. But, Jim, what about Carol?"

"Yes, well, we're on what I believe is known as a break," Jim murmured.

"But last week you were lecturing me about everything I'd left behind and everything you and I had got, and how we shouldn't just abandon it."

"I know, but the thing is you inspired me, mate. That long drive back from here really gave me time to think. I thought about what I was going back to and the further I got up the M1, the less I wanted to get there. It all seemed so, I don't know, deadly, compared to what you've found down here. I've taken a bit of time off work and off my marriage, that's all. I want to spend it with this little wench...and you, of course, mate."

"Of course," Ralph said, shaking his head. "And stay with me, I suppose."

"Well, now you come to mention it, that'd be spot on. Just temporary, you know, while I work on..."

"Yes, alright, we know what you intend to work on. No need to go on about it. Off you trot then, lovebirds. You'd better leave Stanley with me, I suppose."

"Thanks, mate, I appreciate it."

"I knew you'd be happy for us," Anna said as she handed Stanley's lead over. "We'll have to go in a minute though, I need to get the café open. Big Jim, you can be in charge of gravy for the day."

"You see, mate, I've got myself a whole new career just like you. Freelance gravy manager"

Ralph let out a sigh, "What have I done?" he said, just as a big cheer went up and The Rye Rovers had scored the first goal of the game. Everyone cheered and Anna jumped up and down, her enormous pom-pom waving wildly on top of her hat. This was swiftly followed by the final whistle and, by some small miracle, The Rye Rovers had won. Stanley joined in with the players as they dashed to Ralph and his tin of sweets.

"Well done guys, that was sensational," Ralph shouted from the centre of the scrum. "What a goal, Jilly-bean! You must be very proud of our top scorer, Mr Beckett."

"Call me Richard, Coach. You've done wonders with her confidence," Jilly-bean's dad said, as the parents also had a dip in the tin for some chocolate.

"I disagree, strongly disagree," came a thin, but clear voice cutting through the crowd, which parted to reveal Mr Dobson, standing with his rubber-soled shoes planted firmly apart on the frozen mud. "I can understand the misguided euphoria at the recent victorious victory. However, I am aware that many of the players, in which, I sadly include my grandson, are not at all happy or content or utilising many of their skills."

"But we won, Mr Dobson. For the first time in this season and last season we won a match," Sam said, appearing through the crowd.

"Ah, but in your naivety you are equating winning with the fulfilment of these young persons' abilities. My grandson, George, for instance, has clearly been sidelined. He used to play a full role in this team, but has now been left to stand around by his own goal posts waiting to be included. Am I alone in my thinking, Mr Ringrose?" Dobson said as he turned to a large man with unreliable looking eyes.

The man looked nervously round at the group, that

had now fallen silent and turned their attention on him, "Well, to be honest, I was saying that my Joanne seems to have been forgotten a bit. She's never scored a goal and barely touches the ball during a game. It's just doesn't seem right, if you ask me."

Ralph brought Stanley quickly to heel, "Well, I'm sorry you feel like that, it's certainly not intentional."

"I don't doubt that, but I should point out that your bias towards the boys in the team has been noted," Dobson said.

"My what?" Ralph gripped Stanley's lead tightly. "I can assure you..."

"Mr Dobson, I don't think..." Sam started to say.

"Well, we would expect you to support Coach Wright, wouldn't we, Samuel, with your artistic heritage and very public history of immoral behaviour? Now, I have nothing against 'the lavender', which seems all too popular in our somewhat grotesque modern society, but do we really want them in charge of our children?"

Sam took a step towards him, "Now, that's enough."

Mr Ringrose took a step back, "Actually, I wasn't talking about...that. I didn't know that you were...he was...you both were..."

"You have no right..." Sam felt himself shaking as he tucked his cap about as low as it could go over his face, but then he felt a hand grip his elbow and pull him back.

Ralph stepped in front of Sam and spoke quietly, "I know I'm new here, but it is obvious that Sam has done nothing but support this team with both his time and his money. He has made the club viable, so that none of you have to pay for your child to be here, meaning that anyone in this town who wants to play can do so. That is all that is relevant here, whatever gossip you choose to believe."

He looked around at the faces of the little players who looked stunned, some even forgetting to chew their chocolates. Ralph then turned to the parents surrounding him, "As for me, you don't know me, but I am a man who has loved and played football his whole life. I run a bookshop, I used to design websites, I eat four bananas a day, I enjoy painting, I have a dog called Stanley, I drink black coffee and I am a gay man. None of those things make me unfit to help run your football team."

"You miserable piece of...of..." Anna stormed round the edge of the circle to Dobson, who took a step away from her flailing arms and pom-pom. "Of...arse fluff, and I know there are children here and I shouldn't swear in front of them – sorry about that – but you *are* a piece of arse-fluff."

"Kindly restrain yourself, madam. You have nothing to do with this," Dobson squawked. "Step aside and refrain from further profanity. I am merely discussing with other parents, guardians, grandparents, carers, responsible adults and... and...co-habiting co-persons, how unfit this pair seem to be to run a sports team."

"Unfit? *Unfit*?" She yelled. "I'll tell you who is unfit – YOU. That's who is unfit. These lovely, lovely men may be as bent as a nine-pound note – no offence boys - but they are kind and they are sensitive and they are glorious," Anna then pointed wildly at the parents who were watching with mouths open wide. "So, would it be OK for one of them to run a football team? Hm? Even though we know nothing about who they love? Their wives or husbands or milkmen or neighbours in naughty nursey costumes...or... or frigging chimpanzees? Who they choose to love does not make *them* bad people – except for the chimpanzee thing, that'd be weird, but .."

"Anna…" Ralph said.

"No, Ralph, I know I've got a bit lost there, but something has to be said. It's the chimpanzees that threw me, but I'm back on it now," she turned her unstoppable fury back on Dobson. "You are straight, I assume, although god help the sisterhood with your bog breath and your snot and your creepy, creepy quiet shoes, but simply being straight doesn't make you nice or responsible or even normal."

Dobson stood frozen, a dew-drop quivering on the end of his nose until, after a long pause, it fell slowly to the ground, "You, young woman, have gone too far. This is unforgiveable abuse. I always knew that you were damaged, morally corrupt, but this… this…"

Anna clenched her fists, "Listen, Mr Dobson, all I meant…"

"No, you have had your say and I shall have mine," he turned to the crowd in front of him. "I am approaching this matter from a purely unsentimental point of view, I am a businessman of considerable standing, after all. The facts are simple, gays and children do not mix. They should *not* mix, it is common sense. We have to take responsibility. Children do not know best; they do not know what they want."

In the silence that followed a small voice rose from the back of the group of parents and children, "Yes, we do." It was a quiet, but insistent voice and they all turned to see little Elliot, the bespectacled, freckled goalkeeper standing with his muddy knees drying under his baggy shorts and his glasses sitting crooked beneath his spikey hair. His face was bright red and he swallowed hard, but he started to walk slowly through the crowd, never once taking his eyes off Ralph. As he got to his side, he reached up, took hold of his hand and said, "We do know what we want."

There was a small gasp from the crowd, followed by a low murmuring as other little players started to make their way towards Ralph and Sam. First, one appeared, then a second and a third, each taking hold of Ralph or Sam's hands or simply standing next to them, until the whole team, minus one, stood together around their coaches.

"This is nonsense," Dobson blustered, dampness now dripping freely from his nose. "They have been brainwashed, groomed with chocolate fancies, we see it all the time, don't we? The excellent Fiona Bruce has told us via the unimpeachable BBC. We parents and grandparents must not be swayed, we will stand together against what is not right or proper."

Mr Ringrose turned to Mr Dobson, "Actually, this parent won't. I couldn't care less if they were gay, straight or ping pong players, I just want them to be fair to all the team. That's all I was saying. So, yes, we parents may well stand together, but it'll be over there, not here," he walked over to stand with Ralph and Sam, putting his hand on the shoulder of his brave flame-haired daughter, Joanne, of whom he had never felt so proud.

Dew-drop Dobson was frozen to the spot, with short, spherical George at his side, as one parent after another moved to support their children and the two men who both stood with tears shining in their eyes, at the centre of the team. Just as the crowd settled into place, a brown and white shape shot out at great speed and raced across the field. Stanley had sat quietly for some time, sensing the tension around him, but could hold back no longer. It was clear to him, that whatever drama those around him were involved with, that shameless football must not be left to its own devises and he pounded it with his head across the pitch. Then, with one enormous swipe of his nose, he sent it sailing through the air and into the back of the goal, turning in triumph to acknowledge the cheers of the crowd with a barrage of barks.

As he did a lap of honour around the pitch the group of players and parents turned back to Dobson, but all they saw was the back of his old, grey car belching smoke from its exhaust as it sped off out of the car park.

Nothing was left to say as Sam and Ralph's thanks and reassurances were brushed aside, some parents wiping away tears as they all promised to see them as usual on Wednesday for practice.

"I'm sorry, Mr Ringrose, I'll make sure Joanne doesn't get forgotten. I promise," Ralph said.

"I know, Coach, I know, I'm sorry too. Let's forget it. For goodness sake," he said, shaking his head. "We're in the twenty-first century and gay men play football and dogs score goals – it's a whole new world."

CHAPTER 20

The Bahamas, sangria and seaside jollies.

The stars seemed to shine more brightly than ever that night as they reflected off the roof terrace, which also sparkled with ice and fairy lights. The members of the Rooftop Club, tonight including Sam and Jim, were huddled warmly around the new outdoor gas heater that Joe had provided for them.

"Well, isn't this a treat?" Auntie B exclaimed, sitting in her usual sun hat and dark glasses, with her soft blanket over her knees. "It's like being in the Bahamas."

"It certainly is," Anna agreed as she shifted her deck-chair closer to the one that Jim was squashed into. She had abandoned her winter poncho and swapped it for a large patchwork quilt that she had wrapped around herself like a shroud, just her face and a hand holding a large glass of red wine exposed to the night air. "You OK, Jim? Do you need anything?"

"No, absolutely fine," he said from inside his large duffle coat. "I have a pint in my hand and I can feel a good warm glow – which is either coming from you or Joe's contraption. What more could a man need?"

"It's definitely me," Anna giggled.

"I wouldn't be at all surprised," Jim said, sipping his pint.

Anna shivered slightly, not from the cold but from excitement. She still couldn't believe that he had come halfway across the country, leaving his wife and his job for her. His first text had arrived the previous weekend when he had stopped on his way north at a service station on the M25. Back and forth the messages had gone through the day and into the evening, then the next day at lunchtime, then pretty much hourly, moving from friendly banter to heartfelt discussions of life and love, thrilling them both and inspiring distant desire.

Jim's texts talked about feeling restless and being unable to settle back at home. She suggested that her role might be to provide him with an escape from a world he seemed unhappy in. Less than a week later here he was, he had come back to her. That's not exactly how he had phrased it, to be fair, but that was more or less it. She thought he was quieter than he had been when he was here before, less sure of himself, but she knew it was a big thing for him, just as it had been for Ralph, so she needed to be patient - something that was not one of her strengths.

"He does have very quiet shoes," Auntie B was saying as Anna focused back on the conversation. "I've noticed that."

"You see," Anna said, triumphantly. "It's not just me."

Sam was laughing, "I know he does, but my point was that having a go at Dobson's shoes wasn't really relevant to what he was saying."

"Oh, he deserved everything he got, shoes, snot and all," Anna sat back in her deckchair and pulled her quilt firmly around her.

"He's had it coming for a while," Joe said, leaning against the rail away from the group.

"Joe, come and sit with us. You won't feel the heat over there," Auntie B said.

"I'm fine here, thanks. Don't worry about me."

"Well, I do, Joe. You don't seem yourself at the moment; we don't seem to have seen you for ages."

"I'm fine and dandy, Auntie B. I've been around, don't worry. Anyway, we were talking about old Dewdrop, not me," Joe waved at them to carry on.

"He's a miserable git," Anna said. "Dobson, not Joe."

"He's a very unhappy man and he has hardened as he's grown older," Auntie B said.

"Look, everyone," Ralph began. "It was my fault. This wouldn't have happened if it wasn't for me."

"Now, that is just not true," Sam said.

Anna threw her free arm in the air, "It's more than not true, it's bloody bollocks. Sorry, language, but it is. You have done nothing wrong, so, don't you start disappearing again and going all introverted and invisible, just because you've had one little set back."

"Honestly, Ralph, he's a creep, period," Joe added. "He won't show his face around town for a little while from the sounds of it. You and Sam are great together, don't let it get in the way."

"But we're not..." Ralph and Sam said in unison.

"Sorry," Ralph said, blushing.

"No, it's OK," Sam smiled. "Joe, we're not together."

"Really? Why the hell not?" Joe pushed himself off the rail and headed for the little wooden bar. "Drink anyone?"

"Joe, stop being mischievous," Auntie B said. "Ignore him boys."

"I'll have another one of those local bitters, if there is one," Jim said, untangling his long limbs from the clutches of the deckchair. "Anna, you want anything?"

"Such a gent," Anna said, flicking her curls. "Yes, please, I'll have a glass of red, thanks"

"Righty ho, anyone else?"

"I'll have a bitter, please," Ralph said, offering Jim his empty glass.

"Well, you can come and help me then, lazy bugger."

Anna watched Ralph follow Jim to the bar and sighed. How easily he fitted into the group, she thought, he was gentle, calm and made her feel safe around him. She was trying so hard not to rush ahead or move faster than he wanted to go, but she was falling hard for this long, dark man with adorable hair that just cried out to be touched and tamed. As she watched the three men at the bar chat easily, she thought about how much had changed in just a few short weeks; she had a new best friend in Ralph and a new man for herself...probably...hopefully...Oh, god, she hoped so.

Joe had returned to the group holding an empty wine bottle, "Anna, do you have any more red? We're out."

"Yes, I think there's a couple of bottles in my kitchen, help yourself," she said.

"No probs, but before I go let me leave you all with this thought; I knew this lady who gets really annoyed when I mess with her red wine. So, I added some fruit juice to it, and now she's sangria than ever. Sangria? S-angrier? Now, you have to admit that's good, right? Wait let me tell the others. Guys, guys..."

"No, please just get me some more wine, I'm gasping. Save it, they can enjoy that one later...*much* later."

"OK, but there are loads more where that came from."

"That's what we were afraid of, dear," Auntie B said. "Now off you go, make yourself useful."

"OK, OK, but this is comedy gold you know," he chuntered as he disappeared into Anna's flat.

Anna and Auntie B both turned to Ralph and Jim at the bar, hearing raised voices. Ralph looked tense, stepping back as Jim said, "Look, don't get me wrong, I'm not bothered or anything, but this sort of thing, with people like him...well, it's going to happen, isn't it? It just seems that going so public about...you, might not be such a good idea. Keep it below the radar."

Ralph was shocked, "Hide it?"

"Yeah, if you like. Why make your life harder than it needs to be, eh? You're in a new place and you want to fit in, so why make it difficult for yourself?"

"Are you serious?"

"It's just a bit of friendly advice, that's all. Be sensible, don't rush into anything."

"What, like you? Sensible, not rushing into anything."

Anna threw back her quilt and struggled out of the deckchair, as Auntie B said, "Anna, dear, I hope you are not going to get involved. Let the boys sort it out between them."

"I can't," Anna said, finally freeing herself. "They're

my boys." She hurried over to them, the clacking of bangles at her wrists heralding her arrival and momentarily pausing the growing anger between the two friends, "Now, hold on you two. Ralph, calm down, I'm sure Jim didn't mean anything."

"Really?" Ralph said. "Last weekend he came down here to tell me to go home and just accept what I've got and ignore who I am."

Jim stepped up to Ralph, "I never said that."

"Pretty much you did and now with a few horny texts after a boring car ride home you decide to abandon your own excellent advice...oh, along with your home, your job and your wife. For what? A bit of a jolly by the seaside? An adventure with a few freaks, who should really just keep quiet and not cause a fuss?"

"Ralph, enough, that's not what this is," Anna said, putting a restraining hand on his chest, which he threw off with a shrug. "How can you say that about Jim? He's your best friend."

"Friend?" Ralph yelled, unable to control himself, in the face of Anna and Jim standing side by side. "Do you realise what I went through today? After all the years of hiding away in someone else's life, being terrified of being called out for not being good enough or normal enough, within a few days of finally coming to terms with it, *that* happens. A *friend* would understand and not tell me that it's probably best to carry on hiding."

"Well, sod you," Jim slammed his beer down on the bar and stalked off into the flat.

"No, sod you," Ralph called after him.

"Ralph, I can't believe you. I know it was horrible, awful, but we all stood by you...literally. What has got into you? Jim is just trying to protect you, that's all.

What is your problem?"

"I don't have a problem, not anymore. It's Jim, I can't believe he's here and thinks he stands a chance with you. It's ridiculous, he just doesn't get it."

Anna looked at Ralph and she saw red, "Yes, he does get it. In fact, he got *it* this afternoon," she said, even though it wasn't true, but she was on a roll and couldn't stop herself. "You know your problem, don't you? That you thought you were the only runaway and now you don't like that you are not the only little orphan Annie, that someone else might just be as unhappy as you were and has muscled in on your territory."

"What? No, of course not."

"Well, that's what it looks like to me and I think it's a rotten way to treat your friend...both of your friends," Anna turned on her heels, shouting over her shoulder as she disappeared into the flat. "Oh, and I'll be busy with Jim tomorrow with our seaside jollies, so you'll have to find someone else to cater for your event. I can't do it!"

"Here we are," Joe announced as he popped up from Anna's flat with a bottle of red wine. "I've been trying to think of some wine puns, but they are always in pour taste - P.O.U.R...pour?"

Auntie B put down her sherry glass and raised a hand towards him, "Take me in, Joe. It's getting too chilly out here."

"What did I say? It wasn't that bad."

"It's not what you said, it's what you missed, Joe. Come along, I want to go in," she pushed aside her blanket as Joe came to her side. "Sam, Ralph needs a friend and you seem to be it for the time being."

Joe looked at Ralph, "But I'm Ralph's friend, what did

he do?"

Auntie B took his arm, "Nothing, dear, but you are taking me inside and we are leaving Sam and Ralph alone."

Sam looked startled, "There's no need."

"There is every need, Sam dear. Look after Ralph, please, he has had a very difficult day and you do not make it any easier."

"I haven't done anything," Sam protested.

"That is exactly my point," Auntie B said as she and Joe made their way back inside, leaving Ralph and Sam alone for the first time on the rooftop.

CHAPTER 21

The glamorous lady, sausage rolls and flying caps.

Anna found Jim in Ralph's spare room, roughly stuffing clothes and shoes into a battered suitcase, "What are you doing?"

"Packing, obviously," he snapped.

"Please don't," she said, quietly. Jim ground to a halt, stooping over the chaotic contents of the case as it lay on the bed, then he turned and looked at her as she stood in the doorway.

"Sorry. This is not your fault, but I can't stay, Anna, not now."

"Of course, you can. It's just a stupid fight, Ralph and I have them all the time. We fight, he sends Stanley round with flowers or I throw coffee down his front door and bring him cake. It'll be fine."

"Why do you throw coffee at his front door?"

"It's a local custom, but let's not focus on that just

now. You've had a fight with your best mate, isn't that what friends are for?"

"Not us. I've known Ralph since we were eighteen and we have never had an argument. I shouldn't have come down here, I don't know what I was thinking," Jim moved to the small wardrobe and started taking out a shirt and jacket he had hung there earlier in the day.

"Well, that's all the more reason not to go. You can't leave it like this, you have to make up. It's been such an emotional time for Ralph and I can understand that today was pretty traumatic, so he was just a bit strung out, that's all."

"I know and I get that. I also get that this is his space and his time, he doesn't need me arsing about here spoiling things for him. I'm much better to just let him have some room; it's better for both of us."

Anna moved to the bed and sat down, "Not for me it isn't." She took the jacket he had managed to roll into a crumpled ball and started to refold it neatly, "What about a space and a time for us? I thought that was why you were here?"

Jim sighed, "I was, I mean, I am. Oh, shit, I don't know," he slumped down next to her and put his head in his hands. "It all seemed so clear when I was in Barnsley and Carol was sat in her dressing gown watching Love Island with a monster packet of Minstrels. You seemed so...confident and glamorous and...and...well, alive."

Anna gasped and hugged the jacket to her. No one had ever spoken to her like that before, certainly never calling her glamorous, let alone confident. Her stomach was doing somersaults while butterflies were doing joyous circles in the other direction. More importantly to her, though, she had never met a man who was pre-

214

pared to be so honest and straightforward, without her having to drag a feeling or emotion out of him.

"Thank you," she managed to say. "You can still have a new life with me here, a new chapter."

He looked at her and she could see that his eyes were sad, his normally rampant hair limp and her heart sank, "I'm sorry," he said. "I should never have come. I have given you completely the wrong idea. I'm not looking for a new life...just a break from my old one. I thought we'd have some fun for a while, then I'd go back again. I thought you knew that."

Anna looked down at his jacket in her lap, "Oh, I see. So, Ralph was right that you are just here to have your jollies by the sea?"

"Oh, bugger, I've been such a stupid sod. I'm so sorry, I know that's not who you are, you are way better than that...than me."

She laughed, "No, I'm not really. At least, I just told everyone out on the roof that I'm not. I told them that we did it this afternoon, when we got back from the football. Hey ho, just wishful thinking of a glamorous girl in Rye, eh?" She stood up and put the jacket carefully in the case, then she placed a hand on Jim's head and gently smoothed his hair backwards, but it immediately sprang back.

"Good luck with that," Jim said with a small grin. "Many have tried, but none have managed to tame it. It'll take Indiana Jones and his whip to get through that lot," he took her hand in his and pulled her towards him. "Look, I am really sorry. I should have been clearer, I suppose. Texts aren't the best way to explain yourself. I think I am unhappy back at home and a bit bored, but, unlike Ralph, I'm not sure I'm ready to give it all up. I came down here because I liked myself a bit more when I was here, with you, and I thought maybe that nicer bloke might be persuaded to hang around a bit and come back with me to my life. My real life. Does that make sense?"

Anna folded her arms around herself, "It does. As usual, I'm running ahead of myself, getting too giddy. Look, why don't we take a step back and see what happens? See if you find your new you and maybe I'll find - what was it? - a confident and glamorous woman that in me."

"OK, a step back, you say?" he stood up and held out his hand. "Jim Scattergood, nice to meet you."

"Scattergood? Really? That's the most fabulous name I've ever heard."

"Good old mining name is Scattergood, my family adopted it to fit in, would you believe."

She took his hand and shook it, "Well, Mr Scattergood, I'm Anna Rose and I'm very pleased to meet you."

"Miss Rose, now I've heard that name somewhere. Anna? Anna? Oh, yes, according to the Rye Rooftop Club, I am supposed to have made love to an Anna Rose this afternoon after a kiddies football match."

Anna blushed, "Oh, yes, sorry about that."

"Well, look, as we are starting again, do you think I could come back to yours and, maybe, we could get a takeaway...we'll see if this strange prediction might come true, perhaps?"

"I don't see why we shouldn't, as long as you promise me one thing."

"What's that?"

"We don't have fish and chips again."

"Done."

Now that the roof terrace was empty Sam gave Ralph a few minutes to calm down, then stood, pulled his cap firmly onto his head and clapped his gloved hands together, "Blimey, it suddenly got pretty frosty out here, didn't it?" He moved to the railings and looked out across the rooftops, "I wouldn't be surprised if we get some snow soon."

Ralph still stood where Anna had left him. He had no idea why he had flown off the handle with Jim, he knew that he was just trying to protect him. Perhaps it was a delayed reaction to the horror of earlier in the day? Anna and Ralph fighting was nothing new, but this time even that felt different.

"I said, I thought there might be snow soon. What do you think?"

"It's OK, you don't have to stay with me just because Auntie B asked you to. You must have something better to do."

"I don't think I do, actually. Well, not just yet, I've got to be back at the restaurant for closing, that's all."

"Right," Ralph felt drained and unable to say any more.

Sam rested his elbow on the railing and looked at Ralph, "I know today must have shaken you, but look at the support we got. No one cared what Dobson said, he got what he deserved. So, the only harm done is to old Dew-drop. I know Jim meant well just now, but his timing was way off, so I understand why you got upset. Apologise tomorrow, when there's less beer in the air and he'll be fine."

Ralph sighed and looked at Sam, "You must think I'm a complete idiot."

"Here he goes with the idiot stuff again. I can think of lots of words to describe you, Ralph, but that is not one of them."

Ralph moved miserably to the railing and leant over, "Really? How about imbecile? Nincompoop? Moron?"

Sam smiled, "Well, some of those I'm not sure we are allowed to say any more, but I quite like, nincompoop. I couldn't spell it, but it seems cute."

"Here he goes with the cute stuff again," Ralph said, shaking his head. "Don't think it escaped my notice that you said I was cute the other night in your cupboard... sorry, office."

"I certainly did not."

"You certainly did, 'my cute Northern friend' you called me. "

"Did I? It must have been the scotch."

"Thanks a bunch. By the way, didn't we also have words about that cap?"

Sam reached up and touched the peak of his usual grey cap, "I like it."

"You hide behind it."

"I know I do and you know why. Don't try and pick a fight with me just because you're in a bad mood."

"I'm not...am I?"

"Yes, but it's OK. To be honest, I've been pretty freaked out myself since, you know, the other night in my office. I'm sorry."

Ralph looked at him, "Which bit are you sorry for?"

"Well, the kidnapping bit, to start with. Can I ask you a question?"

"Sure," Ralph said. "But I'm no good at geography or science."

"Nincompoop. No, I just wanted to ask, have you told anyone about what we talked about, the other night? What I said?"

"No, of course not, well, only about being locked in the cupboard. The rest was private, I understand that."

"OK, thanks. Sorry to ask, but...thanks."

"If anyone knows about keeping secrets it's me. I've lived in a world of secrets of my own making for years, I suppose that's why I reacted like I did to Jim wanting me to go into hiding again. I won't do it, not again. I missed so much, I mean, I've never even had a proper date."

"Are you serious? Never?"

"Nope, never," Ralph said, blushing.

"Bloody hell, no wonder you nearly kissed me the other night."

"What? I thought you nearly kissed *me*."

"Don't split hairs."

They both stood in silence for a moment, looking out from the terrace, the air full between them. Then they both laughed and looked at each other, their shoulders touching. Sam leant carefully towards Ralph and held his gaze, "I'm not sure this is really wise, but can I kiss you now?" he asked.

"Not in that bloody cap," Ralph said.

Sam dropped his head, laughing, "Last of the great romantics, aren't you? No wonder you've not had any dates."

"Sorry, sorry, I think that was just nerves, but I want to see your face," Ralph reached across and gently took the cap off.

Sam smiled, "So?"

"Yes, definitely, yes."

Sam looked at Ralph, at the dark eyes that still held a little pain, but that had caught him up in their beauty the first time he had seen them. At the soft lips that he had thought so often about kissing. He was also conscious of his own fear of trusting in someone again, but as he looked into Ralph's eyes he felt the fear leave and he leaned forward and gently kissed him.

Sam smiled, "This seems all the wrong way round. I'm a little bit old fashioned, so I think we should go on a date, now that we've kissed," he said.

Ralph looked at him, "I'd like that."

"And this time Dawa won't be there to throw us into a cupboard."

"I knew it was a cupboard," Ralph said, triumphantly.

"Damn, you really are an idiot, you know that?" Sam smiled and they kissed again, this time holding each other, neither wanting to be the one to stop.

Eventually Ralph said, "You can trust me, you know."

"I hope so."

"Well, almost," he stepped back and launched Sam's cap out over the railings and down towards the rooftops of Rye.

"Wait," Sam tried to catch it, but it flew away on the wind. "What did you do that for?"

"No more hiding, Sam. Not here. Neither of us."

Sam looked at Ralph, "You know I have other caps, right? Loads of them."

"Well, they'll all go the same way."

"Jeez, what if my head gets cold?"

"Buy a bobble hat."

"I'm having second thoughts about this date idea."

"Please don't," Ralph said. "How about tomorrow?"

"Tomorrow, aren't you having a book event? I won't be responsible for you skiving, you know."

"I won't be skiving, but I wondered if you'd like to come and do the catering for it? I'm pretty sure Anna will be making me suffer for a few days, so she won't be back on board in time."

"You really are an old romantic, aren't you? Our first date will be me buttering and making a pile of sandwiches and chopping up sausage rolls for the great and good of literary Rye?"

"Well, something like that...except, I don't really want sausage rolls. Anna was going to do sandwiches and mini-cupcakes."

Sam gave Ralph's arm a punch, "Fine, fine. What time?"

"It starts at five-thirty and I'm expecting about thirty people. I'll pay of course, I wouldn't expect you to do it for nothing, but as it's my first event I want it to be really special for people."

"Don't worry, I'll be there, Mr Bookseller, but after that I want a proper date, just me and the nincompoop, right?"

"Deal. He'll be there, he goes wherever I go. Thank you."

"No, thank you," Sam smiled and kissed Ralph again. "See you tomorrow then."

After Sam had left the terrace, Ralph stayed looking out at the frosty stars above him without feeling the cold at all.

CHAPTER 22

*The power of wind, warm wine
and holding hands.*

Joe dropped the cardboard box on the steps and knocked on the sleek glass and steel doors of Cinque. He stood back and waited until a figure appeared inside the doors. A young woman peered out and he heard her muffled voice, "We're not open until lunchtime."

He pointed to the box on the steps, "I know, I've just brought some stuff that Sam wanted, from Let's Screw." At the name of the shop he saw her stiffen, then she held up her hand and disappeared. He waited as instructed and a few minutes later she reappeared with a bunch of keys and proceeded to unlock the door. He picked up the box again and moved on to the first step just as she pushed the door open, punching the box into his stomach.

"You're keen," she said. "I thought you were still over

there."

"I was, then I moved," Joe said, catching his breath.

"So, I see," she said, showing little interest. She was in her mid-twenties Joe thought, pretty, with long fair hair falling in tousled curls around her face and down to her shoulders.

"I'm Joe."

"Yes, I thought you might be. Are you coming in or just causing a draft?"

Joe shifted the weight of the box and stepped inside, "Sorry, I didn't catch your name."

"I didn't tell you it. Sam says he's wrestling with turbot at the moment. Can you wait?"

"Sure, not a problem, if you will wait with me."

"Why would I do that?" she looked at him, unblinking.

"Well, you wouldn't want me just standing here on my own, would you?"

"It wouldn't keep me awake at night, to be honest," but she didn't leave him. "Imogen."

"Pardon me?"

"My name is Imogen."

"Good to meet you, Imogen."

"You own the hilariously titled, Let's Screw, on the high street. Did you think of that yourself?"

Joe looked at her, thrown by a manner that wasn't exactly hostile, but also wasn't the warmest he'd known. He pushed his shoulders back, showing off his impressive chest, "Guilty. It's a winner, don't you think? I mean you knew about it, right?"

"It's been mentioned, by some of the girls here," she maintained eye contact with him, in what may have been some sort of challenge, he found it hard to tell.

"Hey," Joe said. "Knock, knock."

"I beg your pardon?"

"Knock, knock - it's a joke."

"If it ends, 'Imogen what life would be like without me', then it really isn't a joke."

Temporarily lost for words, Joe stood for a moment, "OK, fair comment. Although, I was actually going with, 'Knock, knock.' 'Who's there?' 'Imogen what life would be like without youth unemployment.'"

Despite herself, Imogen smiled, creating small dimples in her cheeks, "Really?"

"No, but it would be a better world without it, wouldn't it?" Joe said as Sam came out of the kitchen.

"Sorry, Joe, fish emergency. Have you got the stuff for the ventilation units?" Sam said,

"Yup, it arrived this morning. I was chatting with Imogen..." he turned, but there was just an empty space where she had been. "Oh, she was here a minute ago."

"She's new. Local girl, but went away to university. We've taken her on for Christmas."

"Right, she's...well, she's..." Joe couldn't quite put into words what he was feeling about this girl who seemed singularly unimpressed by him. "She's sharp."

Sam laughed, "I know. She's not your ordinary kid, although she's not a kid anymore really. She graduated in the summer and has been travelling since then. Thailand and Vietnam, I think. She's got a job starting in the New Year, in Kent at some offshore windfarm. She's an engineer, specialising in wind power, but it's all beyond me, I just do turbot and turnips. She is definitely not to be messed with, so might be one for you to avoid, if you know what I mean."

Joe knew what he meant, but couldn't help looking

into the restaurant as he headed back to the shop, to see if he could catch a glimpse of wind-power engineer, Imogen, but she was nowhere to be seen.

* * *

Stanley had decided to keep well out of the way, since The Bookery was filled with frantic activity in readiness for its first book event, so he was curled up in his bed in the front window, with his chin resting on his paws. It had been a fairly quiet day in the shop, so Ralph had been able to spend much of the time getting things ready as best he could, from answering queries from attendees and adding new customers to the guest list, to unpacking and polishing wine glasses, lining up the guest author's books ready for signing at the end of the evening, not to mention dusting, sweeping and cleaning windows, in-between serving customers.

He had been too busy to go and see Anna to apologise, but he was quite happy to leave her for a few days to cool off. Jim's suitcase and belongings had been missing from the flat last night, so he had either driven home to Barnsley or was just a few metres away at Anna's place. If he was just next door, then he was happy to leave them to it, as he needed all of his focus to make sure that his first event was a success and would worry about making up with everyone later.

Sam arrived at half past four with trays of sandwiches laid out beautifully, separating meat from vegetarian and vegan, with edible flowers and herbs scattered amongst them to add to their appeal. He had also made thirty tiny coffee mocha brownies and thirty squares of lemon and lavender drizzle cake, to further tempt those with a sweet tooth.

Ralph hadn't had time for lunch, but didn't dare ruin the display by stealing anything, "It looks amazing. Thank you so much, I hope your chefs didn't mind doing this."

Sam shrugged, "I made them myself, so they could get on with prep for tonight's service. It was fun, I haven't made cakes for ages."

They laid out the food at the back of the shop, using a couple of the vintage suitcases as a table, ready for people to nibble on after the author had spoken and read from her latest novel, "The Circle of Eight". Then Ralph realised it was time to collect the chairs, which were supposed to be coming from The Cookery when it closed at five o'clock.

"Leave it to us," Joe said, who had closed early to come in and help out. "We could charm the bees from their knees..."

"I think you mean trees, "Sam said, as they hustled out of the shop.

"Do I? Hey, what is a bee's favourite sandwich? A Bee-L-T."

A few minutes later they were back carrying chairs, "What do you call a bee who's had a bad hair day? A Frisbee."

Sam dumped the chairs in the middle of the shop floor, "Please make him stop."

"What did the sushi say to the bee? Wassabee," said a shock of hair that stuck out above another large pile of stacked chairs being carried into the shop.

Joe offered Jim a high five, "Nice one."

"Don't mention it," Jim said.

Sam set off for more chairs, "Not you too, Joe was bad enough."

Joe followed him to the door, "By the way, did Imogen tell you about her Knock Knock joke?"

"No, but she was asking about you."

"She was?" Joe shot off down the street to catch up with Sam.

"Thanks," Ralph said to Jim, standing by the counter with a broom in his hands.

"You're welcome," Jim replied, dusting off his hands.

After an awkward pause, Ralph said, "I wasn't sure if you were still here."

"Yep, you don't get rid of me that easily."

"Our first fight," Ralph grinned.

"I know, crazy, eh?"

"Sorry."

Jim ruffled his hair then stuck his hands deep into his pockets, "Me too." He looked at Ralph, "Is that it? That easy? Jeez, it would have taken me a week to get to that point with Carol. Hey, we don't need to have make up sex now, do we?"

Ralph shook his head, "I've got some dusting to do, so it'll probably have to wait."

"Sorry, mate. I am, honestly."

"Forget it, I'm glad you're still here. Pint later? I imagine you may have quite a lot to tell me."

Jim chuckled, "Too right, a pint it is. Good luck with this author thing, but it's not really my scene, plus Anna's sulking over a wedding cake next door, so I'm probably best-off there. Besides, I'm learning all sorts of new ways to wind up Irene and the process is ongoing. Catch you later," he sidestepped more chairs arriving with Sam and Joe and headed back to The Cookery.

"...Bee-yonce," Joe shouted through his pile of chairs as he passed Jim.

Ralph looked dismayed, "You're not still going, are you?"

"I'm on a roll, baby. On a roll!"

Sam massaged his back, "You'll be on a stretcher if you don't stop, I promise you that."

Ralph started to count the chairs, "OK, we are up to thirty-five on the confirmed list, but I expect a few more will just turn up. We probably need forty, if we can fit them in."

"What do bees use to fix their hair? Anyone?" Joe looked at Ralph and Sam, neither of whom seemed to have heard him. "Anyone? Hello."

"Thirty-eight, I reckon that will have to do," Ralph said.

Sam looked around, "I don't think you'll fit many more in, so some people may have to stand anyway."

"Hello?" Joe said. "Guys, any thoughts?"

Ralph started to move some of the books from the displays, "Sam, can you give me a hand moving this lot out of the way?"

"Sure," Sam said.

Joe threw his hands in the air, "I get it. Well, you will never know the answer. May it haunt your dreams for ever. I bet Auntie B will love that one. Auntie Bee! Do you see what I did there?"

"Bye, Joe," Ralph called. "Thanks for your help."

"Shit, I'm good," and he whistled his way out of the shop and off to check in on Auntie B.

Once the central area at the front of the shop had been cleared, the chairs laid out and the wine brought up from the cellar everything was set. Sam hovered by the door, running his hands through his hair, nervous without his usual cap for protection.

"Erm, listen, is it OK if I disappear for a while? I mean, everything is under control. You don't need me, do you?"

Ralph looked at him, "Are you worried about getting recognised?"

"A bit, I'm not being grand or anything, honestly, but a large group of people like this just makes me really nervous. I'll come back later to help tidy up, don't worry."

"Sam, they are all going to be over seventy, they read Horse and Hound not CelebrityHotties.com. At some point, you've got to start living life properly."

"I know, I know, but can't I take it one step at a time? Look," he pointed to his head. "Freestyle hair. No cap."

Ralph smiled, he could see the effort that Sam was making on his behalf, "Fine, go on, bugger off, but only for a while. I'm going to need help serving the wine and food later. Stanley's service skills are not good enough yet. That'll give you time to go home, get a cap on and come back - for one night only, though. Everyone will be settled and listening to the reading, so they won't even notice you."

Sam saluted, "Excellent, I love a plan. I'll be back in a while."

*   *   *

Two hours later and it was all over. The sandwich and cake trays lay empty and abandoned, except for a few crumbs and two roast beef sandwiches, which Stanley obliged by tidying away for them. The local author had charmed with tales from her latest book and intrigued with her hand-painted eyebrows.

Sam and Ralph sat on the step in the middle of The Bookery sharing a well-earned glass of warm white wine.

Sam, wearing a new blue cap, held up his glass, "Congratulations, Mr Bookseller. I think we can say that your first event was a huge success."

Ralph raised his glass and tapped it against Sam's, "I can't believe it. Everyone seemed really happy, plus we sold twenty-two of her books."

"But the best thing is that The Bookery is now a real centre for local people to come together. Hey, how about doing a singles book night? That'd be amazing," Sam squeezed Ralph's knee. "I might come, you never know who I might meet."

Ralph still reeling from the warmth of Sam's casual touch, looked into his wine glass, "Yeah, why not..."

"I've heard there's a really cute guy running the place now, I might check him out. Hey, mind the warm wine," he laughed as Ralph pushed him sideways.

"You think you're funny, don't you?"

"Not as funny as Joe, obviously."

"No, obviously. Stanley, what are you doing?" Stanley was trying to work his wet nose between the two of them as he felt the need to remind them that not only had he not had his dinner yet - the sandwiches counting merely as an appetiser - but he was also due his evening walk. "I get it, walk time, eh? Come on then," Ralph stood up and stretched. "Do you fancy a walk with me and Stanley?"

"Sure, but shouldn't I stay here and clean this lot

up?"

"No, leave it, you've done enough. I'll sort it out later. I'm meeting Jim for a pint, anyway, so he can give me a hand to take the chairs back to Anna's."

* * *

They stepped out of the shop, well wrapped up against the cold, with Stanley eagerly pulling them past The Cookery, where Anna was still working on a tall cake and Jim waved at them with a large mug topped with a mountain of whipped cream. They headed up towards the old market square and then onto the ancient cobbled paving of Pump Street. Stanley led them past traditional white clap-board buildings and the crooked walls of Tudor brick guest houses, stopping to check-in with each ancient lamppost along the way.

Ralph and Sam chatted easily as they circled the town, telling more about their histories and discovering shared passions for new-wave bands and kid's TV shows from their youth. As they turned past the old Rye Tower, they paused to look across the salt flats below and out to sea. They stood close enough to feel the warmth of each other, then Sam slid his hand into Ralph's and they both smiled. Stanley, however, had other ideas and barked to inform them that he was not about to park his rear on the cold, wet pavement while they made eyes at each other.

On their way back, Ralph nearly tripped over the cobbles as he found himself concentrating on Sam's hand in his, rather than where he was going. He steadied himself as Stanley started to check out the delicious aroma of spilt coffee outside The Old Apothecary Café on the corner of the High Street. Ralph knew that in England two men holding hands was still a rare sight and he felt self-conscious, despite the joy this simple pleasure gave him.

They let Stanley appreciate the full range of different coffee roasts that adorned the stone steps and peered through the café window, debating which was their 'King of Cakes'. Sam had just declared for coffee and walnut, when they heard a car moving with speed behind them and Ralph stiffened at the sound. Suddenly the car was passing them and it blared its horn as Ralph turned quickly, the word 'FAGGOTS!" hitting him full in the face, shouted from the passenger seat by a young skinny guy in a beanie hat. They both froze then Ralph let go of Sam's hand and jumped into the road, "Morons," he shouted at the top of his lungs.

"Ralph, leave it," Sam hissed at him.

"Tossers," Ralph ran after the car, as he saw its red break lights come on up ahead.

The rage he felt at such happy simplicity being spoiled propelled him on and as he got level with the car he kicked out and landed his foot hard against the rear door, which gave a loud crack as the metal buckled under his trainer. A yell came from inside and the passenger door flew open. A small, thin, whippet-like man leapt out and stood for a second looking at the damage. He wore the typical uniform of the thug, baggy jogging bottoms and a dark hoody covering his dirty grey beanie hat, "You fucking faggot bastard," he growled, turning a vicious, hollow-eyed glare on Ralph as he pulled a short-bladed knife from his pocket.

CHAPTER 23

The grey lady speaks, athlete's foot and a knife.

Ralph saw the knife flash just as Sam appeared at his side, pulling him backwards until they both turned and ran, Stanley taking off with them on the end of his lead. They flew up the road, "Why did you do that?" Sam yelled.

A group of teenagers on the opposite side of the High Street had their phones out snapping and filming the whole thing and Ralph could hear Sam moaning, "No, no."

With the thug close on their heels, they sped over the cobblestones and turned sharp right into East Street; although it was uphill their regular morning runs helped them gain ground on their wheezing pursuer.

Unable to shake him, turning left then right, Ralph began to lose his bearings as they turned into a street he didn't recognise lit only by the murky moonlight. They both hesitated, but as the thug's footsteps kept coming they needed to go on. As they started to run, over the top of his panting breath Ralph recognised a heavy, slow dragging sound behind them, which suddenly stopped as a volley of clanking and crashes thundered through the air followed by a pained cry from the knife-wielding thug. This brought them both to a halt, "What was that?" Sam asked, bending over to catch his breath.

"No idea. I've heard it before a few times, but whatever it is, it's done us a favour."

In the silence of the dark street, Ralph started to walk ahead trying to make out a landmark or building that might tell him where they were. It only took a few steps before he realised that he was facing a high wall made of chunks of smooth grey Sussex flint.

"It's a dead end, we've got to go back," he said to Sam.

"Damn, maybe whatever he fell over or...whatever got him, has made him give up and go back."

"Did you see his eyes? I'm pretty sure he's had something stronger than a couple of paracetamols tonight, so, I'm not sure he'll give up too easily," Ralph started to walk back to Sam and heard the thug swear loudly then scream, "Bastards!" behind them.

Sam looked at Ralph, "What now?"

Slowly they began to back towards the wall as the footsteps began to close in on them through the darkness. As they drew level with a doorway to a crooked house, a grey figure stepped out from the shadows, "Down there," she said, pointing to a narrow gap in the wall beside them.

"Thanks," Sam said, pulling Ralph in after him.

"Wait..." Ralph hissed as he and Stanley were

dragged away from the woman.

The gap opened up into a small, square yard, with just enough room for a couple of bikes and two wheelie bins. They threw themselves behind the them, Ralph turned to Sam, "Did you see her? That woman, was she a..."

"Shush" Sam said, trying to hold Stanley still and quiet.

A few seconds later the guy in the hoodie passed the end of the yard, breathing heavily. There was a moment when they thought they had lost him, but then the thug, finding nothing but a solid wall ahead of him, used whatever sense he had and backtracked, peering into the darkness of the yard. He hesitated, then slowly crept in after them, half crouched with the blade held out in front of him.

"Quiet, Stan," Ralph whispered, shifting further behind their shield of bins.

Without warning, Stanley suddenly launched himself up on to his hind legs and barked sharply. They saw the thug crash forwards kicking the first bin aside. As he did so Stanley wrenched himself from Ralph's arms and went straight for their attacker, leaping at him, his lips drawn back, sinking his teeth deep into the thug's thigh. He screamed, dropping the knife and trying to hop away from Stanley, turning his back on him, which was a mistake Stanley was not about to forgive. He released the man's thigh and took aim at his buttocks. The thug was light on his feet and just managed to jump out of the way in time and Stanley's teeth snapped onto thin air just a fraction from his trousers. Ralph came round the bins and called Stanley back, but the guy didn't wait to see if the dog would respond and took off out of the yard, clasping his thigh and looking wildly behind him as Stanley gave chase.

"Stanley, heel. Come here, NOW!" Ralph shouted, following him to the end of the yard. "STAN!"

Luckily, Stanley knew that the fight was over and he stopped on the corner of the street, looked back at Ralph and then trotted, panting, back to his side. Ralph knelt down, checking him all over to make sure the knife had not made contact. Stanley enjoyed the attention, "Calm down, boy, steady now. Well, done Stanley, well done."

"Why the hell did you do that? You kicked his car door in," Sam stood behind him, his face white and his jaw clenched tighter than Ralph had ever seen it.

"Did you hear what he called us?"

"It doesn't matter, you made him come after us."

"It *does* matter, everything was so perfect. He ruined it. I didn't think."

"He had a knife."

"I know, I'm sorry," Ralph went to Sam and they hugged each other tight.

"They got it, they got it. Didn't you see?" Sam whispered.

"Who? What did they get?"

"Those kids, on their phones in the High Street. They filmed it and took pictures."

Ralph stepped back, "Good, we can give them to the police."

"No," Sam shouted. "You don't understand, it'll be all over the internet. What if they knew who I was?"

"Sam, it's dark and you've got your cap on. There was so much happening there's no way they'll be able to identify you, don't worry."

Ralph reached out to him, but Sam pulled away,

"That's easy for you to say, you're not me. You don't know what it's like."

"I'm sorry, I didn't think. Listen, we've done nothing wrong, we were the ones under attack."

Sam nodded, "Yes, yes, you're right. It's just the shock, I'll be fine," he shook himself. "Come on, we shouldn't hang about, he might come back with reinforcements."

Sam walked to the end of the street and looked around the corner, "The coast is clear, no cars, knife men or teenage paparazzi."

Ralph laughed, "Come on, Stan."

As they started to walk down the street they instinctively left a gap between them, the spell that allowed them to hold hands, broken.

"Who was that woman who helped us? Where did she go?" Sam asked

Ralph looked back, but she had vanished as quickly as she had appeared, "I think it was the grey woman, she fitted the description. Anna's convinced she's a ghost."

"A ghost, you're kidding? She spoke to us."

"I know, but Anna keeps seeing her hanging around outside the café."

"Oh," Sam said, putting his hands in his jacket pockets. "Her."

"You know about her?"

"Kind of. Auntie B mentioned her, that's all. I haven't seen her, though...until tonight."

"Who is she?"

"Does it matter? She happened to be in the right place at the right time, that's the main thing," Sam said, tucking his chin inside his scarf.

"If you know something you have to tell me, especially, if we are...you know."

Sam shook his head, laughing, "Wow, that sounds like our first relationship rule...no secrets. Are you blushing, because I said the R-word? Relationship?"

"Me? No, it's just the cold. Anyway, it's the *second* rule, the first one is no hiding behind hats, remember?"

"Oh, that one, I hoped you'd forgotten that. Number three definitely needs to be about not kicking the doors of small cars containing drug-fuelled knife men."

Ralph shook his head, "I'm sorry, I don't know what came over me."

"It's one of the first laws of being gay, don't let the haters get to you," Sam said as they turned back into the High Street. "The others are; never be seen in public without hair product and you must be able to list all of Kylie's hits in chronological order."

"Bloody hell, all these new rules and laws, I'll never get the hang of it," Ralph said.

"Learning the gay laws are all part of the training before they let you in. The gays take it very seriously," Sam laughed.

"I think I was off with athlete's foot the day they had those classes at school. That's why I failed the exam and I'm married to a woman," Ralph heard himself laugh, but Sam seemed to have stopped.

"You're married?"

"Well, technically."

A cold edge crept into Sam's voice, "Either you are or you aren't."

"Well, I am, yes. Helen. She is my wife, but...." before he could finish Sam had pulled the peak of his new cap low over his face, turned around and run away from him.

"Sam, wait," Ralph called, but Sam had already vanished.

Ralph looked back up the empty street. How could an evening that had started so well end in such disaster? Ralph cursed himself, he was the one going on about having no secrets and not hiding - how did he think he was going to be able to do this? All the stupid, cowardly choices he'd made in the past were still clinging to him, infecting everything he did. He wasn't ready for someone like Sam, but the emotions he had experienced in the last few days had made him feel so alive that to lose it all so suddenly was almost more than he could bear.

CHAPTER 24

The pink camels, more scampi and
Mystic Evelyn has regrets.

Anna slammed her fist down on a purple fondant dragon and flattened it in one angry movement, "Who the hell puts a dragon on their wedding cake? It's not right."

From his position on the kitchen worktop, Jim looked down on her and the large pink cake, "Oh dear, does this one look like another pink camel with wings?"

She sighed, "This one was more of a hippopotamus with flat feet...and don't laugh, it's not funny."

Jim couldn't help himself and chuckled as he eased himself off the counter and put his arms around her, "I'm not laughing, honest. Why don't you call it a night and start fresh in the morning?"

"No, I've got a golden wedding cake to do in the morning and a new recipe pie to work on."

"What is it this week?"

"Turkey and coconut cream."

"Hm, very..." he paused, looking for the right word. "Exotic."

She rested her head against his stomach, which is as far up his tall frame as she reached, "I'm sorry, this is no fun. I really wanted to spend time with you, but I still have my business to run."

"Look, I understand, it's fine. I promised I'd have a pint with Ralph tonight anyway," he said, as he heard some loud thumps from the bookshop next door. "Sounds like he's back, so why don't I leave you alone to finish off the fantasy safari cake and I'll come back later."

Anna clipped him with a tea towel, "It's a dragon themed wedding cake and you know it, so clear off. Enjoy yourself...and bring my chairs back, Irene will go mad in the morning if everything is not back exactly as it was before."

Jim sauntered through the café, putting his duffle coat on, "Very good, m'lady. As you say, m'lady."

When he arrived at The Bookery the door was open, but just the lights in the window display were on. As he went inside he only just ducked in time as a silver serving tray, formerly used for sandwiches, flew over his head and landed with a crash against the wall.

"Steady on, mate, that could have sliced my head off."

Ralph froze with another tray raised above his head ready for lift off, "Shit, sorry. I didn't see you." He hesitated, then let rip with the tray anyway and sent it flying against a set of shelves on the opposite side of the shop.

Jim held his ground, "I've never been keen on washing up, but this is a little extreme, don't you think? Didn't it go well, this author thing?"

Ralph sank down onto his stool behind the counter, "Oh, that was fine, it's not that."

"What is it then?"

"It's just...why am I here? Really? I mean, I've only been here about a month and one minute it feels like I actually belong, then the next minute it all feels wrong and I want to just pack up again and run."

"Well, I suppose you can't expect it to be all tickety-boo straight away, can you?"

Ralph looked at him, "Tickety-boo? When did you start to say tickety-boo?"

"Not sure, I think it's all the southern water down here, it's having a really strange effect on me. I need beer."

Ralph stood up wearily, "OK, come on then."

"Hang on, we need to get these chairs back to Anna first. It's more than my life is worth to not have it all back for Irene's inspection in the morning."

"Yes, right."

"I'd suggest carrying them round though, rather than throwing them, if that's OK?"

"Fair enough," Ralph said, forcing a smile. "Is Anna still angry with me? I'm not sure I can face another fight right now."

"I think she has other things to worry about at the moment, so I'd just carry on as if nothing has happened, if I were you. And for goodness sake, don't mention pink camels."

* * *

When they arrived at The Mermaid Inn about half an hour later, they both felt the welcoming warmth of the fire in the giant hearth. Ralph went to the bar, while Jim headed to the same table they sat at last time. As he squeezed into the seat, he caught his scarf around the back of the chair of a familiar elderly man in a V-neck jumper at the next table, propelling him forward suddenly and frightening his wife, who let fly a large piece of scampi that had been heading for her mouth. The scampi flew into the air, watched by all three of them, then Jim's long fingers shot out, caught it mid-flight and gently dropped it back on to her plate.

He grinned at them, "Sorry about that – they're nice and hot, aren't they? Good to see you again, have you finished your crosswords?" Before he could sit down, though, Ralph arrived with their drinks.

"Joe and Auntie B are in the other bar; they want us to join them. Oh, hello again," he smiled at their stunned neighbours and then made his way back around to the other side of the bar.

"Bon appetite," Jim said as he followed Ralph.

Joe and Auntie B were sitting on an high-backed wooden bench, packed with tapestry cushions, in a quiet corner at the back of the pub. They had two empty plates pushed to one side of the table and Auntie B had her customary glass of sherry in front of her, while Joe was drinking from a bottle of beer.

"Evening, gents," Joe said. "How's tricks?"

Ralph and Jim looked at each other, "Let's just say it was a day of two halves," Ralph said, as he pulled up a chair. "Nice to see you out and about, Auntie B."

Auntie B leant towards him, "Yes, Joe, invited me out for dinner. It's been quite a treat. I've learnt such a lot about wind farms, it's Joe's new interest apparently."

Joe shrugged, shifting slightly, "You have to keep up with the new trends, save the planet and all that."

Auntie B reached out and found Ralph's hand, "How was your event, dear?"

"My what? Oh, yes, the book event, really good, thanks. It seems like a long time ago now though."

She kept hold of his hand, "I feel some tension here."

"Here she goes, the great Mystic Evelyn Bondolfi, strikes again," Joe said. "Leave the guy alone, he looks fine."

"Well, he is not fine," she snapped, causing all of them to start. "Ralph, you have been up and dow, with such highs and lows in the last few weeks, I'm worried about you. Did anything happen tonight?"

Ralph took his hand back, "No...well, not really. Sam and I, we went for a walk, then...we had a bit of a shock, and I...well, I'm just not sure I'm ready."

"He feels like running off again," Jim said. "Sorry, mate, but these people are your friends, they need to know."

Joe put his beer down and moved the dirty plates to the empty table next to them, "Listen, Ralph, I'm no mystic and have no special powers, but I know this – you belong here. Right here. You and Sam might get it on, you might not. That's cool, but, honestly, you cannot leave. Remember what you told me? You have found your path, no matter where it leads, you need to stay on it."

"Mate, he's right," Jim said. "I can see what you've got here and it's great. It's really special. Besides, I need you to be around when I have to go back home."

Ralph looked at him, "Why? What do you mean?"

Jim looked embarrassed, "Well, I know I'll have to go back eventually. I mean, Anna is amazing, but I'm not like you - I'm not brave. I can't just start again, reinvent myself."

"But surely Carol won't take you back, not just like that?"

"Mate, she thinks I'm at a conference - a tax seminar in Eastbourne. I've got to be back on Saturday."

Auntie B picked up her drink and sat back, "Oh, dear."

"Ouch," added Joe.

"But you said you'd left her or taken a break. That's what Anna thinks," Ralph whispered.

Jim ran his hands through his hair, "I told you I wasn't like you, brave enough to be honest."

"You have to tell her. She thinks you could be *the one*."

"No, no, we talked about it...a bit...I think...she knows this is just a bit of fun."

Auntie B looked stern, "Are you sure, Jim?"

"Take it from an old hand," Joe said. "I may have the reputation as a guy with few morals...Hm, I left a gap there for someone to disagree."

"We would hate to disagree with you, dear," Auntie B said.

"Well, you're paying for your own scampi then, old lady. Anyway, Jim, I've dated - not as often as you guys think - but I've dated. I learnt from my mistakes and I'm honest right from the get-go, if we are heading for the sack then it's a one night only thing - I don't go deeper than that. If they want more then that's not my problem, my conscience is clear, they knew the deal. I may be many things, but one thing I am not is dishonest. Anna is a nice girl. She doesn't have anyone much except us, the Rooftop Club, so if you mess with her, my friend, you mess with all of us."

Jim took a swig of his pint, "Look, I don't want to hurt her, I really don't."

"Then it's time to go home, Jim," Auntie B said, quietly but firmly. They all looked at her, as she placed her glass carefully back on to the table and turned her empty gaze on Jim, "Go back to your life. If it's something you want, then go back to it and make it work. Ralph's journey is different, he is not on the same path as you."

She then turned towards Ralph, finding his hand again across the table, "Ralph, my dear boy, I know your biggest fear was rejection and somehow being made to feel less than others, but you have fought that fear so well and with such strength, please don't let moments of conflict send you into hiding. They will happen, it's inevitable. Fight back, Ralph. What you feel now is nothing compared to the feeling of regret you will know later if you don't stay and fight for what you want. Stand up for who you are and stand up for who you love. My goodness, I wish I had learnt that lesson years ago - I have so many regrets."

"Auntie B, what regrets do you have?" Joe said. "I mean, what should you have stood up for?"

"Joe," she said turning to him. "You have no idea the regrets that I hold inside me. My life was blessed, but not as you think. I was a coward and far too sensitive, I failed because of that. So, I urge all of you boys to be better than you are, to be stronger than you are and to be as honest as you can possibly be with the world. I include you in that Joe. I love you more than you will ever know, but you need to grow up. You need to let someone love you properly and fully, and not keep moving on from woman to woman but going nowhere. You are a beautiful young man, but beauty fades and what is left is the person behind it. You are waiting to belong and it is time you realised that. So, get on with it, you won't be pretty for ever," she sat back, exhausted as the three men looked at her.

Joe picked up his beer, "Well, that told us."

"I'm sorry," Auntie B said. "But sometimes things simply need saying. You all know what you have to do."

* * *

Ralph, Jim and Joe each left The Mermaid Inn reeling from the honesty of the ninety-two-year-old woman. A woman who appeared so wise when addressing them and yet her wisdom seemed not to have allowed her to put her own demons to rest.

Jim returned to the flat above The Cookery, listening to Anna's eager footsteps coming down to the front door to let him in, steeling himself for the conversation he knew he needed to have with her and then the long, difficult journey back to his marriage.

Joe stood on the beach at the end of his short garden with the wet, salty wind whipping around him. He felt battered by the weather and a whole host of questions that tumbled through his head. Was Auntie B right? Was he missing a sense of belonging? Is that what had been worrying him lately? Was it belonging to somewhere or someone? Every fibre of his being fought against the idea of belonging to another person or them belonging to him. But wasn't that what people said when they found someone special, that they belonged together? That wasn't him, was it? He turned his face into the wind, hoping its ferocity would clear his head.

Ralph let himself into his flat, threw his coat over the banister and flicked on the kettle, before checking on Stanley, who was fast asleep on the sofa. He quickly shed his clothes, hoping that removing them might shake off some of the events of the day. He padded back to the kitchen and made himself a cup of tea, took it into the living room and sat on the floor beside Stanley, gently fussing the sleeping dog's soft ears. He knew that Auntie B was right, he couldn't take flight every time he hit a bump in the road. He had made Rye his home and there were so many reasons for him to stay. One of those reasons was Sam Ross, who he knew in his heart was worth fighting for.

CHAPTER 25

*The lost children, three-ply napkins
and Dawa's duty.*

I rene opened another packet of Christmas napkins and handed one to Anna, "You'll have to stop soon or this is going to cost you a fortune. These are three-ply."

Anna blew her nose and sobbed, "I just thought he was different. He said he wasn't ready for anything long term yet, but he did say - *yet*. And I thought *yet* meant not now, but later. Soon, maybe."

"Listen, he was huge. He was a danger to all them knick-knacks you've got upstairs, wasn't he?"

Ralph crept into the empty café, "How is she?" he whispered to Irene.

"Second pack of three-ply and it's only half past nine," she replied. "We're never going to open at this rate."

Ralph knelt down in front of Anna and took her

hands away from her face, "Sweetheart, you have to stop this. It's been two days since he went."

"But...but..." Anna hiccupped. "Why did he have to go? He could have stayed all week, Carol thought he was in Eastbourne until Saturday. He didn't have to go back, not until the weekend."

"But would that have made it any better? He needed to be honest with you, so isn't it better he did it sooner rather than later?"

"I suppose," she sniffed. "Have you heard from him?"

"Yes, he's living at his mum's house at the moment. He obviously decided that telling lies to Carol wasn't on either, so he told her the truth and she threw him out."

Anna's head shot up, "Really? So, it's over? He can come back then."

"No, Carol has agreed to them seeing a counsellor together, they start next week. It might take some time, but Jim reckons there's a chance they'll get through it."

"Well, you're a bringer of glad tidings, aren't you?" Irene snorted, holding out a new Christmas napkin for Anna.

"I'm fine," Anna said, bravely. "Come on, we need to get this café open," she stood up and started to put on her apron.

"Don't you think you should change out of your Snoopy pyjamas first and maybe jump in the shower?" Ralph said, gently.

She looked down at herself, "Oh, yes, probably. I won't be long." She threw her apron on to the counter and headed out of the kitchen, swiftly returning and snatching the packet of napkins from Irene before disappearing again.

"Can't you use the two-ply?" Irene called. "Honestly,

men have so much to answer for."

Ralph took one look at Irene's face, made his excuses and left.

* * *

The short trip to Cinque had now become a well-trodden path for Ralph and here he was again, heading there to try and see Sam. He had rung at different times, called in when he could in the evening or at lunch times, but was always met by the same polite response from Dawa Singh, that Sam was not there just at the moment. He felt that if he could explain about Helen, that his marriage wasn't what Sam thought it was, that he wasn't deliberately keeping secrets, he could make things right between them. Last night, Ralph had had a long talk with Stanley about it and the conclusion was that he would make one more effort today then that was it, he was not going to continue to make a fool of himself. If Sam wasn't prepared to even listen to him, then what hope was there for them?

The restaurant wasn't open at this time of the morning, but he knew there was always activity inside preparing for the day ahead. He knocked on the door, his growing frustration making it a good, strong knock. Through the glass he saw Dawa appear in the distance from Sam's office/cupboard. He looked immaculate, as always, today in a dark blue suit, with matching tie and turban.

"Good morning, sir," he said, as he unlocked and opened the door.

"Dawa, please call me, Ralph. I've asked you every

day."

"I am afraid my answer is the same, sir, Sam is not here at the moment," he started to close the door, but Ralph took Dawa by surprise and squeezed into the reception area.

"Look, Dawa, I know you think that your job is to protect him, but..."

"My job *is* to protect him, sir. I provided personal protection for his father and promised I would do the same for his son. That is why I am here."

"Oh, I see. Really? You were Damien Ross's bodyguard?"

"Personal Protection Officer."

"Well, that's great, but the thing is he doesn't need protecting from me. I just need to talk to him, to explain things."

"He's not here, sir," Dawa remained by the door, holding it open, each statement from him suggesting that it was time for Ralph to leave.

"I don't know whether he told you what happened, but it was a mistake."

"A mistake? You were mistaken that you are married?"

"Oh, so he told you...well, no, not a mistake then, just a misunderstanding. I am still married, but we are separated. She knows, about me, about...you know. So, it's not like before for Sam, not like...what was his name? Steve, the lawyer. Please, Dawa, this means a lot," he looked at Dawa, who remained unmoved in the doorway.

"Right, I see," Ralph knew he was defeated. "I'll go. Just tell him that I'm really sorry. I thought that we might have something special," he stepped out of the door, buttoning up his jacket.

He heard Dawa take a deep breath, "Wait. He's not here because he went back to London, to stay with his mother for a few days."

Ralph saw a flash of hope, "Really? Well, could I have his mobile number then I can speak to him?"

"I'm afraid I couldn't do that. Perhaps I could take your number and give that to him. I can't guarantee that he will call, but I would be happy to pass it on...if it is genuinely a misunderstanding?"

"It is, honestly, but the thing is I don't have a mobile phone. I left it behind with my marriage," he saw Dawa raise a curious eyebrow. "I know, it's all a bit crazy. I have a landline in The Bookery, but he could have called me there already if he wanted to. So, I guess that's it. Thanks anyway, don't worry, I won't pester you anymore. I'm going to try and cling on to my last tiny shred of dignity now. Goodbye, Dawa."

Dawa watched Ralph walk away, his head down and hands stuffed into his jacket pockets.

"Ralph," he called. Although Dawa would never admit to being a romantic, the look on Ralph's face told him that this young man was genuine and he knew that his duty here was to bring these two unhappy people together, not to keep them apart. "Sam is coming back on Saturday. He should be here by mid-afternoon. However, I would not advise just turning up as you have been doing, Sam does not appreciate being ambushed. You need a different approach."

Ralph walked eagerly back towards Dawa, "What do you suggest?"

"Have you never been to the movies?"

"Pardon?"

Dawa shook his head, "Don't you know how these things go? Invite him to meet you at a certain time and a certain well-chosen location. As the injured party he has the right to leave you standing alone and heart-broken, or to arrive just a minute or two late and fulfil both of your dreams," he paused. "I believe, that is the traditional approach."

"Brilliant," Ralph said. "OK, so can you please tell him...no, ask him, to meet me at seven, at the Rye Tower on Saturday night. If he comes, I know there is a chance for us and I can explain everything to him. If he doesn't, then this wasn't meant to be. How's that?"

"Perfect," Dawa said, trying not to give away the emotion he felt at the back of his throat. "I will tell him...and Ralph, good luck," then he turned, went back into the restaurant and locked the door behind him.

❉ ❉ ❉

When Anna returned to the café, looking more her-self in a sparkling berry-red kimono, everything was set and ready to open, "Thanks, Irene," she said. "What would I do without you?"

"Good question. Now, just so you know, my kidneys are up today so I won't be handling the mince pies."

Anna couldn't help but smile, "Whatever you say, Irene. Now, would you like to try today's special pie?"

"What is it?" Irene said suspiciously.

Anna headed into the kitchen, "It's a mince-pie pie."

"What's one of them?"

"Well, it's mostly mince, to be honest, with tomato and onion and...a few other things."

"I know you, it's those *other things* that have caused me all sorts of problems down below before, so I'll say thank you, but no. Let's try them on the customers, it's not a big problem if we lose one or two of them, but you'd be hard pushed to replace me."

Anna leant on the counter and looked at Irene, "That is so true, Irene. How long have we known each other?"

"Feels like a lifetime some days," Irene said, beginning to plump up the cushions on each chair.

"Seriously, it feels like I've known you all my life, but it's only been, what? Two years?"

"Something like that. You'd had that other woman here, with the hair that made her look like broccoli, but she left to move to Wales or Woking. I'd just parted company with the tourist information board over the bendy bus situation and saw the sign in the window. What are you smiling at?"

"Nothing, I was just thinking that even when I'm down I can always rely on you. You are always there, always the same."

Irene bashed a cushion extra hard, "Now, don't get all soppy on me. You always get like this when you've been hurt by a rotten fella. Why do you do it to yourself? You do perfectly well on your own. You have made this place from nothing, you make beautiful cakes for people, your pies are not for my innards, but other people like them. You employ staff...and me. Why you think you need some lummox with a scrotum around the place I have no idea? Look after yourself, that's what I say."

Anna banged the counter with the flat of her hand, making Irene start, "From now on, I am only going to listen to you, no one else - especially myself. You're like a mum to me, you know that?" and she came out of the kitchen and placed a kiss on Irene's cheek.

"Now, pack that in, you know I can't handle it, not with my cholesterol. Besides, you've got a perfectly good mother of your own, so don't go adopting me. You should be going to see her, it's nearly Christmas."

"Not that again, Irene. You say that at Christmas, Mother's Day - not to mention the fourth of July, for some reason. I've got enough grief at the moment without dealing with her."

"That didnt last long! You just said you were going to listen to me. I know it's none of my business, but a girl needs her mother. I should know, I've got enough daughters to sink a ship – and at their size it wouldn't take many of them."

"It's difficult with my mother. She wasn't there when I needed her, she let me down again and again."

"Well, none of us are perfect. I've left more children outside shops in their prams than you've had hot dinners. In fact we had the same policeman turning up so often, with one mislaid child or another, that he ended up marrying my eldest."

"You are right, Irene, I don't need anyone but myself. I don't need a man and I definitely don't need my mother. Besides, it's been six years, I probably wouldn't even recognise her if I saw her."

"Just think about it, that's all I ask."

"Fine, OK, I will," Anna said, turning on the heat under a saucepan to make today's gravy, knowing that she thought about her mother far more than she would ever admit.

CHAPTER 26

*The slow road to Eastbourne, three
fig rolls and where it all began.*

As the Christmas season truly got underway, all
the shops in Rye were busy and the usual leisurely weeks were a thing of the past. Anna and
Ralph both benefited from this by taking their minds
off their romantic lives and the week flew by. Early
on Saturday morning Ralph knocked on the window of
The Cookery and Anna, liberally doused in icing sugar,
opened the door.

"You're up early," he said, Stanley pulling him frantically towards the delicious smells in the kitchen.

She looked flustered, "It's a Christmas log crisis.
Stanley, please get down this is supposed to be a hygienic environment. We ran out of chocolate logs yesterday, I told you people wouldn't be put off by the
Marmite in them. Oh, ye of little faith."

"Fair enough, each to their own. Is Irene feeling better?"

"Yes, the doctor said it was just trapped wind. She was mortified, said they don't have wind in her family and is threatening to sue. It's perishing out there, I didn't think you'd be running today?"

"No, I haven't done, they said we might get snow today. We've cancelled the Rover's last match of the season on Sunday, well, tomorrow, because of it. I think the parents were relieved to be honest."

Anna suddenly put down her icing bag, "Saturday."

"Correct, can you name the month too?"

"No, it's Saturday. *The* Saturday. *Sam* Saturday." she said, grabbing him by the elbows with excitement. "He's back in town today and you have your romantic rendezvous tonight at seven. Oh my god, it's just like a film. I might hide in the church yard and watch."

"Please don't, the squirrels look pretty nervy at the best of times."

"But aren't you excited?"

"Of course, I am, but I've ruined things before, who's to say I won't do it this time? That is, if he even turns up.".

"Of course, he will, it's meant to be. You've got this, just don't be a…a…you know, and kick any mobster's car doors this time."

"Thanks for the advice. I'll try, if you promise not to leap out from behind a gravestone at us."

"Deal. What are you wearing? And don't say, this. As soon as we close, I'll come round to yours and we can go through your wardrobe. This is so exciting, I'm kind of glad you haven't got a mobile, or else you'd have sorted it all out by now and this wouldn't be happening. I love it!" She skipped around the kitchen, waving a tea towel at him.

He stepped sideways, avoiding being clipped by it, "Well, you've changed your tune from earlier in the week. You'd have sooner gone to visit your, so-called, evil mother than get involved with romance again."

"Well, this is yours not mine, that's different. Anyway, she is not *so-called,* she really is evil."

"Anna, I'm sure she's not, I'm sure..."

"Enough, I don't want to talk about her, I'm too excited. Right, clear off you two, I have chocolate butter icing to mix with Marmite and the ratio is very important to get right. Too much Marmite could be explosive."

Ralph dragged Stanley out of the café on his stomach as he was refusing to use his legs in protest at leaving without being offered any of today's baking.

✳ ✳ ✳

After lunch The Bookery had its first lull of the day, which allowed Stanley to settle down in the children's corner to rest before he had to guide more visitors around. For what must have been the hundredth time, Ralph checked his watch, just three hours to closing, then plenty of time to shower and change - even with Anna's interference - before he would see Sam again. After a week apart Ralph knew what he wanted - and it was Sam. Auntie B had been right, he needed to stay and fight, but he was scared that he might ruin it all again. So, he had carefully worked out in his head what he needed to say to Sam and even practiced it a few times. He had convinced himself that if he stuck to his plan, nothing could go wrong.

"Ralph, Ralph," Joe called as he charged into the shop. "Have you seen Auntie B today?"

"No, why?"

"She's not in the flat. She's always in the flat," Joe paced up and down.

"Well, perhaps she went out with someone, a friend?"

"No, all her friends are too old to take her out. They go and see her upstairs."

"What about Sam? Perhaps he came back early and they went out somewhere."

"Yes…no, he always calls in to collect the key from me when he comes to see her. She must have gone out on her own."

"But how can she?"

"Christ knows, she has no guide dog, she hasn't even got a white stick. She always refuses to go out by herself, she says she's too frightened. I'll have to call the police, then start hunting round the town."

Ralph followed Joe to the door, "Right, I'll close up too and start looking. Call me if you find her. Shit, no, wait you can't. Well, call Anna and she can find me,"

Ralph locked up, scribbling a hasty 'Closed for an emergency' notice for the door, before hurrying Stanley upstairs. He rushed next door to The Cookery, but Anna and Irene hadn't seen Auntie B either, so he set off along the High Street, looking up every side road and into every shop hoping to see the big wide hat bobbing along amongst the shoppers, but there was no sign of her. He ended up at the taxi rank on Cinque Ports Street and worked his way along all the cars to see if any of them had seen her. He was despairing by the time he got to the last one, "I don't suppose you've seen a very small, very old lady, with white hair, have you?" he asked.

The driver raised a pair of unruly black eyebrows, "Hundreds of them, fella. This is Rye," he chuckled at his own joke.

"Yes, I know, but this one probably had blue coloured dark glasses and a big, white floppy hat."

"Like a big sun hat sort of thing?"

"Yes, yes, have you seen her? Which way did she go?"

"I gave her a ride. She rang the office and I picked her up a couple of hours ago, from the High Street. Lovely lady, such a shame she's blind and everything."

"So, where is she now?" Ralph asked, losing his patience.

"Well, still in Eastbourne, I expect."

"Eastbourne?"

"Yes, I took her where she wanted to go and then she said she would probably be there for a while, so I didn't need to wait."

Ralph banged his hand on the top of the taxi, "And you just left her there?"

"Listen, fella, she told me to go, so I went. She seemed to have all her marbles, how was I to know?"

Ralph opened the back door of the car, "Right, take me there, as quickly as possible - exactly where you dropped her. Do you remember?"

The driver started the engine, "Of course, I'm not daft. Calm down, I'll get you there. It was a street, now what was it called, something Hurst? I know it was number two or was it three? I can't think of the name of it."

"You must remember," Ralph shouted.

"I'll be doing nothing if you keep up that tone."

"Sorry, sorry, I'm just worried about her. She never

261

goes out; she can't see a thing."

"Alright, alright, don't panic, I can't remember the name of the road, but it'll still be here in the satnav, plus I can pretty much remember where it is. We'll find her, don't you worry."

The driver pulled out and set-off heading west out of Rye. Eastbourne was about thirty miles along the coast and it would take at least an hour to get there, the driver thought. It wasn't until about twenty minutes into the journey that Ralph realised that he hadn't told Anna or Joe where he was going or that he knew where Auntie B was. He thought of borrowing the driver's mobile to call one of them, but he didn't know either of their numbers. So, he sat tight and focused on just willing the taxi to move as fast as it could through the country lanes and coastal roads of Sussex.

❋ ❋ ❋

The icy conditions and slow-moving traffic meant that it was nearly an hour and a half later that they arrived on the outskirts of Eastbourne, where the Victorian seaside resort nestled in beside the imposing cliffs of Beachy Head. They drove passed 19th century terraced houses and villas transformed into B&B's towards the long, spindly pier that stretched out into the stormy English Channel. As they headed further into town, with each turn and delay at traffic lights Ralph became more anxious.

"Is it close?" he asked, perched on the edge of the seat, looking out as seagulls screeched overhead.

"Just round this corner, fella. I remember it well, the

lady, she asked me to describe things to her as we arrived in town, just so she could picture where we were."

Ralph started to get his wallet out of his pocket, hoping that he had enough cash to pay for the journey, "Did she say why she was here?"

They turned into a wide street, with fat red-brick houses on either side, "Oh, yes, she said she was revisiting an important place from her youth. Where she'd met someone really special, that's what she said. She met someone really special here for the first time. Here we are, fella."

The car pulled up in front of a simple two-storey house on the end of a terrace. Ralph looked out at what seemed like a perfectly ordinary family home, with a large bay window at the front, next to a covered porch. No sign of Auntie B though. He quickly paid, using up everything he had in his wallet, allowing just a slim tip, which the driver's unruly eyebrows showed was woefully inadequate.

As the car took off Ralph looked up and down the street, but it was quiet except for a ginger cat a few doors down, sashaying along showing off its skills at wall walking. He took a deep breath and went up the short path to the solid looking front door inside the porch and rang the bell. He didn't have to wait long until he heard footsteps approaching and the door was opened by a large lady, who looked to be in her sixties with the tightest perm he had ever seen.

Her smile, however, was warm and softened the severe hairdo a little, "Well, hello," she chirped. "I imagine you're here for Mrs Bondolfi, are you?"

"Yes, I am. Is she alright?"

The woman stepped back to allow him in, "She's

absolutely fine. She's on her third fig roll, so all seems well. Come through." She closed the door behind Ralph and then squeezed past him in the neat little hallway to lead him through to the back of the house. They entered a tidy kitchen and then turned sharp right into a small conservatory, where Auntie B sat on a wicker sofa, with a cup of tea at her side and a black and white cat curled up on her lap.

Ralph let out a long breath, "Auntie B, thank god!"

She looked up, still wearing her dark glasses, but her large sunhat lay on the coffee table in front of her. Without it she looked smaller than he had ever seen her, "Ralph? Oh, how lovely. Have you met Mrs Dorey?"

"Yes, I mean, no," he turned to Mrs Dorey. "Sorry, I'm Ralph, I'm Auntie...Mrs Bondolfi's neighbour."

Mrs Dorey patted his hand, "I know, dear. Mrs B has been telling me about you and the rest of the Rooftop Club, it sounds like you are quite a team. I wish I had so many lovely young people around me. It'd certainly brighten my day - it's just me and Barbs here, you see. Not that I'm complaining, she's just about the best company a woman can get, aren't you Barbs?" The cat stirred at the mention of her name, then settled back down to her duties of keeping this new little lady comfy and safe, with her warmth and soft purrs.

"Now, where are my manners," Mrs Dorey continued. "Would you like a cup of tea or coffee perhaps? A man likes a coffee I tend to find, after a shock, rather than a tea."

"Coffee would be amazing, thank you."

"Let me see," her small, enthusiastic eyes appraised him. "Black, no sugar. Am I right?"

"Yes, spot on."

She clapped her hands together, "I knew it. It's my little party trick. Too many years running coffee mornings at the Central Methodist's, I'm afraid. I may not be an expert at many things, but sizing up a man for his hot drinks is my speciality," she chortled as she busied herself back in the kitchen.

Ralph pulled up a wicker chair next to the sofa and sat down, "You gave us a proper fright, Auntie B. None of us knew where you were. Joe's probably still running around Rye looking for you."

She looked down and gently stroked Barbs' soft fur, *"Is it better to have had a good thing and lost it, or never to have had it?"* she quoted quietly to herself.

"Auntie B? Are you OK?"

She turned to him, "Yes, I'm fine. I'm so sorry to be such a nuisance, but I just felt I had to come back, you see. Back to where it all started."

CHAPTER 27

The greatest mistake, manly digestives
and a gift for Ginger.

B ack to where what started?" Ralph asked Auntie
B, the winter sun warming him through the
glass roof of the conservatory. "Back to see Mrs
Dorey? Is she a friend of yours?"

"No, we haven't met until today," Auntie B said,
stroking the purring cat in her lap. "She has been so
kind, letting me come into her home like this. Such a
nuisance, such a nuisance."

Ralph frowned, "Then why did you want to come
and see her? I don't understand."

"I didn't come to see Mrs Dorey, I came to see the
house, or feel it, at least, as best I can."

Just then Mrs Dorey trotted back in, triumphantly
carrying a small tray on which sat a mug of black coffee
and a plate of biscuits. She placed it carefully down onto
the coffee table.

"Thank you, that's very kind," Ralph said.

"I'm going to make myself scarce. Mrs Bondolfi has told me her story and it's a personal one, so you won't want me around. Take your time, there is no rush. I've got a damp cloth and some pantry shelves with my name on them, five of the little devils to be precise, so I've got plenty to be getting on with."

Ralph sat in silence for a few minutes, sipping his coffee, while Barbs snored contentedly and more seagulls cried high above them. Auntie B shifted slightly in her seat and Ralph adjusted the cushion behind her back, "Thank you," she said. "You see, when you all say I am strong and wise, it is simply not true, Ralph. Until I met Mrs Dorey today, I have only told this story to one other living soul, my husband. It has been my secret and the greatest mistake of my life," she paused and took a sip of her tea.

"I was the eldest of five children. My parents were good people, but distant. Today we would probably think of them as cold, but that was the way things were then, in the 1930s and '40s. We never wanted for anything, but they were strict about doing things right and proper. Well, that wasn't really my way, I wanted more adventure than our little village could offer, especially after the restrictions and dark years of the war. When I was seventeen, just after the war ended, I met this lovely chap, Robert. Bob, I called him. Oh, he was so glamorous. He had such a moustache and a dangerous charm to match, so, of course, I fell for him. Like Alice down the rabbit hole, whoosh, down I went. When I came back up, I was pregnant and he was gone.

Remember this was 1946 and my parents were shop owners, established people. I concealed it for as long as

I could, but Mother soon worked out what was happening. They were good church people too, so there was not even a question of getting rid of it, which I certainly would never have done. I was young and foolish, but I knew one thing above all else, that this tiny person inside me was going to be loved for the rest of their life. I dreamed that we would have such adventures together and make a wonderful life for ourselves. Let's just say, that is not how my parents saw it.

They insisted on the baby being adopted, given away to strangers. I may have been physically small, but I had enough strength to fight them on that. If the baby was to go away, then so was I. I would disappear and they would never see us again. We fought and fought for weeks and in the end they came up with a compromise. When I became too big and the baby couldn't be covered up anymore, I would go away. My mother would get out her old maternity clothes and let the world know that she was expecting another baby. She made a special cushion that would tie round her waist and could have extra stuffing added to it as the weeks moved on. Once the baby was born, they would bring it up as their sixth and youngest child and no one would ever know that it was mine. No shame would be brought on the family or on me.

At the time it seemed like the only way out. I didn't have a penny to my name, no useful skills and nowhere to run. At least this way I got to be with my child every day and, I hoped, one day we could still go off together and see the world. So, it was all settled. Mother and I grew bigger together, her bump on display and mine hidden under layers of clothes. Then it was time for me to disappear, confinement they called it then; mothers would go away and rest somewhere quiet for the last few weeks or months of their pregnancies. So, I came here.

In 1946 this house was the Bell Hostel for unmarried mothers. Tucked away in a quiet side street, out of harm's way, with a live-in matron. There were four girls here at a time and I shared a bedroom with Julia, who had the largest breasts I had ever seen in my life. Breasts that had got her into the same trouble I was in, but she was fun and decadent and chaotic and we got on like a house on fire. After we had our babies we wrote to each other for a while. She found a new chap and moved to London. I don't think he treated her well, because her letters became fewer and shorter, until in the end they stopped altogether.

Mother came to stay in a guest house just round the corner from here, telling everyone that she was visiting her sister until the baby came, so as not to disturb my father's work in the shop he ran in the village. They'd already told people that I was with my aunt anyway, helping out around the house. Then on Christmas Eve 1946, in the front bedroom of this house, just up there, I gave birth to the most glorious little girl in all the world. She had enormous, furious eyes and the prettiest golden hair you have ever seen. I was allowed to name her and called her Virginia, after Ginger Rogers. She was my favourite film star back then, she was feisty, sexy and did everything the men could do, but backwards and in four-inch heels. My parents always called her Virginia, but to me she was always Ginger.

Two weeks later we were back home, in our village. Everyone cooed over Ginger and congratulated my mother and father, they said I must be a very proud big sister. Sister? It crashed in on me - that's all I was now. This precious little girl would never call me mother. She would never run to me first if she fell or was frightened. I did as much as I could for her, but my mother always took over, she always knew best. After a while, I think she even forgot that she wasn't Ginger's real mother, just her grandmother. So many times I thought of just picking Ginger up and running away, but what could I offer her on my own? There she had a large family to care for her and protect her. She was free of scandal and gossip. Could I really be so selfish as to take her away from all that, to who knows what? Time went by and I got to be with her every day and help her with her chores and her spelling when she started school. We drew and painted together, and I like to think that we had a special bond above my other sister and brothers.

When I was twenty-one and she was four, I met Clifford Bondolfi. His father was an Italian prisoner of war brought here from the Middle East and being a master baker, his skills were useful to the war effort. Eventually, he made a life for himself here, so his wife and son came over to join him, eventually. Cliff started off life as Dario, but after the war people were still suspicious of foreigners, so they changed his name to something English to help him fit in.

When she was sixteen, Ginger came to work for us, we had our own little bakery then in Joe's shop, next to The Bookery. That was the happiest time of my life. It felt like we were a family, just the three of us. Cliff was the only person I ever told about Ginger. He was so kind, he didn't seem to mind at all. We tried for our own family, but it just didn't happen. A doctor told me that there must have been some complications after Ginger was born and he didn't think I was capable of having any more. Cliff always said that he preferred older children anyway, who you could have a decent conversation with, but deep down I think he cared that he was never a father.

Ginger had a stubborn streak in her, maybe a little like me when I refused to have her adopted, or when I went down the rabbit hole with Bob. So, I suppose I shouldn't have been surprised when she started up with a chap like Gordon Wells. He was a wild boy, always in trouble, always tearing around at a hundred miles an hour, with bigger dreams than his shoes could carry. We tried to protect her, but the more we tried the further she would pull away from us. I remember one day, when we had refused to let her go out to a party, her screaming at me over the kitchen table, "You are not my Mother. You can't stop me living my life!"

Imagine if I had told her the truth then? I was so close to doing it, but I thought it would just make things worse, she was angry enough with me. What if she was even angrier that she had been lied to all her life, that everything she held to be true was not as she thought? So, I said nothing. I was a coward again; I chose not to be her mother for the second time. A few months later she announced that she and Gordon had got an assisted ticket to go to Canada, to a new life. She wanted to see the world and have an adventure, she said. Oh, didn't I know that feeling? I remembered it all too well and although it broke my heart in two, she had to go. Cliff fought against it, but I didn't. I always wanted it to be us two having the adventures, Ginger and me, but just because I couldn't go, how could I deny her the right to do it without me?

We stayed in contact, I made sure of that. Even when she didn't reply, I kept on writing, kept on chasing her to find out where she was and sent her birthday and Christmas cards. She started her own family, had two beautiful children, Nicole and Christopher. I have some lovely photographs of them growing up. Then as a surprise fortieth birthday present for Ginger, Joe came along."

Ralph's coffee had gone cold as he sat in silence listening to Auntie B tell her story, "Did you never go out to Canada to see her or your grandchildren? Didn't they come here?"

"No, they didn't have much money and couldn't really afford it. I offered to pay for their flights, but Gordon wasn't too keen, I think. I don't blame him, we weren't very nice to him when he was in Rye. Cliff didn't like to leave the shop for long and wasn't a big one for travel, but he often said I should go over on my own. But I never did."

"Why not?"

"I suppose I was hoping that she might ask me to go. That she would say that she wanted to see me, but she never did. After all, I was just one of her sisters, not her mother. What did she need me for? She was happy, I could tell that from her letters. Even up to the end, she seemed content. Then my Clifford died. Ginger was in her sixties, a grandmother herself. Her husband, Gordon, Joe's father, had died a few years before in a car accident. My parents were long gone, and I was the last of the brothers and sisters. I realised that if there was ever a moment to tell her the truth, this was it. Joe was with us in Rye by then, stopping off on his tour of the world and just never moving on. He had no idea, of course, that I was actually his grandmother. I told Joe that I was thinking of going over and visiting his mother, and he thought it was a great idea and that we should go together and surprise her. We had it all planned, we even had the tickets. Then two weeks before we were due to fly Joe got a call from his older brother, Christopher, to say that their mother had died. She had never once mentioned that she was ill, to Joe or to me, or that she had gone through chemotherapy many times before, until there was nothing more they could do. We were told she didn't want Joe to know in case he cut short his trip. She still believed in people having their big adventures, I suppose.

Joe used his ticket to fly home for her funeral. He wanted me to go with him, but I said, no. I didn't need to see my daughter buried in the cold ground. At the day and time of the funeral, I sat out in the middle of the Rye marshes with an easel and my paints. It was the most glorious Spring day, all around me new buds and plants were being born. I began to paint a picture for Ginger and for me. A present from a mother to a daughter. It's the one I still have over my mantelpiece."

"With the bright gold flowers?" Ralph whispered.

"Yes, the prettiest golden flowers for the prettiest golden-haired girl. My Ginger," she bowed her head and Barbs felt the movement and looked up. Then the cat raised her head and gently touched her nose to Auntie B's.

After a moment Auntie B turned to Ralph, "That is why I am always encouraging you all not to waste your lives and your opportunities, like I did. Live now. Be who you want to be now. I had so many chances in my life to be a mother. To be who I was, who I believe I truly should have been, but I lost them all. Today, I had a feeling that I needed to come back where I first met Ginger, when it was just her and me for the last time. The few precious hours I spent in the bed upstairs with her in my arms and the only time anyone ever called me Mother, when I was with the mid-wife and matron. I just wanted to be close to her again, just for a moment. I am sorry to have caused such a fuss."

Ralph brushed away a tear and knelt down beside the tiny old lady, who suddenly looked very frail, "Any amount of fuss is worth you being here. And for what it's worth, I think you did the greatest thing any mother could do, you gave your daughter a chance for the best life she could have. Even if it meant a massive sacrifice for you."

Auntie B shook her head, "Thank you, Ralph, but I know that I let her down," she patted his hand and then gently felt for his cheek. When her soft hands reached his face, she held him still and leaned forward and gave him a delicate kiss, "Now, I'm very tired. Do you think that we could go home, please?"

CHAPTER 28

The Queen of the Universe, Mr Timberlake
and mothers' mistakes.

Ralph was guided by the warbling of something he vaguely recognised as an old Cliff Richard hit, to a large pantry at the end of the kitchen, "Hi, Mrs Dorey?"

"Oh, you startled me. Are you ready for some more coffee?"

"It's been really kind of you to look after Auntie B and to take us in, but I need to get her home now. I don't suppose I could make a phone call, could I?"

"I just hope she found what she was looking for by coming here. I had no idea of this house's history until she told me. Now, the phone is in the hallway, do you know the number?"

Ralph halted, "Erm, no, actually, I don't."

"Well, if it's a taxi you need, I have the number of a very good firm that I use occasionally, just to take cakes and so on to church."

"Just a moment," he popped his head back into the conservatory. "Auntie B, I don't suppose you have any cash on you, do you? For a taxi?"

"No, dear, I used all mine to get here. I hadn't thought far enough ahead about getting home."

He smiled sheepishly, "Snap. Don't worry, I'll sort something out."

Mrs Dorey was waiting in the kitchen doorway, "If it's a question of money, I do keep a little..." she began.

Ralph held up his hand, "Absolutely not. You have been more than generous already, I'll sort something out. This is a long shot, but I don't suppose you have a computer and the internet here, do you?"

"As a matter of fact, I do. We had a lovely man from Seaford, called Mr Timberlake, come to talk to us at the Women's Fellowship group, he has no left leg, you know. It was fascinating. Mr Timberlake kindly came and fitted me up, it's just at the top of the stairs first door on the right. It's all switched on, I was checking the weather for next March before Mrs Bondolfi arrived. There's a telephone extension up there too, next to the computer, so just help yourself. I'll put the kettle on."

Once Ralph had settled into the little box room that held an old card table with a green felt top, a bright orange kitchen chair, the phone and a laptop, he quickly found the number for The Cookery. It was Irene who answered and told him that Anna was out with the police, but she would get hold of her and call off the dogs, then get her to jump in her car and come straight over to collect them.

He came back into the conservatory, where Mrs Dorey and Auntie B were both fussing Barbs, "Anna's on her way, but I'm afraid it may take her a while to get here, Mrs Dorey. We can always go to a café or a pub nearby."

Mrs Dorey leapt to her feet, "You will do no such thing, not while there is water in the kettle and fruit cake in the Queen Mother's memorial tin. I'll be two ticks; sit down, you must be exhausted with all your adventures, the pair of you."

It was two cups of coffee and three large slices of fruit cake later when Anna arrived and joined them in the conservatory as the daylight was beginning to fade.

"But what made her come all this way? One of us could have brought her over to see her friend, she only had to ask," Anna whispered to Ralph.

Ralph looked at Auntie B, fast asleep with her head against the back of the sofa, Barbs the cat still wrapped into a ball on her lap, "She didn't come to see Mrs Dorey. She got it in her head to re-visit an old haunt, so off she went. It's a long story, but it's not mine to tell. I have a feeling she'll tell you when she's ready."

"Fair enough," Anna shrugged and picked up a pile of raisins from her plate. "This is great cake, I must ask her for the recipe."

Ralph rubbed his stomach, "I know, I won't need to eat again until Easter. You got here quickly, it took my taxi driver ages. The roads were icy in places."

"I know, I'm hoping I won't get too many speeding tickets. I did hit a patch of ice just outside Westfield, near Cock Marling – no cheap jokes, it's a real place – but a well-placed holly bush saved me. It was quite Christmassy actually, for a moment, being wrapped inside a holly bush..."

Ralph sat up and stared at her, "You came off the

road and drove into a holly bush? I told Irene to tell you that we were alright, there was no hurry; you could have killed yourself."

Anna picked up another piece of cake, "I didn't think that your life would actually flash before your eyes at moments like that, it was weird."

"Why are you being so calm about this?" Ralph asked.

Anna shook her head and looked down at her plate, which was shaking a little in her hand, "I don't know, I just wanted to get here to see Auntie B, to make sure she was OK. So, I just reversed out of the ditch and drove on."

Ralph put his arm round her, "You idiot. So, did you see me when you saw your life flash before you? Was I front and centre?"

Anna gave him a weak smile, "Well, there was someone who looked a bit like Irene, but she was smiling, so, I don't think it could have been her. Then my dad, I think. Only briefly, but I'm sure I saw him. Oh, and Mum."

"Blimey, that's amazing."

"It was only for a split second, but they were both there...I haven't seen my dad's face since I was ten and there he was, right in front of me."

"Do you remember where you last saw him?"

Anna looked up at the darkening sky through the glass ceiling, "There's barely a day goes by when I don't think about it."

"Do you want to tell me?"

She crossed her arms over her chest, either as protection against the memory or the cold shiver that ran through her, "I was ten, oh, I've said that. Anyway, he was working late, so I was in bed. He was always working late; he was the editor of the local paper - The Rye and Battle Observer. It was quite a big deal, but as far as I was concerned my Daddy was never there to kiss me good night and that's all I cared about. He told me that when he got home, he made sure he always came into my bedroom and gave me a kiss, but I was asleep so I reckoned that didn't count.

Anyway, on this particular night I was angry with him for not being there again, he'd promised me he would be back in time to read me a story. I heard him come into the house, then up the stairs, kind of slow and weary. I was annoyed, so, when he got to my room, I pretended to be asleep and turned away to face the wall. He came in and kissed me on the back of the head and then crept away again. Just as he got to the door I opened one eye and saw him standing there and he was smiling at me, but he also looked sad, then he went. About two hours later he had a massive heart attack and died. It was on the kitchen floor, just downstairs. The first I knew was that Mum was sitting on my bed, waking me up and she told me."

"Oh, Anna, that's awful. Your poor mum."

She looked at him, confused, "Mum? Don't you see, I rejected my dad just before he died? He was already under stress at work and then his daughter turned her back on him, causing him to have a heart attack."

"But Anna, you were a kid, he broke a promise to you. You had a right to be angry, besides, people don't have heart attacks because their kids are in a strop with them. If they did, parents would be laid waste all over the country. It was not your fault."

Anna picked up her coffee cup, "I know, but I didn't think that when I was young. I carried that guilt with me for years, and I blamed myself."

"Is that when your mum started drinking?"

"Pretty much. I didn't notice it for a while, but by the time I started secondary school it was becoming obvious. So, there I was carrying round the guilt of my father's death and there she was carrying a bottle of Shiraz. She's useless, she just doesn't care."

Ralph took his arm away from Anna's shoulders, "That's not true, she does care. Why else would she come and try to find you?"

Anna's frowned, "What?"

"She was grieving," a voice said from the other side of the room and Auntie B sat up on the sofa, the moonlight on her face. "I'm sorry to eavesdrop, Anna, but she was your mother. She was also a wife who had lost her husband. Imagine what she went through with him on the floor of your kitchen, unable to help him, desperate for the ambulance to arrive, but all to no avail? That poor woman, then had to go up those stairs and wake her daughter, to tell a little girl her father was gone. It must have been unbearable."

"It was her job to help me, to tell me it wasn't my fault, but she never did," Anna gulped.

"No mother is perfect, Anna," she said with a fleeting look at Ralph. "Did your mother know that you thought you had played a part in your father's death?"

"Yes, of course...I'm sure she did...she must have done."

"But you never told her?"

"Well, no, not really," Anna wrapped her arms around herself again.

"My dear girl, mothers are many things; good, bad, cruel, lazy, loving, drunks, but above all they are human. They hurt and they grieve and they do the wrong thing, but sometimes I do hope that one or two of them may be forgiven for their mistakes, especially those who do not have the power to be mind-readers. Perhaps as a favour to me you would think about that a little."

"OK," Anna nodded, then she turned to Ralph. "What did you mean she came to find me?"

"I'm sure Ralph just misspoke," Auntie B said, shifting forward and moving Barbs from her lap. "Now, I do believe we should get going as time is moving on."

Anna leapt to her feet, frightening the cat who shot into the kitchen, "Blimey, yes, come on we need to shift."

"What's the big hurry, we're all safe and sound now?" Ralph asked.

"Don't you know what time it is?" she said, helping Auntie B with her sun hat.

"No idea, why?"

"Ralph, it's five to six."

"So?"

"So, you have to meet Sam at seven or he'll think you've changed your mind or something."

"Oh, shit, I completely forgot. Well, that's it, we'll never make it in time," Ralph slumped back into his seat.

"No, that's *not* it. We might make it, it's still possible. Even if you are a few minutes late he'll understand."

"He won't, why should he? I invited him to meet me, I'm the one with the explaining to do. Look, there's always something getting in the way between me and Sam; Big Rachel's hen party, some thug in a Ford Focus, the small matter of my marriage and now this. Let's face it, something in the universe is sending us a sign. We are not meant to be together," Ralph looked forlornly out on to Mrs Dorey's neat little garden.

Anna abandoned Auntie B and started dragging Ralph up out of the chair, "Don't be so defeatist, come on. We can do this!"

"Ralph, "Auntie B said, "I am aware that you think that something in the universe is telling you that your romance is doomed, but I am nearly as old as the universe, therefore, I am qualified to tell you not to be so stupid and to get your cute little rear end in the car and go and get your man," Auntie B took aim and slapped Ralph perfectly on the bottom. "Well, that was a well-aimed guess, wasn't it?" she said proudly. "Now, vamos!"

Anna shook herself, "Ye gods, she's talking in tongues now and she thinks she's queen of the universe. We'd better do what she says, come on."

They guided Auntie B to the front seat of the Anna's small, pink Fiat 500 and Ralph folded himself into the back. Anna roared away from the house as Mrs Dorey waved them off from her front gate, promising to come and see them when her friend Mr Timberlake next wanted some begonias and she could persuade him to drive as far as Rye for them.

Auntie B slammed her hand onto the dashboard in front of her and shouted, "Don't spare the horses woman, get a ruddy move on," thoroughly enjoying herself.

CHAPTER 29

*The dueller's ghost, dancing in the snow
and an eight-inch baking tin.*

T he clock on the tower of St Mary's was ready to
strike seven-thirty, as Ralph raced around the
churchyard and through the square to Rye Castle. He knew his search was futile, but he still circled
the castle's towers and went down to the Gun Gardens
below. But Sam was long gone, and Ralph leant against
one of the ancient canons that still gazed out to sea, as if
hopeful of one more chance to join the battle.

"One last chance, eh?" he said dismally, patting the
cold metal. "We've blown that, my friend."

"Everyone gets one more chance," a deep, gravelly
voice said, from behind him.

Ralph leapt away from the canon, turning to search
the darkness until his eyes could make out a pile of bin
bags tucked under the base of the stone walls of the castle, "Bloody hell, you made me jump."

The bin bags produced an arm and then a foot, as the man beneath them settled himself to block out the cold, "There is always one more chance, old thing. That's my motto, it has to be or I'd have flung myself off that tower weeks ago. We can't give up, we really can't."

"I might as well, I only had this chance."

"For what?"

"Love," Ralph sai, sheepishly.

"Love? My dear old thing, love is allowed more chances than anything else. Didn't you know that? At least six, last time I checked."

"Really? You think it's worth a try?"

"Good god man, of course! It's love we're talking about, not trying to get Yorkshire puddings to rise. Never give up, if you mean it."

"You're right," Ralph set off up the steps, but stopped half-way and turned back. "Erm, sorry, what's your name?"

"Thank you for asking...it's Martin."

"Thank you, Martin. I'm Ralph and I appreciate the advice. What are you doing tomorrow?"

"Well, I've got an appointment with my bank manager at twelve, then my stylist is giving me a cut and colour..."

"Yes, right, sorry, of course. What I meant was, do you know The Bookery on the High Street?"

"I may do, yes?"

"Well, that's my shop. Please come down tomorrow, about nine o'clock and I'd be very happy to buy you breakfast, as a thank you."

"Well, that's very decent of you, Ralph, I might well do that if I don't have other plans. Now, clear off and find that love you're looking for...and shut the door behind you, there's a rotten draft in here," Martin settled down again, barricading himself in as best he could with his bags that clinked and rustled as he drew them around him.

Ralph ran back through the square and on to Cinque, bursting in through the front doors in a flurry of cold steam and scarf, "Hi, sorry, I'm Ralph," he said to a waitress hovering by the door.

"Hello, are you OK? I'm Imogen. Do you have a reservation with us?" she said.

"No, I don't have a reservation, I was hoping that Sam was here."

"It's too late," Dawa Singh said as he emerged through the double doors from the kitchen. "I believe you had a reservation at seven o'clock, but it is too late now, sir. Thank you, Imogen, I'll take it from here," he drew himself to his full considerable height and took Ralph's arm, steering him back on to the street.

Ralph squirmed, trying to release Dawa's steely grip, "Wait, wait, you don't understand, I was just late. I'm sorry."

"You had your chance and you didn't take it, that is all," Dawa effortlessly moved Ralph closer to the door and pulled it open. "Please, do not make a fuss."

"Why not? I've never made a fuss in my life, but now I want to make a fuss," he said as he struggled against Dawa's strength. He took hold of the edge of the door with both hands and hung on with all his might as he was pulled through, "Please, Dawa, just let me see Sam."

"He does not wish to see you. Please let go of the door, Ralph."

Ralph fought to stay attached, "I know I was supposed to meet him at seven, but this guy, Martin, said

285

I had another chance, although I've had quite a few, I know, but I think this may be my *last* chance. Am I making any sense at all?"

Dawa was straining to remove Ralph, "Not a great deal. Look, I need to serve other guests, please go." He took Ralph by the waistband of his jeans and lifted him off the ground, so he was more or less horizontal, but still holding on to the door by his fingertips.

"Don't make me fight you, Dawa" Ralph said in desperation.

"I would not recommend that," Dawa said as he pulled Ralph further into the street, the door slowly closing onto his fingers.

"Aaargh," Ralph yelled, wriggling in one last attempt to free himself. Then a hand appeared around the door and held it steady.

"Ralph, what are you doing to Dawa?" Sam said, through the glass of the door.

Ralph, still held at full length in the air, panted, "I think you'll find it's more what he is doing to me."

"Please go away."

"No, I won't. I really need to talk to you, to explain."

"I have nothing to say, I waited for you. I trusted you, again. That's all. That's the end."

"But it isn't, honestly, I can explain...but, do you think I could do it whilst being vertical? My shoulders are about to leave their sockets."

Sam paused, then said to Dawa, "Put him down."

Ralph found himself being lowered gently to the ground. Dawa stood for a moment and looked at Sam, then went back inside to restore some calm to the curious diners who had gathered to watch the unexpected cabaret.

"Ralph, please don't cause a scene...well, more of a scene. Go away. You know I need to trust people and you let me down. It's over, just move on."

"I can't move on," Ralph said from his position on his knees at the bottom of the steps. "You need to listen."

Sam walked up the street away from the prying eyes peering through the windows of his restaurant, "What I *need* is to be able to trust someone, preferably someone who is not married."

Ralph went after him, "And I need to be able to trust that you are not going to run away before asking a simple question and finding out the truth," he said, the pain in his stiff fingers stoking his anger.

Sam didn't turn to Ralph, "What question?"

"The other night, here, when I said I was married, you just disappeared. You didn't ask why I hadn't told you about my marriage. You didn't let me explain that I had run away from it, that we're separated and she knows I'm gay and am never going back. You just needed to ask a question and stay put, then none of this would have happened."

Sam turned on him, "So, this is my fault, is it?"

"Yes. No. It's both our faults. I know you've been hurt before, I know you're scared..."

"I told you about what happened to me and I thought you were different, but apparently not," Sam leaned against the corner of the restaurant building, his arms firmly crossed and dark red cap pulled low over his eyes. "Every promise that was ever made to me was broken; my dad said he'd always be there for me and he wasn't. My crush at school said he'd keep our secret, but he told the world about it. Steve, the lawyer, just lied from beginning to end, and you weren't at the tower when Dawa said you had begged me to be there."

Ralph stood on the curb looking up the street at Sam, "But I didn't break my promise, I was just late. I went to the tower, but you'd gone...and, I know, that's not your fault, but it's not mine either. Auntie B disappeared today, we had to track her down and I went to Eastbourne to bring her back. That's why I wasn't there, not because I don't love you. I didn't break my promise."

Sam looked at Ralph, "What did you say?"

"Auntie B got lost, but she's home now - Anna drove us back."

"No, after that."

"Oh, well, I think I said, I didn't turn up because I didn't love you. That bit?"

"That's what I thought...a double negative," Sam mumbled.

Ralph stood on the pavement and shivered. Neither he or Sam moved, they were alone and the only thing between them was a few metres of pavement and tiny, swirling snowflakes that had started to fall. Ralph couldn't tell whether Sam's eyes, in the shadow of his cap, were full of anger or hurt, but he took a step forwards.

"If you say 'sorry', I'm not sure what I might do," Sam said, looking Ralph straight in the eye.

"I won't...except...bugger, I had planned exactly what to say and it started with sorry," Ralph scratched his head and felt the snowflakes laying damp in his hair. "OK, look, I'll just tell you the truth. All my life I've been afraid, but since coming here I'm getting braver. Braver and more *me*, every day. But that process has only just started, so I may have met you a couple of days too early."

Sam muttered, "Maybe a week."

"The thing is, we've both been scared for too long, but that's no way to live. I feared telling the world who I was, but now I have I won't go back. Sam, I've learnt that you can't spend your life worrying about what other people are going to say about you. Your life is *your* story, not theirs. You need to take it back. You need to decide how it ends, or at least what the next chapter is going to be. I am not going to let fear ruin my life anymore and I'm going to do something about it. That's why I've been thrown around half the roads in Sussex at ninety miles an hour, nearly getting killed, then belting round Rye like a lunatic trying to find you and fighting Dawa Singh."

"You weren't really fighting him, he was carrying you out of the restaurant by your trousers."

"That's true, but I would have fought him if I'd let go of the door. I was prepared to."

"Really? You'd have fought Dawa for me?".

"Yes, of course," Ralph nodded and took a small step forward. "You know the thing I was most scared of tonight?"

"What?" Sam said.

"That if I couldn't find you, someone else might get to kiss you and not me," with a courage that felt new to him, Ralph closed the gap between them, took Sam's face in both hands and kissed him passionately, then carefully stepped back again.

Sam looked at him, but before he could speak the sound of a car made them both turn. It was the grubby car with a tell-tale dent in its back door and the thug grinning in the front seat. As it jerked to a halt, they both stepped back, bumping into the restaurant wall behind them.

"Well, well, well, it's my lucky day," the thug said, jumping out of the car and standing unsteadily in front of them with an open can of cider in his emaciated hand.

"Now, listen..." Sam began.

"No shitty dog to protect you now, gay-boys? So, it's just us and my little friend," he grinned as he threw the can aside and pulled a vicious looking kitchen knife from the back of his sagging tracksuit bottoms.

As he leered at the blade and back at them with drunken menace in his eyes, they heard a whistling sound and a large black bin bag flew out of nowhere and landed with a clatter right in the side of the thug's head, catapulting him sideways to the ground. Ralph and Sam stared as he lay in the gutter, then a man in a long dark overcoat, a tartan hat with fur earmuffs and long grey hair dash in front of them to reclaim the bag.

"Martin?" Ralph said.

"Evening, old thing," he said, picking up the bag that clunked as if it contained something heavy and metal. "I think we should take the opportunity to exit stage right, don't you, gentlemen?" Martin set off with a loping run, followed by Ralph and Sam. They ducked into a doorway in the shadows at the end of the street and looked back to see if they were being followed, but the thug still lay on the wet ground, snow beginning to settle on his back. Then the driver's door opened and a thin young woman wearily got out, moved round the bonnet of the car and prodded the body with her foot. She bent down and pulled him upright by the scruff of his hoody and leant him, groaning, against the front wheel of the car. She picked up the knife, looked around and then dropped it casually down a sewer grate at the side of the road. Finally, she opened the passenger door, dragged him to his feet and dumped him unceremoniously inside, then slammed the door shut and returned to the driver's seat. The car then started up and drove slowly away.

The three onlookers let out a collective sigh and Sam slid down onto the step of the doorway. Martin bent down and opened the top of his bin bag to examine any damage to its contents.

"What have you got in there? He went down like a fat kid on a see-saw," Ralph said.

"Four saucepans, a frying pan and an eight-inch baking tin," Martin said.

Sam looked up, "Why?"

"When my wife asked me to leave, she said I should take whatever I could carry, so I went for the things I liked best. I'd always had a passion for cooking, so I took these. Never having had much experience of living al fresco, I realise now that perhaps it was not the most practical of choices."

"No, perhaps not, but they don't half pack a punch, so thank you."

"No need for thanks, that young toe-rag has caused me several sleepless nights in the last week alone, so it was my pleasure. He was no better at school, although the worst I could do to him there was give him detention. Sadly, we were not encouraged to hit pupils with frying pans, more's the pity."

"You were a teacher?" Sam asked.

Martin stretched his back, "I once received a card at the end of term that said, *It takes a big heart to shape little minds*, but in my case it also took a bottle of brandy a day." He then deftly collected his many bags in both hands and started to walk away, dragging the heaviest behind him, creating a sound that Ralph had first heard the day he arrived in Rye.

"The dueller's ghost!"

"What?" Sam said.

Ralph ignored him, "Wait, Martin, do you tend to move around the town a lot? At night?"

Martin turned back, "Usually, yes, partly to keep warm, but more often to keep out of the way of young scroats like that young fellow. Why? I hope I haven't ever disturbed you."

"No, not at all. I think I may have heard you, but...look have you got somewhere to stay tonight?" Ralph said.

"I believe the Waldorf has vacancies this evening, so fear not, old thing. I shall see you for breakfast, if your kind invitation still stands."

"Of course, but..."

"Good night, gents," Martin said as he strolled down the high street with extraordinary dignity, his bags of pots and pans clinking around him.

Sam watched him go, "Who is he?"

"Another one of Anna's ghosts, I just met him up by the tower. He told me about love having more chances than anything else..."

"Love again?" Sam said, looking down at his feet.

"Yes, that's why I'm here," he turned, hesitated for a moment then crouched down and removed Sam's cap. He looked into his eyes, "Listen, I'm quite likely to be hard work, I can't deny that, and I have no idea whether I'm even worth it, but I'm really hoping that you will give me another chance."

Sam shook his head, "Things always seem to get in the way..."

"...but there's nothing in the way now."

"I'm not straight-forward either. I may have beautiful eyes, but I'm damaged goods..."

Ralph laughed, "I thought we agreed they were striking?"

"No, we took a vote, remember? And beautiful won."

"OK, fair enough."

"Seriously, though, I've got a long way to go before I stop worrying about being plastered across the papers or the internet, but I am going to try, I promise."

"People are always going to be interested in others who look like they have more than they do, and then they'll try and bring them down - but it really has nothing to do with us. We are going to be way too busy holding hands and dancing in the snow to worry about them."

"Are we?"

"We are."

"Dancing?"

"Yes, dancing."

"Where?"

"Here," Ralph stood back and held out his hands to Sam. "Just how brave are you feeling, Sam Ross, second most eligible bachelor in Britain?"

Sam hesitated, glancing quickly at the diners in the windows of his restaurant and ruffled his hair, now free of the cap, "Try me," Sam said.

So Ralph took him in his arms and they danced slowly in the middle of the street, as if the world turning white around them was theirs alone.

CHAPTER 30

The end of an addiction, Christmas fairies and Sleeping Beauty.

I rene finished throwing salt on to the pavement outside The Cookery to clear the remaining snow, "It's not as bad as I thought. When I looked last night on my way to my midnight tinkle, it was coming down quite heavy then."

She locked the door and came to check on Anna, who was trying to thicken a turkey and coconut milk mixture for her new pies without much success, "Can't you chuck in some mashed potato? That'd soak up all the juice."

"I think I've got it, thanks, Irene," Anna puffed as she continued to beat the sauce furiously. "The corn flour should do the trick, we just need to be patient and keep the lumps out."

"We'd better not open this morning then if you don't want any lumps coming in," Irene quipped. She was in a good mood as she was wearing her annual Christmas jumper for the first time, which would now remain in place until the end of December. It was bright green and displayed Santa clinging to a pole, while around her stomach ran the words *North Pole Dancer*.

There was a knock on the door, so Irene hitched up her bra and straightened Santa, who had been sent sideways by her readjustment and went to unlock it. Seeing Ralph and Sam outside, she said, "Here are the Christmas Fairies come to help," and opened the door.

"Pardon?" Ralph said. "I missed that."

"Probably for the best," called Anna. "Irene, I'm going to have to dock your wages next time you discriminate."

"I can't even spell it let alone have a crack at it," Irene grumbled. "Don't tread slush across my floor, you'll cause a hazard."

"Well, look at you two," Anna cooed. "I take it Sam was still at the tower last night? Tell me everything. Was there moonlight? What did you say?"

Ralph looked at Sam, "Well, it's a long story..."

"Great, I want to hear it all. Here stir this, my arm's about to fall off," she handed Ralph the spoon.

"Sam's the cook, not me."

"Yes, but he looks exhausted, what have you been doing to him? Actually, don't answer that question." She looked into Sam's tired eyes, "Have you forgiven him? He doesn't want to be married, honestly."

Sam grinned, running his hands through his hair, "Yes, I get that now."

"There's something different about you. Oh, you've got hair, I've never seen it before."

"He made me throw my cap away," Sam said, pointing at Ralph.

"We're making a few changes with our lives," Ralph added.

"Well, it suits you...both of you," Anna's voice was thick with emotion. "This is so amazing, you are made for each other. Tell me what happened?"

"Actually, we don't have time to tell you everything, because we want to come for breakfast and bring a guest who should be arriving any minute. To cut a traumatic story short; Sam wasn't at the tower and I think I've twisted the hinges on the door to the restaurant because it won't shut properly."

Sam continued, "Dawa Singh needs to see an osteopath for his back, we got attacked by the chav again, this time with a huge kitchen knife, then he made me dance in the snow with him..."

Anna's eyes were wide, "You had to dance with the knife man? In the snow?"

"No, with Ralph. I danced with Ralph. Why would I dance with the knife guy?"

"I don't know, that would have been strange."

"I saw an osteopath with my kidneys once and he said I was, *beyond his scope*. Cheeky devil," Irene said, before disappearing into the loo with a mulled wine scented air-freshener.

Ralph, still stirring the sauce, turned to Anna, "Look, we're about to bring in a homeless teacher for breakfast who has saucepans in his bin bags, is that OK? I'm paying."

"Have I ever told you that since you got to Rye, you have been getting weirder and weirder?"

"I think you may have done. This is getting thicker, I think," Ralph stepped away and handed back the spoon.

"I'll be back in a while then, with Martin."

Irene returned from the toilet just as Ralph disappeared out onto the street, "He didn't last long...mind you, that's the story with most men."

Sam laughed, "He'll be back in a minute. Any chance of a coffee, I need the caffeine this morning."

"Sit down, I'll start up the engines," Irene said, gingerly approaching the coffee machine. "What's the matter with you?"

Sam settled himself at a table near the kitchen, "After everything last night we went back to the restaurant and spent the evening chatting in the bar. Ralph told me about his past and his wife, then I filled him in a bit more about my bizarre family and, before we knew it, it was two in the morning, there were three empty bottles of wine on the table and Ralph was fast asleep with his head on my lap."

"Aww, that's just so lovely," Anna said.

"Hm, the thing was that Ralph was knackered after chasing Auntie B and then trying to find me, so I didn't want to disturb him. Besides, he was sleeping so peacefully, he looks amazing when he's asleep...anyway, I sat there and waited for him to wake up."

Irene was incredulous, "All night?"

"Well, what was left of it. I think I nodded off a few times, but not often. So, we've come here for coffee and to meet up with Martin."

Anna took the saucepan off the heat to allow it to cool, "Which one's he? The knife-man or the homeless guy?"

"The homeless guy - he was amazing, he got rid of the moron with the knife for us. Thanks, Irene," he said, as she put a steaming mug of coffee in front of him.

"Well, I'm just so pleased for you both. I knew you were made for each other," Anna said. "I always wanted something like that, someone special."

"For goodness sake, how many times do I need to tell you? You do alright as you are," Irene said as she wiped down the counter.

"Don't you miss your husband, Irene?" Anna asked.

"I do not, that's why I've got jigsaws," Irene said, looking at Anna. "What are you doing now?"

Anna had taken her phone from her apron pocket and was typing a message, "Hmm? Just sending a text."

Irene shot across the kitchen, "Oh, no you don't," and swiftly took the phone out of Anna's hands and threw it in the microwave, shutting the door and standing in front of it. "I'll press the cook button if you so much as touch that door, I swear I will."

"What on earth is the matter with you?" Anna said, as Irene led her out of the kitchen and pushed her down onto a chair next to Sam.

"I'm not having this," she said as she headed for the door, which an elderly couple had just pushed open, "Sorry, we are shut for an emergency, build a snowman and come back later." The couple were propelled back on to the street and the door locked behind them before they knew what had hit them.

Irene stood with her back against the door her arms held out blocking the exit, "I'm staging an intermission."

Sam looked at Irene, "I don't think you mean an intermission, unless you fancy an ice cream or some popcorn."

"What do I mean, then?" Irene asked.

"An intervention, maybe?" Sam said.

Irene pulled another chair up to the table and sat down, "That's the one, yes, an intervention."

"Why?" Sam asked, his lack of sleep not helping him make sense of the situation.

"She was going to text that big bloke, Jim. Weren't you?"

Anna hesitated, "Actually, I was..."

"I knew it, why? I've told you before..."

"It's not what you think..."

"Of course, it is," Irene sighed. "It's always the same. You are addicted to romance or your silly idea of romance. It's not good for you. Tell her," she said to Sam.

"Well..." Sam started to say.

"Exactly," Irene continued. "You are a busy woman, with a full life, nice friends – odd, but alright - a good little business that you have built all on your own, you employ staff – not always properly appreciated, but you pay our wages - and I know you have a head full of plans for expanding this place that you never stop talking about. What on earth makes you think you need anyone else to interfere with that? It's been a long time since women have needed men to make things happen. Tell her I'm right."

"Actually..." Sam said.

"You see? Let me ask you this," Irene waved her hand in the air. "Which parts of this business or your life are you prepared to give up for a man you hardly know? Because if you go out and, by some bloomin' miracle, find one, something will have to give to make room for him."

Anna smiled, "None of it. I don't want to give up any of it, in fact, I want more. It's all too precious to compromise a bit of what I have."

Irene looked surprised, "Oh, right...well...good, don't

spoil it then by getting involved with some bloke like Jim, who lives hundreds of miles away with his wife."

Anna shook her head, "Irene, you're amazing and I love you, but I'm not."

Irene looked at her, "You're not what?"

"Getting involved with Jim again."

"But you were just texting him."

"I was replying to a text he sent me yesterday morning. He sent a message asking if I was alright and saying he missed me. I didn't know what to say, so I hadn't replied. But when we got back last night, I talked to Auntie B and she told me about her life as a girl, growing up when women had so few choices. I mean, did you know that as late as the 1980's, pubs could refuse to serve a woman if she was spending her own money?"

Irene shrugged, "I always let the man buy me a drink, they had very few uses otherwise."

"Stanley stayed with me last night and we went for a long walk to do some thinking, and I realised that I would love to be loved, but I don't *need* love in order to be happy. It would just be a bonus really and I am certainly not going to let anyone interfere with the life I've built for myself. Then just now, when I saw that romance was back on with these two, I was so happy for you, but it didn't make me yearn for a man – I was fine about it. So, I was messaging Jim to say, although I wished him well, I was not missing him at all. I was too busy helping my rooftop family and making my life a success."

"And it is a success," Sam said. "Don't forget that you have us for support too, everyone in the Rooftop Club."

"I know and I have Irene," Anna reached out and took Irene's bony hand in hers.

"Yes, well, let's not get silly," Irene sniffed, gently taking her hand away and turning to Sam. "Did you know that your father once signed my husband's crash helmet with a felt tip pen? You have his chin. Your father's chin, not my husband's, he had no chin to speak of, but a nose like an ornamental door knocker..."

As if on cue, there was a knock on the door and they turned to see Ralph outside with a nervous looking Martin. He looked haggard and dishevelled, but a pair of expressive hands attempted to smooth his hair around his noble face. Anna came and opened the door for them and gave Ralph a long hug.

"I've only been gone a few minutes," he said.

"I know, but I just needed to do this."

"OK," Ralph said, raising his eyebrows to Sam over her head.

Anna let him go, "All done now. Come in."

Ralph stepped in from the cold, but Martin hesitated, "What is it?"

"I'm a little concerned that I'm not really suitably dressed to actually sit in a café and eat," Martin said.

Anna smiled at him., "Have you seen the way I dress?" gesturing to her Christmas robin dungarees under a Christmas Elf apron. "All comers are welcome here."

So, Martin stepped into the café, insisting on washing his hands and laying a newspaper on the chair before he would sit. Anna prepared the food and Irene moved the charity collecting tins into the fridge and hovered with an air freshener. Once they were all tucking into their full English breakfasts they chatted easily and even Irene pulled up a chair, when she learned that Martin had been an art teacher at her children's former school.

"My history is not a distinguished one," Martin said, wiping his grey whiskers with a Christmas napkin. "After a long career as a teacher and brandy drinker, I was preparing for retirement when some ill-advised investments went down and conversely my brandy intake went up, leading to the loss of my job. My wife took this as a long-awaited opportunity to strike, and I was ejected from our house and our marriage. I had a few friends with available sofas, but one doesn't want to outstay one's welcome, so I'd soon run out of furniture, and...well, you know the rest."

"Where did you stay last night?" Ralph asked.

"The Waldorf had some sort of event on and was fully booked, however, the bus station provided a glamorous alternative. Sadly, the facilities were a little lacking; no bar, no dry roasted peanuts or turn-down service. Still, the plus side of all this is that even if the bus station did have a bar, I couldn't afford the booze. I have, in fact, been sober for nearly three months. The irony is that as a result I have never felt better, whilst simultaneously never feeling more miserable. That, dear things, is life, is it not?"

Irene leaned across to Anna, waving a Charlie Chaplin pepper pot at her, "Just so you know, my kidneys are going to struggle to handle the table clearing up to Christmas, so we are going to need some help. We need someone like him," she pointed Mr Chaplin at Martin. "Just saying."

Anna smiled, "Irene, I am seeing a whole new warm and fuzzy side to you today."

"I don't know what you are talking about," Irene said, getting up to welcome some new customers. "If you've got wet feet don't walk heavily or you can tip toe, I'm not mopping all day."

"Ah, that's the Irene we know and love, she's back," Anna sighed. "But she's right, we will need some more help over Christmas."

"Me too, I had no idea it was going to be as busy as it is and I could really do with an extra pair of hands at busy times. Would you be in a position to help us out?" Ralph asked Martin.

Martin looked overcome and wiped his face, "Well, I could start tomorrow, if that was convenient for you both."

"Perfect," Anna said. "That's going to help me enormously. Why don't you start with me in here, for breakfast – food comes with the deal, by the way - then you can go back and forth between The Cookery and The Bookery for the different busy periods. Does that work for you, Ralph?"

"Sounds perfect," he said.

Martin looked at them, "You are good people and I will not let you down."

"That, I do not doubt," Ralph said. "We're all sorted then."

"There's just one thing," Martin said, shifting in his chair. "There is a local charity that runs a hostel for people who have run out of luck like myself. They require a peppercorn rent each week, just a few pounds, but they also require a written statement of some sort to show that you have the where-with-all to pay and are able to cover the costs."

"Right, that's easy," Irene said, appearing at the table again. "You two need to clear-off upstairs, get that computer logged-up and sort out some paperwork for the hostel saying you're paying him. Come on, chop, chop."

Ralph and Anna did as they were told and headed for the door to Anna's flat, but Irene waved her Babbacombe Model Village tea towel at them, "Oy, what are we going to do with sleeping beauty here?" She pointed to Sam, who was sitting back in his chair, his chin resting on his chest and snoring quietly in a deep, contented sleep.

CHAPTER 31

The terms of a date, pudding
races and belonging.

The next morning Martin was at the door of
The Cookery even before Anna had made it
downstairs. She barely recognised him, he was
cleanshaven, freshly showered and his long grey hair
held back in an elastic band at the nape of his neck.
He was wearing some rather too large raspberry coloured corduroy trousers and a cardigan with blue suede
panels down each side of the long zip.

"I apologise for my somewhat colourful appearance,
but Zandra Rhodes was on duty at the hostel's second-
hand clothing cupboard last night and was convinced
that these were my colours," he said.

"She was right, you look amazing. Colours are my
thing, so you'll fit in perfectly. I love your shoes as well,"
she was looking down at a very fine pair of brown leather brogues.

"Ah well, these are the models own, as they say," he explained, grinning. "When my wife insisted that I left my home I filled some bags with my saucepans, but also found room for my shoes. I think the brandy may have had something to do with my choices, but I have recently found myself grateful for both."

"Bloody hell," Anna exclaimed as Sam suddenly appeared behind Martin in the doorway. "That's a sight to boost my sausage roll sales!"

Martin turned to see Sam smiling sheepishly as he stood shivering in nothing but Ralph's green shop apron and a pair of trainers, "Good lord, is everything alright, old thing?"

"Sorry, it's just...well, I'm trying to make breakfast for Ralph before he has to open up, but he hasn't got any eggs. Actually, he hasn't got anything except food for Stanley, his fridge is like an arctic wasteland."

Anna waved him in, "Get inside, before someone sees you or you get arrested for indecent apron exposure," she shot into the kitchen to find some eggs. "I thought you did everything you could not to stand out in the crowd? Now look at you."

"Hmm, Ralph's got me on a new regime, to try and worry less about what people think."

Martin looked him up and down, "Is there a chance you may have gone too far, too fast?"

* * *

Over the next couple of weeks Martin proved himself to be invaluable to both The Bookery and The Cookery. He and Irene became a formidable team, with Martin using his considerable charm to smooth out some of the spikey excesses of Irene's customer service skills. During quiet periods in the café Martin joined Ralph in The Bookery, with the erudite art teacher proving to be a knowledgeable, easy-going guide for young and old. Ralph was soon able to leave Martin alone in the shop while he ran errands and managed the arrival of new stock down in the basement. Stanley contributed by continuing to be a great attraction, especially for the children of Rye. Ralph had a pen and ink sketch Martin had drawn of Stanley printed onto cloth book-bags, which became a big seller, requiring rapid reprints twice in just a few weeks.

The downside of the busy season was that as Ralph finished work, Sam was just gearing up for his long evening service in the restaurant. Given the troubled start to their romance, they both agreed that being forced into building their relationship slowly was not such a bad thing. However, Ralph soon found himself happily spending more and more time at the restaurant. In the end, once Dawa Singh had apologised for waving him around by the trousers and Ralph had apologised for stretching the door hinges, they began to work together in harmony to meet and greet the customers that flocked to the restaurant in their Christmas finery. Dawa could not be persuaded to join in with the festive theme and remained immaculate in his single colour suit and turban combinations. That is until, after days of badgering from both Ralph and Sam, he agreed to wear a small, striped candy cane badge on the well-pressed lapel of his suit.

As Christmas grew closer, more and more shimmering trees went up in the ancient squares around town, in time for the traditional Rye Christmas Festival. One evening buskers and stilt walkers heralded the arrival of Father Christmas himself, who started the annual Christmas High Street Races with manic Santa relays and highly competitive pudding races. It meant that all the shops, cafes and restaurants were full, day after day. Ralph had never known anything like it, he extended his opening hours, but he and Martin were still rushed off their feet and Stanley lay exhausted in the window at the excitement of it all.

Cinque was hitting its peak season when a powerful run of flu raged through the waiting staff, even Dawa succumbed to it, leaving the restaurant struggling to cope. As Sam contemplated the only option that seemed available, to cancel some of the bookings and serve fewer diners, Ralph popped his head around the kitchen door, "Evening, Chef."

Sam looked up, "Hey, how much money have you got?"

Ralph frowned, "About six quid, why?"

"Is that enough to buy a sheep farm in Alice Springs?"

"Only a very, very small one, why?"

"I don't think I want to be a chef anymore," he lent on the kitchen counter and put his head in his hands. Ralph came up and put his arms round him, "You haven't got the flu too, have you?"

"No, I'm just knackered. We're two down in the kitchen, three waiters short and no Dawa to hold it all together. We've done another full house at lunch and already have a waiting list for tonight's sitting and it'll be nose to nipple in there right through until after New Year. I was just thinking, Australia is a long way away from this sodding kitchen and I reckon I'd look alright in one of those hats with corks hanging off it. You grew up on a farm, you must know about sheep?"

"Hm, well, I know they have a hoof in each corner and lots of cotton wool, but after that I wouldn't be much help," Ralph said, pulling Sam up so he could look into his tired eyes. "On a scale of one to seventeen and three-quarters, how much more would you love me if I could solve your problems?"

Sam smiled, "Eighteen and a bit."

"Correct answer. Come with me," Ralph took his hand and pulled him out of the kitchen into the restaurant's reception area.

"Ralph, I don't have time, honestly..." but he stopped as he saw three people lined up in front of him. Martin and Joe smiled at him, but Rosie, the goth Saturday girl from The Cookery, couldn't be bothered to smile until she was on the payroll.

"Ta da! Meet the new members of your team," Ralph announced. "Martin is an experienced cook, all be it in his home kitchen, but he comes with his own set of only slightly dented pots and pans."

"Hello, old thing," Martin said, stepping forward shyly. "Ralph said you were in need of an extra pair of hands in the kitchen and I'd love the work if you have it. Any night...in fact, every night would suit me. I seem to have mislaid my reference from the Ritz, but they were very pleased with my mashed potatoes, if that's any help."

Sam laughed, "Martin, when can you start?"

"Well, if I cancel my yoga class and can find somewhere to park the Bentley, would now be convenient?"

"Absolutely, head straight into the kitchen, ask Paul

to find you a uniform. Thank you, so much."

Ralph brought Rosie forward, "Sam meet Rosie. She is now on her Christmas holidays from college and has extensive waitressing experience from The Cookery, trained under the strict apron of Irene, The Terrible."

"She frightens me," Rosie said.

Sam grinned, "You and me both."

"Rosie is looking for as many shifts as are available, as she is saving up for a giant magpie tattoo on her back," Ralph said to Sam with a smile.

"Really? How big?" Sam asked.

"I want each shoulder blade to be a wing and the beak to be coming up my neck," Rosie said with enthusiasm and a tiny smile that lit up her face under the funereal make-up.

"Sounds amazing," Sam said. "So, rule one, clean fingernails and no chipped nail varnish."

Rosie held out her small hands to show ten newly painted black nails.

"Excellent. Rule two, smiling is required at all times, but it will buy you a magpie tattoo if you can keep it up from now until January."

Rosie paused, then broke into a smile showing a fine set of teeth encased in shining silver braces. Sam and Ralph looked at each other and started to applaud Rosie, "Congratulations, you just got yourself a job, Rosie."

"Oh, there is one thing, I don't want to be called Rosie here. I hate it, I want to be called by my Klingon name. Irene wouldn't let me, 'cos she knows my mum."

Sam hesitated, "OK...so, what would you like to be called?"

"Tholkog," Rosie said and stared at the two men. "But you can call me Thol, if you want."

"Fair enough. Imogen!" Sam called and she appeared from the bar behind them. "Imogen meet Tholkog, who we can call Thol if we want to. She is starting work here tonight, can you show her the ropes and find her a Cinque shirt, please?"

"Hey, Tholkog," Imogen said, tying a lose strand of hair back into her ponytail.

"Hey, Kred'onn," Rosie said, breaking out her rare smile again.

Imogen took Rosie by the hand, turning to Sam as she led her back to the bar, "I used to babysit for her and we watched old Star Trek episodes back-to-back for most of the time."

Joe stepped forward, "Imogen, how are things?"

Imogen looked briefly over her shoulder at him, "Busy," she said without breaking her stride.

"Ouch," Joe said, shrugging at Sam and Ralph. "She's hates me, doesn't she?"

"Absolutely."

"Totally."

"So, Sam," Joe said, rubbing his hands together. "I understand that Dawa has left a gap in the hospitality sector for someone with my particular skill set. You need a hand, my friend?"

"Really? Are you sure? I mean, yes, please, that'd be amazing," Sam said. "But what about your social life in the evenings?"

"Who was it once said, don't believe everything you read in the press? Oh yes, you," Joe smiled and took off his jacket, revealing a smart black shirt, that remained just this side of decent as it stretched over his toned physique. "I'm all yours for as long as you need me, once Let's Screw is closed in the evenings, of course."

Sam gave him a hug, "You are a life saver. Are you OK to work with Ralph tonight? He's hosted loads of times now, so he can show you what's what. But if you don't like it or whatever, just say, I won't be offended."

"Boys, it's fine," Joe said, laying a hand on each of their shoulders. "Look, it's a whole new audience for me and my finely honed comedy skills - of course, I'm going to like it."

They both groaned, "I did hesitate before asking him," Ralph said, apologetically.

Joe turned and made his way behind the small welcome desk, "Hey, the waitress said to me, 'You wanna box for your leftovers?', I said, 'No, but I'll arm wrestle you for them!'"

Ralph looked at Sam, "I'm so sorry, I was only trying to help."

Sam laughed, "I know, any port in a storm, eh? Right, I'm off to introduce Martin to the European roast potato mountain. Have fun, guys," he stopped at the swing door into the kitchen. "Erm, Ralph?"

Ralph hung his coat on a hook and came over to him, "Are you, OK?"

Sam smiled shyly, "You are amazing, you know that?"

"I bet you say that to all the boys."

"True, true, but I don't do this to them," and he put his hand around the back of Ralph's neck and drew him in for a long kiss.

Joe coughed, "Aren't there hygiene rules about that sort of thing in a food environment?"

But Sam didn't let Ralph go, he just swung his other hand up with two strong fingers extended towards Joe. When he released Ralph, he turned and disappeared into the kitchen. Ralph stood for a moment catching his breath and waited for his knees to regain their strength, before turning to Joe, "I think he's feeling better."

"You don't say?" Joe laughed as he flicked open the diary to see what was ahead of them.

* * *

Over the next few nights the new temporary staff members got into their stride at Cinque. Rosie enjoyed being part of a team of people around her age who accepted her for exactly who she was and her confidence soared. Martin proved to be a natural in the kitchen and he learned to plate up the starters and deserts with his own artistic flair.

Joe soon found that he too was in his element, using all the sexual charm at his disposal to woo diners from across the spectrum, with few people complaining about waiting for a table when it meant spending time with him at the bar. He also found a ready audience among the waiting staff for his endless stream of festive jokes. Every night he had a new one and they would all, boys and girls alike, hang on his every word. Except one - Imogen, the wind-power engineer.

Despite using everything he had in his canon he could not break her, she would not respond. She always stood at the outside of the group at the end of the shift, while the others gathered round him. Yet, as she kept to herself, she drew Joe's focus entirely, driving him mad, until one night he caught up with her outside the restaurant.

"Imogen? Can I ask you a question?" he said.

"It's a free country," she replied, continuing to walk as Joe came up beside her.

"What's your problem?"

"I wasn't aware I had one," she said, pleasantly. "You on the other hand have a considerable problem."

"I do?"

"Yup, me," she turned a corner abruptly, forcing Joe to misstep and scurry to catch up with her.

"What? I don't follow," he puffed.

Imogen stopped suddenly and Joe found himself backtracking to where she stood, "It's simple," she said. "You want me, badly. Just as much as I want you. Correct?" She looked at him straight in the eye, with a steady amused gaze.

"Wait, hold on, I...you...you want me?" he stammered, her directness leaving him breathless.

"Why not? But you're a player and I will not allow myself to fall under your spell and become another easy score for you."

"That is not me, you've got it all wrong."

"Really? Joe Wells, thirty-five years old. Canadian. Nephew to Evelyn Bondolfi. Owner of the pitifully titled, Let's Screw. Pierced left nipple. Acceptably pert buttocks...how am I doing?"

Joe gaped at her, "Holy shit, what are you, FBI?"

Imogen shifted her bag from one shoulder to the other, tucked her hair behind her ears and began walking again, "No, just an engineer who likes to know what she is dealing with. This a small town, don't guys like you think that women talk to each other?"

Joe watched her walk away, then lurched into action running past her, turning round and facing her, but she did not stop so he was forced to walk backwards, "Your research has one mistake, however - she's my Grandmother. I'm her grandson, not her nephew."

"Interesting. I didn't know that," she said, her brows crinkling slightly.

"To be fair, neither did I until recently, so don't beat yourself up about it."

"Thanks, I won't."

"So, you hate me because I'm a player, but you also said you want me. How does that work?"

"Watch out," Imogen said a fraction too late to stop him hitting an iron lamppost first with his shoulders and then with the back of his head. The impact knocked all the breath out of him and for a second the world turned upside down and Joe slid heavily onto the pavement.

"Are you OK?" Imogen said, sounding a note of genuine concern.

"Yep, fine. Nothing to see here. I think one of my acceptably pert buttocks just deflated on impact, but otherwise no problem," he groaned and shifted gingerly into a more comfortable position on the ground.

Imogen crouched down in front of him, "Left or right buttock?"

"Erm, left."

"Shame, that was my favourite."

Joe looked up and felt dazed by both the lamppost and this young woman, who refused to take him seriously or be in anyway impressed by him, "Would you like to go for a drink sometime?" he asked.

She smiled with real warmth for the first time, "Yes, Joe, I would love to. I thought you'd never ask. But I won't sleep with you, not yet. It'll be one drink and I will pay and we will see if we like each other, then we will go home – to our own homes. If we do decide we like each other enough to have another drink together then you can pay for the drinks next time. Let me be clear, if we take things further, we will be exclusive until we both agree it's over, whenever that may be. Then you will be released back into the wild to do as you want."

As Joe thought how to respond, he knew that his restless energy that had been searching for a place to land was entirely focused on this woman and her strength drew him in like a magnet.

"Is this how things work now, people agree terms before the first date?"

"Not usually, but you are not a usual man, Joe Wells, and I am certainly not your usual woman."

He shook his head, "You can say that again."

"If you agree to those terms, then I am prepared to believe that you belong in a different bracket to those men whose brains are nestled in their Spiderman underpants. So, think it over," Imogen ran her finger briefly along his bearded chin, before setting off and leaving him sitting alone on the icy pavement.

It took two more shifts at Cinque for him to convince her that he would accept her deal and abide by it, then and only then did she go for a drink with him. This led to a second date, when Joe did indeed buy the drinks, then to dinner, twice. Then and only then did Imogen slip into his bed. After that, although he still charmed the customers and the corny jokes continued to flow, it was clear that he was happiest at this strong, clever, witty woman's side. Joe also knew for the first time what it was to belong somewhere and together with someone - and he liked how it felt.

CHAPTER 32

The season of open-heartedness,
gifts and tiny velvet slippers.

I t was decided that Christmas Day for the Rooftop
Club was going to be a group affair. Joe had offered
to host at his place by the beach, as Imogen would
be spending the day with her parents. Martin had been
persuaded to attend and would wear his new Christmas
snowman jumper, knitted for him by Irene, which had a
small kitchen funnel attached to the front, as she'd lost
the plastic carrot she was planning to use for a nose.

With the restaurant closed for the day, Sam was
happy not to cook and he and Ralph were going together. However, Ralph had made it clear that once the
pudding was served and the crackers pulled, he was taking Sam away for a special treat as a part of his present.
He had arranged for them to stay the night in the very
best room at The Mermaid Inn. Just them, champagne,
the log fire and an antique four-poster bed - a much-

needed time for them to spend together and alone. Like Sam, Anna was also happy to not be cooking on the big day and would be bringing Auntie B, under the strict understanding that speed limits would be adhered to the entire way.

On Christmas Auntie B insisted that the moment the shops were shut everyone should gather on the roof terrace for a short while. Anna brought Stanley up, ahead of their now regular evening strolls and he was wearing a rather fetching purple tinsel collar, which matched the colour of the enormous mohair cardigan she was wearing that stretched from the back of her neck to the heels of her shoes and was fastened at the front with plastic buttons in the shape of Santa's reindeer. Joe and Ralph quickly showered and changed, looking dashing all in black, ready to go over to Cinque for the full-to-bursting evening sitting, but Sam had been excused as he really needed to be at the restaurant to hold things together.

By the time they had all arrived, the sky was deep blue and a brilliant moon poked its face out from behind a foreboding wall of cloud. Auntie B made sure that they were all gathered around the table and she sat in her usual chair with a large box beside her, where she could easily reach it. Joe opened a bottle of pink champagne and poured it into vintage teacups, brought up from The Cookery.

"There you are, Grandma...jeez, I still love saying that," Joe said, sitting beside her and giving her a kiss on the cheek.

"You have no idea how long I have waited to hear you say it," she said. After returning from Eastbourne, she had sat Joe down and told him the story of her life and the truth about his mother. Both shed tears of sorrow and of joy, but the bond that was already strong between them became unbreakable that night, and Joe's roots in Rye grew that little bit deeper.

Now, as she sat with her grandson beside her and the rest of the Rooftop Club around her, she felt almost total peace, something she had not experienced for a very long time. She intended to enjoy it for the rest of her life, along with her position at the head of this, her own little family.

She tapped her cup on the edge of the table to call for silence, "I know you have so many other things to do, so thank you for indulging an old lady, but I wanted to take a few moments to give you your Christmas gifts," she said.

"Presents tomorrow," Joe protested. "Bring them with you and we'll put them under the tree."

Auntie B shook her head, "If you don't mind, I would rather do it tonight, here. This rooftop has been a very special place for all of us and especially for me. Hearing you all coming and going, living life to the full, has been a joy to me in my last years. So, I wanted to say thank you all, tonight, up here above the rooftops."

She reached down and felt her way into the box and pulled out a glittering red envelope, with a single sprig of holly attached to one corner. She held it out, "Anna, this is for you."

"Thank you, Auntie B. Shall I open it now?" Anna said, taking it.

"Yes, please do."

Anna turned the large envelope over and slid her fingers under the flap. Inside was another smaller envelope, which was blank and the back was open. She turned it over, opened it and pulled out a Christmas card decorated with a simple wreath of holly, ivy and tiny red apples. Above the picture, in a flowing script, were printed three words, 'Merry Christmas, Mother.' She opened the card, to see that it was blank inside and looked back at Auntie B, "I don't understand. You're not trying to tell me that you are *my* mother too, are you?"

Auntie B laughed, "Good heavens, no. You have a mother, who is missing her daughter this Christmas. A mother who needs you, just as much as you need her. It is time to show her the woman you have become and make her as proud of you as I am. It is time for you to forgive her, to bring her back from the shadows of your life. Promise me you will."

Anna nodded and clumsily tried to put the card back in the envelope, her vision blurred with tears, "Thank you," is all she could say.

"Now, Ralph, these are for you," Auntie B reached out and laid her hand on two large, narrow, square packages wrapped in candy-striped paper. "You will have to come and collect them yourself, I'm afraid."

Ralph moved round to the box and lifted out the parcels. He knelt beside Auntie B and pulled the paper off what he found to be two white picture frames, identical to the ones that he had in the shop surrounding her paintings, "Aren't these yours?" he said.

"They were mine, but Joe cleverly took my paintings out of them, so now they are yours. It is time for you to express yourself again, Ralph. You once said that when you were a child you painted to escape, but now you are finally free your painting can take on a whole new life. I want you to fill these frames with whatever your heart sees and your brush directs. Promise me you will."

Ralph leant across and hugged Auntie B, "I promise, thank you."

"So, that just leaves Joe. My restless Joe, who seems of late to have become a lot less restless," Auntie B said, placing her hand on his shoulder.

"Hey, look, I really don't need anything, not this year. You've already given me the best present by letting me be your Grandson," he said.

"That is very sweet, but you will learn that Grandmothers always get their way. Your present is in two parts. First, you get to tell us a Christmas joke, without interruption, complaint or criticism...and we will laugh. Won't we?" She said sternly to Ralph and Anna.

"Yes, of course," they mumbled.

Joe's face lit up, "Your spontaneous enthusiasm moves me, guys, it really does. Right, hold on, which one to choose? I need to pick a doozy...let's see, 'Santa Jaws'? No, erm, how about 'Claus-trophobia'? Nope."

"Don't push your luck," Anna hissed.

"OK, OK, I've got it," Joe rubbed his hands together. "This'll sleigh you...that's just a warm-up, that's not the joke. So, what does Santa do with over-weight elves? He sends them to the elf farm!"

Auntie B giggled with genuine glee, which made Ralph and Anna both laugh for real too. Joe was beside himself, "I knew that would be a winner. I was saving it for Christmas Day, so I'm going to have to bring out the big guns tomorrow."

"Don't think you'll be treated so kindly tomorrow," Ralph laughed. "Normal rules apply after tonight."

Once they had quietened down, Auntie B continued, "There is a gift in the box for you as well, Joe. Please take it out."

Joe reached to the bottom of the box and pulled out a small square present, wrapped in beautiful soft, golden tissue paper. He laid it carefully on the table in front of Auntie B.

"This is something that has been the most precious comfort to me, but it is not mine. It was for Ginger, although I was never able to give it to her. Now it is yours."

Joe took the parcel and carefully tore the paper, revealing the white frame, brilliant greens and shining gold details of the painting that had hung over her mantelpiece. The painting that Auntie B had created on the day that her daughter was laid to rest thousands of miles away from Rye.

"But I can't take this..." Joe began.

"You can and you will. It was for your mother; I was merely the custodian. I could not put it into her hands..." she paused as her delicate voice broke. "So, now you have it and I hope you will treasure it. Please promise me you will."

"Always," Joe said, gently tracing the painted surface of the picture with his fingers. "It will now be my most precious thing, until I hand it on to my son or my daughter."

"I would like that very much," Auntie B said.

❊ ❊ ❊

When the champagne was finished, Ralph hugged Auntie B and Anna before taking his empty frames back to his flat above The Bookery. When he got to Cinque he stood for a moment looking through the glass panel in the door to the kitchen and saw Sam in complete control of his domain and his team of cooks. He couldn't believe that after so long he had not only found his place, but he had also found someone with whom he could truly just be himself. Sam turned and saw Ralph through the glass and smiled. Ralph's head spun for a moment as he saw an image of a painting in a white frame, a painting of Sam.

Sam came through the door, "You look like your blushing," he said, putting one hand on Ralph's cheek. "What are you thinking about?"

Ralph looked down, "You, but you were...never mind, it's embarrassing. I was just being an..."

"Idiot?" Sam finished. "I doubt it. Tell me later, when we're alone. Gotta get on," he kissed Ralph gently on the lips and returned to the kitchen. Ralph turned, laughing to himself as he headed off to the warmth and frenzy of another night in his extraordinary new life.

✽ ✽ ✽

Anna left Stanley sleepily listening to a carol service on the radio and slipped out of her flat. Twenty minutes later her little pink car drew up opposite a narrow three-storey house in the neighbouring town of Winchelsea. She sat for a long time in the car looking at the building. No Christmas lights, no shining tree, just a soft glow through the folds of soft muslin at its bay window. Suddenly, she felt a bolt of electricity pass through her as the familiar grey shadow of a woman passed across the pale curtains. Her ghost. The exact shape and movement she had seen so often outside the shop or out of the corner of her eye as she had moved about the town.

Now she knew why the sight of the grey figure had made her feel an odd sense of familiarity and even comfort. She waited to see if she would reappear, but there was nothing.

After a while Anna let out a breath and took the blank Christmas card from her pocket and signed it carefully, adding a single kiss under her name, and tucking her business card from The Cookery inside. She put the card in the envelope and hesitated before writing, 'Mum', on the front of the envelope. Then she got out of the car, crossed the road and quickly posted it through the letter box. Just as quickly she returned to the safety of the car, started the engine and drove away, emotion catching in her throat, knowing that before too long she would meet the ghost from her past, face to face.

* * *

Once Anna and Ralph had left the rooftop, Joe tidied away the wrappings and Auntie B's present box, then returned to help her inside. She didn't want to lock herself way from the night just yet and asked him to move her chair next to the steps that led back into her flat, that way she would be able to simply turn herself around and go back in when she was ready. He tucked her up well with her soft blankets and she sent him off for another night at the restaurant and with Imogen.

Auntie B sat on her small iron chair, feeling the light, chill wind on her face, feeling immensely content and tired in equal measure. She thought of Ginger and the same night over seventy years before when they had met for the first time in that small bedroom in Eastbourne. Her beautiful, golden-haired daughter; she hoped that she'd had a happy life, even without her true mother at her side.

She thought of Ralph and the new man he had become in this strange, ancient little town and the potential of the sensitive artist she knew he could be with Sam at his side. Of Anna and the newfound confidence that seemed to have blossomed in her, that she hoped would bring her contentment and then love in years to come when she was truly ready for it. Of Joe, who had the adventurous heart of both his mother and his Grandmother beating inside him, that she knew would guide him wherever he chose to go next.

Then she thought of her constant companion, Mr Charles Dickens, who had provided words and comfort for every occasion of her life. She started to speak quietly, sending his words over the red roofs of Rye:

"It was the season of hospitality, merriment and open-heartedness. The old year was preparing, like an ancient philosopher, to call his friends around him and amidst the sound of feasting and revelry to pass gently and peacefully away."

Auntie B remained at her door, warm in the soft embrace of her blue and yellow blankets, her unseeing eyes closed. Then the smallest, most delicate snowflakes began to settle on her tiny velvet slippers, but she did not go inside. Evelyn Bondolfi's life had been long enough and she was free of it at last, free of its joys and its secrets. She was ready for a whole new adventure.

Thank you for reading Book One in The Rye Rooftop Club series.

If you enjoyed this book, please review it on Amazon.co.uk - it really helps other people to find their way to The Rooftop Club!

The Great British Rom-Com continues in the second book in the series:

The Rye Rooftop Club: *Mothers Day*

A story of friends, relationships, gnomes, skinny dipping, breaking into other people's houses, sausage rolls, forward rolls, nice shoes, motherhood and untold secrets.
Available from Amazon.

To keep up to date with news on further books in the series and more of Mark Feakins' writing follow us on Facebook:

My Writing Life

Acknowledgements

Thanks to all the lovely friends and acquaintances who have had their names recycled in this story. Although I have used their names, I have not used any of their characteristics and any peculiarities of the characters are entirely of my own creation.

Thanks also, to my brilliant team of early readers Gillian, Josée, Marie, Rosie and Sue for your enthusiasm, encouragement and guidance.

Particular thanks to my proof reader and editor-in-chief, Joanne Ringrose, who read this book more times than is probably healthy. I admire both your staying power and your attention to detail. Love and thanks as always.

Finally, to Martin, who makes everything worthwhile, and read this book at every stage of its journey and never failed to pull me up when I'd gone astray, encourage me when I faltered and let me disappear for hours on end into the world I had created, without complaint or question. Thanks will never be enough.

About the Author

Mark Feakins grew up on the Sussex coast and has been a frequent visitor to Rye throughout his life. He moved to London to go to drama school and, after a brief time as an actor and running his own theatre company, he began working in theatres; as the Programmer for The Bloomsbury Theatre and the General Manager of the Young Vic. He then travelled further north as Executive Producer of Sheffield Theatres before creating his own photography business. He has a degree in Librarianship, danced around a maypole on BBC TV's Playschool and won Channel 4's Come Dine with Me in 2010.

Mark now lives happily in the region of Valencia in Spain, with his husband Martin.

E: markfeakins@gmail.com
Facebook: My Writing Life

Books By Mark Feakins

The Rye Series

#1 The Rye Rooftop Club

#2 The Rye Rooftop Club: Mother's Day

Printed in Great Britain
by Amazon